The Pain
Nurse

Books by Jon Talton

The David Mapstone Mysteries
Concrete Desert
Camelback Falls
Dry Heat
Arizona Dreams
Cactus Heart

Other Novels
The Pain Nurse

The Pain Nurse

Jon Talton

Poisoned Pen Press

Poisoned Pen Press
6962 E. First Ave., Ste. 103
Scottsdale, AZ 85251
www.poisonedpenpress.com
info@poisonedpenpress.com

Printed in the United States of America

For Susan

Paying My Debts

Many people generously helped in the research and writing of this novel. Eddie Lueken, RN, first intrigued me with the idea for this book, then she spent many hours with me explaining pain management nursing. Ellie Strang, RN, helped refine my ideas and keep the details accurate, and gave invaluable insights into the daily life of a hospital and its nurses. I'm also grateful for the excellent suggestions of Dr. Verna Corey.

On the law-enforcement side, retired Phoenix Police detective Cal Lash provided me a veteran's perspective from both the homicide and internal affairs details. Retired Mesa Police Officer Skip Redpath gave me additional insights. My Cincinnati friends and writers Sue MacDonald and Kathy Doane helped fill out my knowledge of this singular, magical, haunted city. Blame me for inconsistencies, deliberate changes in procedure or descriptions, or errors.

My abiding thanks go to Barbara Peters, my editor, for her perfect pitch in helping me bring to life this nocturnal world of nurses and cops.

Chapter One

The pain always gets worse when the sun goes down. As often happened, it brought Cheryl Beth Wilson back to Cincinnati Memorial Hospital that December night. And like most nights, Cheryl Beth beat the pain. Mrs. Dahl told her how she loved her, tears in her filmy, gray eyes. She started telling a story Cheryl Beth had heard four times before, but she sat and listened. Then the old woman instantly dropped into sleep, the stencil of cancer momentarily leaving her face. Mrs. Dahl, who an hour before had been screaming from the postsurgical mess that had once been her belly. Cheryl Beth eased the old woman's hand down to the sheet, checked her IV flow one more time, turned down the light in the long fixture on the wall at the head of the bed, and walked out into the quiet, darkened hall. The room's persistent smell of decaying flesh, ointment, and deodorizer faded.

She walked to the nurses' station. With most of the hall lights off, it stood brightly lit in the distance like a truck stop on the interstate. After making notes in Mrs. Dahl's chart, she turned to her own notebook, drawing a happy face next to the woman's name: her shorthand for a patient in pain, just that. She knew she could fix that easily. In another situation, she might draw a face with slits for eyes—someone who was oversedated. She could fix that, too. Then there was the face she would draw with wide eyes and wide mouth, an addict seeking pain meds. To this she would add her FC scale—one through ten—for "fucking crazy." Fucking crazy and mean can get you in trouble. The faces told it all.

"Saved again by the pain nurse." Cheryl Beth saw the heavy brown hand on her shoulder and turned to smile at Denise, a large woman in green scrubs who had worked on this floor for the past two years. Tonight she was the RN in charge.

"I don't know what we would have done without you," she said.

"You guys did the hard work." Cheryl Beth had a pleasing, musical voice with a hint of the Kentucky drawl she had worked hard to lose. "I just helped."

"You always share the credit. I know how you work." Denise smiled at her fondly. "Pizza?" She indicated an open box in the adjoining storeroom.

"That's a big no-no. Don't let Stephanie Ott catch you." Cheryl Beth walked back and took a small piece, holding it on a paper towel and taking a bite. She needed something in her stomach besides liquor.

"I don't have to worry about that," Denise said. "Ott doesn't even come to the floors, much less at this time of night. If the suits don't like it, they shouldn't close the cafeteria at eight. They can't close things fast enough at this old place. At least you helped poor Mrs. Dahl."

Cheryl Beth spoke between bites. "The woman's been in pain every night. Then when her doc comes by in the morning, she's finally fallen asleep. He says, 'What's the problem? She's sleeping.' He didn't see how bad it had been the night before."

"Did Dr. Miller enjoy you calling him during his Christmas party?"

"I'm lovable. It just pisses me off when people suffer. We had a nice chat. He hadn't wanted to adjust her meds." She washed and sanitized her hands. "But he didn't like her lung sounds. I gently reminded him it was because she was too exhausted to try sitting up and walking. So I finally convinced him to change her meds and he signed the order to use a fentanyl patch. We'll have to monitor the dose carefully."

"Well, he wouldn't have done it for me," Denise said. "No wonder you were Nurse of the Year. Thanks, baby girl."

Denise had called her that for years. At forty-four, Cheryl Beth felt far from being a baby girl. She was older than many of the docs now. She had watched as more patients turned up who were her age or younger. It was a battle now to keep weight off her average build, keep her hair something approximating the light brown she had been born with. On close inspection, a net of wrinkles was etching its way around the edges of her eyes. When she was younger, people had told her she looked like Jodie Foster, and she had sometimes believed there was a passing resemblance. But that was a long time ago.

She said, "The truth is, if I waited for every doc to return calls I'd never get anything done. That's why I have my guardian angel docs who will sign off on my orders."

"You know more than half of them anyway. You ready for Christmas, baby girl?"

"I haven't begun."

"Christmas, 2000." Denise shook her head slowly. "Can you believe it? A whole new millennium and old Cincinnati just seems the same."

Cheryl Beth laughed. "About the best I did today was to rake the leaves out of my flower beds and buy a couple bottles of wine. Is that Christmas-y?"

"I'd love to go have a drink with you right now. But since they stuck me on this night shift, about all I can do is drink a little scotch on my days off. Salve my pain, pain nurse."

"Actually, tequila has the best pain management properties. And that's data driven, not Cheryl Beth driven." She finished her charting and replaced the pen in her white lab coat, which tonight she wore over her street clothes. She slid the chart in its place, which at Denise's station was neatly kept.

"Dr. Lustig called for you." Denise dropped a pink message slip on the desk beside Cheryl Beth. She checked the pager on her belt, but it was blank. Why hadn't Christine just paged her?

"Can you believe we're still using this 'While you were out' shit?" Denise folded her arms over her large breasts and surveyed the station's file drawers, shelves, chart caddies—all the paperwork grown high around them. "My kids have better technology than this place. We're still doing charts by hand like when I got out of nursing school. If we weren't buried in paperwork all the time we could actually commit medicine."

"I hear they're working on a big new system, put all the records on computers. Dr. Lustig's one of the big movers behind it."

"Well, I guess she's working late tonight. I can't believe they put people in those offices off in the A-wing basement, especially a woman. Want me to walk with you?"

Cheryl Beth did a fake karate move. "I don't scare easily. Anyway, it's just where the residents go to screw in privacy."

Denise gave a knowing nod. "Not just that, baby girl. Used to be the morgue down there, the mental health wing. There's lots of stories. Some say it's haunted. Back in the day, they started having the toe tags disappear from the corpses down there. About a year later, they found out this girl who was working there had taken them and made them into an art project—it was on display in some gallery!"

They were both still laughing as Cheryl Beth walked to the elevator.

Dr. Lustig. Dr. Christine Lustig. Christine. The name conjured a mess of emotions inside Cheryl Beth as she rode down in the big empty elevator. She was glad for the distraction when the door opened two floors down and one of the patient transport guys wheeled in a heavy gurney. He was a tall, thin man with very dark skin. She had seen him before but couldn't remember his name.

"Where to?"

"To one," he said. "Imaging. But they already told me on the way back I got to go through the basement. Can you believe that? Got to go the long way. They brought a shooting victim to the ER and they're going to close off the first floor in a few minutes. 'Security concerns,' they say. What they mean is they don't want black folks coming down to see what happened." He gesticulated fiercely. "This man in ER was shot by the cops. Man was unarmed. What is it? Fifteen black men shot by the police the past five years? Nights I go home I think I could be next, know what I'm saying? They disrespect the whole black community. Last month, police pointed guns at my neighbor right in front of his kids."

He shook his head in disgust, then stared at Cheryl Beth. "Now everybody's going nuts, afraid his friends and family are gonna come down and start trouble." He looked around the elevator, up at the ceiling, then back at Cheryl Beth. "Some day this town's just gonna blow, you know? Down there on Main Street, all them white yuppies coming to the new nightclubs, coming in from the suburbs. A block away you got six kids living in a room of a tenement, no heat, and a black man can't walk on the street without a beatdown from five-oh. How long before those black folks look over on Main Street and see how goddamned poor they really is? Then what's gonna happen, huh?"

Cheryl Beth looked at the patient on the gurney. He was a big man with wavy dark hair and a handsome face, even with the nasty blister on one lip. He must have been through a long surgery. He briefly looked at her, smiled, then closed his eyes. His eyes were tired and afraid. She had seen the look thousands of times. When the elevator opened at the first floor, she held the door while the patient was wheeled out. The transport guy was moving fast. He probably had a dozen more transports waiting for him, even at this time of night. Then she rode down another floor alone.

In a few moments she stepped out into a dim corridor. The floor was a uniform checkerboard, aged and scuffed. It was narrower than in the more modern parts of the hospital, and most of the lights were off to save money. This had been a main part of the original hospital, when the twenty-story, art deco tower had been a proud civic monument and Cincinnati Memorial had been one of the top hospitals in the Midwest. Generations of docs had trained here. Now the hospital was struggling and the basement was mostly forgotten. It still had a black-and-white tile floor that seemed right out of the 1930s. The wall was plaster, fading white with an institutional green stripe running horizontally. Cheryl Beth liked to imagine the medicine that had been practiced here once, when nurses had worn white uniforms and neat caps, when pain management had been, if someone was lucky, morphine.

It was better than thinking about Christine. Why was she even coming down here? What more was there to say?

The darkness of the corridor seemed to swallow sound. Other hallways, narrow alleys, and double doors led off at regular intervals. The doors had small, darkened windows. Old beds and laundry carts were lined along the walls and tucked into intersecting hallways. Then a metallic crash, muffled, short-lived, somewhere behind her. She jumped and looked back. Had the sound come through those two dark doors off to the left? She stood for a moment in the gathering silence. It was silly. Cheryl Beth was not the jumpy type. She liked walking the old corridors, taking shortcuts. The old building made its own sounds, never mind the reality that the basement also attracted horny staff members and the occasional transient. And for some reason, Christine had moved her office down here. In the distance, she heard an elevator bell sound, heard anonymous hums of large electric machines.

She could see warm, golden light breaking out of Christine's office door, which was partly opened onto the corridor. Christine hated the overhead lights and often worked with only her desk lamp lit.

"Hey, it's me." Cheryl Beth knocked as she opened the door.

For an instant, the world seemed out of phase, not right, almost comically not right. Red spatter on the floor. Christine on the floor, undressed. Among the tide of emotions washing in was almost a millisecond of laughter: this was a practical joke. Then heavy breathing. Cheryl Beth's own.

"Christine?" It took Cheryl Beth a moment to recognize her own voice.

Dr. Christine Lustig lay on her side, completely naked, her pale skin luminous except for the blood. Everywhere. Cuts lashed her arms, legs, side, face; in places, the skin had been viciously avulsed, like work a butcher might do. Cheryl Beth's training effortlessly overcame the hysterical instinct boiling up in her and in two strides she was at the doctor's side, reaching for a carotid pulse. Her fingers sank into gore. The knife had found its fatal target in Christine's neck. Around the other side of her neck the skin was unbroken and pulseless. Her finger felt her thigh, the femoral artery; again, no pulse. She felt a ballerina's spinning light-headedness. She felt disembodied but no, connected to another body, one that would take barely a breeze to float away. So much blood—maybe there were other victims. The average human contained 5.6 liters of blood. Then she realized how much blood she was standing in. It betrayed the unevenness of the floor, pooling here, flowing like scarlet canals between the aged tiles. It inundated her red patent leather Danskos. Suddenly she felt a touch slither against her neck.

Her disembodied hearing heard a sharp breath, a small *"oh!"* Her own.

Cheryl Beth pulled the stethoscope off her neck and stuffed it into her lab coat. The white coat was now streaked with Christine's blood. Behind her was the doorway, with the empty black hallway beyond. The entire world seemed monstrously soundless, even the distant electric hum gone. Cheryl Beth sprang up, crossed the room, and closed the door, locking it. She carefully walked to the desk, her shoes now hopelessly hydroplaning on the bloody floor, and grabbed the phone receiver. Even before her ear registered the dead device she could see the cord ripped from the wall. Her own cell showed no signal.

Panic finally threatened to overwhelm her. Her breath came harder and she reached into her pocket for the small inhaler, shook it, and took a puff. She made herself breathe slowly. Buried beneath the vast hospital, the cell phone stubbornly refused to find a signal.

"Oh, shit." She leaned against the wall and looked back at Christine. That's when she saw the strange shape of the woman's left hand. Christine's ring finger was gone, leaving a dark red tangle of tissue.

Cheryl Beth walked quickly to the door, unlocked it, and ran down the hallway toward the elevator, but not before finding a disposable scalpel in the cabinets of Christine's office, unwrapping it, and brandishing it before her like life itself.

Chapter Two

He was alive.

Later he would learn that the surgery had lasted more than ten hours, but to him it was one lost instant that began after the anesthesiologist had opened his leather case and said, "Bar's open. What's your pleasure, Detective Borders?" Will had laughed and called for good Kentucky bourbon and a Christian Moerlein chaser. Next he was awake on his back, looking at a lighted ceiling, and at Cindy's face, telling her how much he loved her, how grateful he was to be alive. They could start fresh. They would have Christmas. He would live to see another Christmas. He had just been babbling, a long series of moans, but these words are what his brain so clearly heard him say.

Can you wiggle your toes? Can you feel this? Yes, yes!

He was alive. This elation kept him going through the hours in the ICU, when he sweet-talked the nurse into giving him more ice than she probably should have. His thirst was primal. The ice was salvation. He could feel his feet and toes, kept wiggling them anxiously. Then he had been wheeled up to a patient floor, a good sign surely, and Cindy had sat with him for a while. Then she had poured him water and left. The persistent sleep that had annihilated the past few days again took him. Everything else could wait. He was alive.

Suddenly this madman had appeared, vowing to take him for an MRI. It was midnight. Will had protested ineffectually as they slid him to a gurney and wheeled him like tardy cargo through the empty halls of the hospital. For the first time since waking from the surgery, Will was afraid. The nurses hadn't heard about this trip to the imaging department. He overheard a hushed conversation. And the attendant seemed so careless, so quick to take a fast turn with the gurney that might have sent Will sprawling onto the floor. The corridors were empty. Could the MRI even be operating this late? Yet he was a prisoner, flat on his back, barely able to move below the waist.

He felt profoundly vulnerable: part of his vertebrae was missing and a long, fresh wound was cut down his back, held together by sutures that could easily rip apart. The drugs and exhaustion had made him feel oddly disembodied. From the safety of his bed, he had studied the assorted tubes coming out of his arms and chest with an abstract disregard. Now they looked like menace, like death attached.

He felt utterly alone.

It didn't help Will's apprehension that he was at the mercy of a young black man who hated cops. The man had made that tendency clear to everyone he encountered. There had been another shooting of a black by a police officer, no doubt a white officer. Will Borders was a white police officer. He feigned sleep and hoped that his tormenter didn't know his occupation.

After an hour of being banged inside the futuristic coffin of the MRI—thank God, he wasn't claustrophobic—he was again loaded on the gurney and wheeled to the elevator. This time they took a long, circuitous route, through bleak corridors that looked as if they hadn't been used in years. Will was growing sleepy until the gurney jerked to a halt and he looked ahead to see a hallway blocked with yellow tape. It was crime-scene tape.

"Can't go this way."

"What? I can't use the A-Main corridor. The cops blocked that, too. I got a man who needs to get back to his room."

It was the first time the orderly had shown any more concern for Will than for a cart of someone else's groceries.

"Wait."

Will strained to see in front of him. He could make out two uniformed police officers standing outside an open doorway, their regulation white shirts and badges glowing in the reflected light. Will was too exhausted to be curious. The thrill of being on the other side of police tape had passed years before.

"Let him through...stay over this way."

The gurney moved again and Will opened his eyes, just in time to look through the door. It was an office and blood was on the walls and floor. A technician stepped carefully to take photos of the scene. The body was still there, a woman, nude, and badly slashed. Will studied the view with a trained eye, suddenly engaged. His stomach was turning to ice. His throat threatened to close.

"Stop!" Will tried to pull himself upright, got his trunk a quarter of the way up, and fell back. "Stop!" he said again.

"Are you nuts, man? You move around too much and you could reopen your sutures." The orderly looked alarmed.

"That woman in there," Will said. "Look at her left hand."

"Yeah, she's stone cold..."

"No, look at her left hand. What do you see?"

The orderly's voice rose an octave. "Shit, man, somebody cut off her finger!"

"Come on, move along."

Will knew the voice instantly and a tired, sour feeling enveloped him.

"What, you don't see enough blood in your job...what's this?" A broad ebony face bent down and surveyed Will. "Well, well, Internal Investigations will do anything to sneak up on real working police."

Homicide Detective J. J. Dodds assumed his usual lordly stance. He was not merely big but downright fat. He grew fatter every year, regularly outgrowing his suits. Will didn't know how he passed his annual physical. He did know how to dress, though. Tonight Dodds wore a blue pinstriped suit, starched dress shirt, and a burgundy tie.

"What the hell happened to you, Borders? Having a boil removed from your ass?"

"It's a little more complicated than that."

"Oh, yeah, what? You look like shit."

The orderly asked, "You guys know each other?"

"Yeah, I arrested him once," Dodds said. "Morals charge."

Will ignored him and nodded toward the room. "That victim. Did you see her hand?"

"I saw. Why are you here? Enlighten me." A moment before the cops had been rushing them by. Now Dodds' meaty hand held the gurney fast. The orderly sighed loudly and lounged against the wall. A few feet away stood the pretty nurse he had seen on the elevator going down. Her clothes were streaked with blood and her face was ashen.

"What ailment, Borders? Surely not something in the line of duty."

Will's throat was still sore from the intubation for surgery. He swallowed hard and wished he had some water. "A spinal cord tumor, okay?"

"Spinal cord what?" Dodds' exotic, cynical eyes widened. Then he blinked the moment away. "I've got a bad back, too."

"Her hand, Dodds. Her hand."

"I saw it." He lounged nonchalantly against the rails of the gurney.

"Dodds…"

"What are you telling me, Borders? That you believe in ghosts? The Mount Adams Slasher died at Lucasville last summer."

"Maybe he wasn't the Slasher."

Dodds lifted the sheet and studied Will. "Shit, you've got tubes coming out of you. That's gross. You in pain?"

"Who was this woman? Do you have a suspect?"

"They'll just go lay it on an innocent brother like they always do," the orderly grumbled. Dodds ignored him.

"This is none of your concern, Mister Patient." Dodds carelessly replaced the sheet. "You're the only one in town who ever had a doubt over that case, and as I recall you left the Homicide Unit. You make a living ratting out police officers."

"He took her ring finger, goddammit. Just like the Mount Adams cases."

"So it's a copy cat."

Will hissed, "We never released that information about the crime and the media never reported it!" His back was starting to hurt, a low, spreading fire of pain. "I bet you found her clothes folded neatly, too. Dodds!"

"Borders…"

"You know who did this. You know it." Will heard an unfamiliar pleading in his voice. "Look for the knife!"

Dodds tapped the gurney. "Get him out of here." The orderly pushed and the scene receded. Out of the gloom, he heard Dodds' voice, "Hope your back feels better, Borders."

Chapter Three

It was only safe to cry at home. She never cried at work, never broke that professional boundary. Only at home. But this time Cheryl Beth didn't make it that far. A guard had walked her to her car, she had locked the doors, inserted the key into the steering column, but then sobs heaved through her body. She stayed like that a long time, trembling, wrapped in her trench coat, her arms clenched tightly across her chest, the halogen lights of the parking garage burning into her tired eyes. For a long time she didn't trust herself to drive. The drive home only took three minutes if she hit the lights right. Her house in the Clifton district was so close that on summer days she often rode her hot-pink bicycle to the hospital. It made people smile.

Her little bungalow sat dark at the end of the street. The porch light had been burned out for a week. It was only tonight that it took on a sinister dimension. Her stomach tightened into a cramp and her breathing kicked up. She clicked on the bright lights as she approached. They swept the empty yard and spindly winter bushes.

Then, out loud, to herself, "Don't be silly."

She parked at the top of the driveway and stepped out, the chill helping to center her. The street looked coldly benign in the moonlight. The moon looked like it had been shot out of a cannon.

It came quickly from her left, shadow and blurry motion.

"No!"

"Cheryl Beth, it's okay. I didn't mean to startle you."

"Gary." She felt her heart slowly withdraw from her throat. "What are you doing here?"

"The hospital told me."

"Come inside."

She clumsily unlocked the door, led him in, and turned on some lights. When she turned around he was right there, pulling her greedily into his arms. At first she resisted, guilt and empathy fighting inside her. Then she let him hold her. After a moment, she even held him back. Dr. Gary Nagle stood a foot taller than she, but his body was hard with muscles, lacking even a careless hint of fat. He was a killer squash player.

"Oh, Gary, I am so, so sorry."

With that she started sobbing again and cleaved against him until the coat made her oppressively hot, the heat reminding her of the impossible awkwardness of this. She broke away, tossed her coat in a chair, and went silently to the kitchen where she made herself a Bushmills on the rocks. He was already fixing himself a scotch. He knew where the bottle was kept.

"They told me you found her."

He followed her back into the living room and waited, standing while she put a fake log in the fireplace, thinking the light and flame might be comforting. It bloomed into unnatural light as she told him what had happened. She was accustomed to telling the story now that she had told the police four times. The big black detective, she didn't like him. He had aggressively questioned her every sentence, almost as if he suspected her of the crime. Several of her RN friends had married cops, but she had little personal experience with the police. If this was any indication, it was no wonder so many of those marriages had failed.

"She was just cut so badly," Cheryl Beth said. "There was nothing I could do. She bled out. He cut off her ring finger."

"If it was a he."

"I didn't think she was even wearing a wedding band now. This makes no sense."

His voice seemed so matter of fact. By this time she was sitting on the small sofa in front of the fireplace. Gary sat next to her, the flickering flame accentuating his blue eyes and wolfish mustache. He started stroking and twirling her hair.

"Stop, Gary. My God, your wife was killed tonight."

He pulled his hand slightly, to the back of the sofa, still resting on her shoulder. "Ex-wife," he said. His face fell into a boyish sulk.

"I'm surprised you're not down there," Cheryl Beth said.

"The police want to talk to me. They left messages." He took a deep pull on the scotch. "You know how they always suspect the husband. The ex-husband is even worse. You know how the police think. I'm considering getting my lawyer."

Cheryl Beth regarded him silently. She had several rules concerning Dr. Gary Nagle. They were designed to keep her clear-headed about him. One was already broken: he was sitting too close. Another was getting emotional. She resisted blurting out the obvious: *man, your wife, okay ex-wife, somebody you loved enough to marry, was killed tonight, murdered, horribly murdered, what the hell's the matter with you?...* After a breath, she said, "I don't know why you came here. It's three a.m."

"I wanted to know what you told the police."

"What are you talking about?"

"You might have been the last person to see her alive," he said. After an impossible pause he added, "Other than the murderer."

She turned toward him, felt her face redden. "What do you mean?" But she knew exactly what he meant. "You were on Main Street tonight?" She realized it was last night now, but made no effort to clarify. She shook her head. "You were spying? Following me? That's very bizarre."

"If an ex-husband sees his ex-wife and ex-lover having a drink together, he's going to take notice."

"Especially if he's stalking."

"You two were together around nine last night. Why in the world were you both back at the hospital later? Christine was working on a computer system, for God's sake, not doing patient rounds any more."

"We did have a drink. I left. Then I got paged. I do have patients. She didn't tell me she was going back to the hospital." Oh, she hated his neurosurgeon's arrogance. She couldn't imagine the time when she had mistaken it for an edgy confidence and had been attracted to him. "I was on one of the floors when they gave me a message from her at the nurses' station. She said she was in her office and asked me to come down. Then I went down and she was, she was…. Why…?" She felt herself getting angry. "Why am I explaining myself to you? I don't owe you anything."

He ignored her mood and finished off the scotch. After a few minute's silence, he said, "I warned her about that office. That hospital's not safe. They ought to shut it down, and they would without the neurosurgery unit carrying everything else."

"Gary, you need to go see the police. Now."

"Chris was going through the postdivorce wilds. Having a great time being away from me. Playing with residents. They're young and idealistic and horny. And playing with nurses, I hear."

"As I remember, you left her."

"It was over a long time ago, way before any judge ruled. As I remember, you once wanted me to leave her to be with you."

A wave of nausea swept over Cheryl Beth. "That's not true." She spoke quietly but heard her words echo off the walls and mantle. "What we had was a…fling. My bad judgment."

"Oh, the pain nurse, always making nice." He stroked her hair again, ran one of his high-priced hands down the side of her face, down her neck. He smelled good. Damn it.

"Stop, Gary." She moved to a chair facing him and took a gulp of the whiskey. His face was strangely blank, the handsome planes of his cheeks, strong chin and sensual lips. He would look thirty-five forever. Then he leered at her, his dusky blue eyes morose and appraising. She knew her face was red and her eyes puffy, her makeup a mess, but he looked as if he hadn't parted with one tear. Some days she hated blue eyes, swore she would never trust them again.

"Well." He set down the glass and stood. "I'm going to have to tell the police that you two were together before she was killed. But I assume you already did."

"I did." Her mouth filled with cotton.

"Did you tell them about us?"

"No," she said softly.

"Cheryl Beth, always discreet. Always the good girl, even when she wasn't."

"Why are you being such a jerk?"

"Because I'm not going to let Chris get me from the grave." He pointed adamantly down, as if she were buried beneath the house. "Like I said, the ex-husband is always the prime suspect." The leering smile returned. "But so is Chris' romantic rival. Who knows what she might have said to you tonight. But, you told the police everything, right? Well, almost everything."

He paused, then, "What else happened at the hospital tonight? Did Bryant come down there?"

She said the chief executive had come down. He had been very solicitous and gentle with her, and had told her to take two days off.

"Come here, babe, I'll give us both an alibi." His body language was all too clear.

She edged him toward the door, afraid of all the raging things she might say. "I don't need an alibi. And you need to call the police, talk to them. I can't even believe you were alone tonight, spying. What about Amy, that child physical therapist you were fucking."

"Oh, I love to hear you talk dirty, Cheryl Beth. Gets me so horny." He smirked. "But your mother would disapprove of that language."

She knew he was pushing buttons. He was so good at that. But the words still lashed her. Why had she ever let him into her life, especially into the deeper parts that could wound?

"Please go."

"Maybe I was with Amy tonight. You don't know. And she's hardly a child. She's twenty-two." He looked around the familiar room.

"I need you to go now."

"I hope you close those curtains after I leave. Those big windows. You should really be more careful."

"Gary, you're really…" She didn't finish the sentence. She just held out her hands defensively and he slipped out the door. When she had locked it, she spoke to the door. "Gary, you're really creeping me out tonight."

Chapter Four

"You're a hard man to find."

Will Borders sat in the wheelchair, against the wall in a hallway behind a cart with red drawers, an EKG machine and menacing-looking defibrillator paddles, and there was Scaly Mueller walking toward him. Captain Steve Mueller was the commander of the Internal Investigations unit.

"But good men are hard to find."

He talked that way, lapsing into motivational clichés. It was just another Scaly Mueller joke. All the cops made fun of him behind his back. Will said hello, but the unspoken answer to Mueller's question was that Will's only peace was anywhere but inside his room. After a week in the neuro-rehab unit, he had barely slept. Moving meant pain. Even raising his arm to dial his cell phone meant excruciating torture. Immobility meant pain to come. Once he was down for the night, he was strapped into what looked like vibrating socks—prevent blood clots, they said. They also killed his ability to sleep. But the biggest problem was three feet away from his bed.

His roommate was a quadriplegic from a car crash. He was trussed up in a contraption of wires and tubes. Every few minutes a nurse or technician would come in with a different, invariably noisy treatment. The commotion and stench made rest impossible. Hospitals were noisy places. When the poor man was conscious, he only wanted to watch back-to-back episodes of

Judge Judy, with the volume on high. The room itself offered no view. The neuro-rehab unit was located in a first-floor addition that shot off the main part of the hospital. But Will's window looked back into the old blond-brick building, across a small stretch of hibernating grass. The heliport was located on top of the neuro-rehab wing, and late at night medevac choppers would land, causing the windows to shake as if an earthquake were happening. The night-shift nurses joked darkly with him about the likelihood that one day a helicopter would crash on them. "The first thing you'll see is the aviation fuel running down the walls, before it ignites and we're all toast," one said merrily.

At least he was off the morphine. It had masked the pain but it had brought dreams. Morphine took him to an old amusement park in Newport, Kentucky, right across the river from downtown. He had no memory of such a place ever existing—but it must have, the drug told him so. It was fenced off and deserted, but Will had walked through the gate. It was twilight, the sky on the verge of rain. He was alone, surrounded by rusting kiddie rides. All around was a quadrangle of old wooden buildings, their reddish paint flaking off. He walked inside one and saw straw on the ground, as if it had once been a stable. The morphine told him that children had been killed here, many children, murdered horribly. His dreaming self fought to find a way out, a way to wake up. The souls of the innocent dead followed him until he had crashed back into his broken body, staring at the harsh light over his bed. After that, he was happier to have the pain than the morphine dreams.

As he slowly got better, Will would dress in the bed and call a nurse first thing in the morning to transfer him from the bed into a wheelchair. The wheelchair was comfortable and moved easily. It had the brand name Quickie, which seemed like a sick joke. He might never be able to have a quickie again.

He stayed out as long as they would let him. With difficulty, he began to slide himself from the bed to the wheelchair, wheelchair to toilet and back. He needed a nurse there to help, of course. His right leg seemed unable to bear any weight, although he could move it easily. Will had quickly realized that he was one of the better-off patients. When the nurses weren't taking care of what everyone called "the quads," they were writing endless paperwork, as bad as cops, worse even. He called the nurses less often, did things for himself.

"You look good."

Will knew it was a lie. Mueller started to clap him on the shoulder, then seemed to think better of it. His hand hung between them awkwardly. They awkwardly shook hands. Steve Mueller was around forty, wearing chinos, tie, and wool sport coat. He had a close-cropped halo of blond hair ringing his baldness and the look of a faded high school football player. He had a bristly peach-colored mustache. Growing up on the west side, he had played football for Elder, and had never been farther than Chicago. In other words, he had the resumé of nearly everyone who rose to command in the Cincinnati Police Department. It was one more reason Will would never move ahead. He was Scots-Irish Protestant in a German Catholic town.

"Can I wheel you somewhere, so we can talk? Where's that pretty wife of yours?"

"She's working. I can wheel myself." And Will could, until he started hurting too badly. "There's a Starbucks down by the lobby."

"How are you two doing? You and Cindy."

"We're okay. We're good."

"That's good." Mueller sounded skeptical. Then: "Love conquers all, huh?"

After a few minutes, they had navigated the crowded hallways, out of neuro-rehab, down the corridor behind the emergency room and into the bright, glassy expanse of the main concourse.

"So Dodds is working this homicide?" Will asked after they had coffees. He clutched his cup in both hands.

"How you doing?" Mueller countered.

This innocuous question had assumed the complexity of quantum physics. Before the tumor, Will could give the expected answer without a thought. Nobody really wanted more. *Doin' fine.* Now everything about his life was contained in the unstated. No matter how hard he worked, he could barely move his left leg, his most violent command from the brain translating into a murmur in his toes, like a broken clock pendulum. Vast tracts of his belly, buttocks, and right leg were dead to the touch, as if a deranged dentist armed with Novocain had repeatedly attacked him. He was put in the shower so rarely, and getting in was so painful, that he could smell himself like some street person he used to roust. He was constipated. He hurt for hours. Every movement was difficult. Nobody wanted to hear all that.

He said, "I'm okay. The docs seem pleased. The tumor was not malignant. They think they got it all. I need to get into rehab." He knew he was lucky or blessed to be alive, that he could have been killed or put into a wheelchair permanently. Yet he felt exhausted. He was working hard to keep it from showing.

Mueller half nodded. Will's mind went back to the homicide, an easy leap from thinking about pain, a dead leg, and *Judge Judy.*

"Dodds needs to follow the MO," Will said. "This woman was killed…"

"I know. On the surface it appeared similar to the Mount Adams Slasher. Dodds told me he saw you. You know, big guy, I had my appendix taken out last year, and for the first day I hardly knew where I was. Don't take this the wrong way, but you were probably kind of out of it that night…"

Will put the coffee on a table and shifted in the wheelchair. The maneuver required him to push down with his arms and swivel his hips. Instantly his back flared in agony. He whispered, barely in control, "I know what I saw. If Dodds…"

"I don't want to hear about you and Dodds. You're like an old married couple fighting. He feels like you deserted him when you left homicide. Anyway, that detail's got its hands full right now. Three nights ago a P&G executive was shot and killed on a street in Over-the-Rhine. You know Procter rules this town. Mayor's going nuts. Dodds' partner, Linda Hall, she's off on maternity leave. So he's working solo. This doctor was probably just a victim of a random crime. I see the street people just wandering through the halls. Gangbangers. Dodds will clear it." He looked around. "Should you even be out here?"

"Who knows?" Will said, forcing a conversational voice. "Better to ask for forgiveness than for permission."

"An interesting statement from an Internal Investigations cop." Mueller didn't smile. "I talked to your doctors." He paused as a loud procession of family members went by, bearing stuffed animals, headed to the children's wing. He nervously scratched the back of his right hand. As a patrolman, Mueller had been nicknamed Scaly, because of some kind of skin ailment that made him itch constantly. Officers complained that the seats and steering wheels of patrol cars inhabited by Mueller on a previous shift always had a dusting of flaked skin. At some point, he had gone to a doctor, but the name had stuck: Scaly Mueller. Now he only scratched when he was in uncomfortable situations.

"I talked to your doctors," he repeated.

"They say I will walk again."

Mueller lowered his eyes and sucked in his lips. "Come on, Will," he said finally, "you're in a wheelchair. I know that's hard to accept. I can't even imagine… Best case, you'll always use a cane. And that's okay. My gosh, things could have been so much worse. But you face a tough rehab and you'll never be able to be…"

"You talked about a desk job," Will quickly interposed. "Why not? We have wounded officers who are technically disabled, but the department finds a place for them. I can still do internal affairs, white-collar crime. I'm good at what I do."

"You weren't wounded," he said. "Those guys, they have a story to tell, the public loves them and we benefit from their continued service. You know the way of the world. Why are you so fired up to keep mucking out this sewer anyway? Had a deal down in Walnut Hills last night. You see the paper? Dispatch lost contact with two uniforms on a domestic. One of them ends up shot dead. Young guy, twenty-three, one kid. Jeez. Now the hospital killing is yesterday's news. There's going to be hell to pay at communications. Chief is already all over my ass for a report. Why would you miss that? Hey, today is the first day of the rest of your life."

Will said nothing. His life now was lived in front of his face, in the next moment. Get his meds. Follow the rehab group down to the gym. Keep from shitting on himself. The painful process of pulling on socks. Trying to find the humor in the way that the human foot was such a stubborn hook that he fought to get his underwear off it. He didn't want to think beyond that, yet this killing wouldn't let him alone. He sipped and put the coffee down again. His hands were shaking. He hadn't touched caffeine since before surgery. He concealed the shaking by wheeling himself.

"Hey," Mueller said, following. "Want to go up to the solarium? That would be nice. See downtown probably, all the leaves are off the trees."

They crowded into an elevator with people in green and purple scrub clothes. They looked comfortable. They could stand. Will was now looking at the world from most people's belly buttons, something new to a man who stood—*stood!*—six feet, two inches. They rode up two floors and the car emptied out. But when Mueller started to step out, Will stopped him.

"Let's go to the basement."

Mueller looked at him oddly and they rode down in silence.

Will led the way when the doors opened.

"What are we doing down here?"

Will ignored the question, hearing Mueller's shoes click behind him. The hallway was dim and deserted. Only one overhead lighting fixture was illuminated. Taking his bearings, he tried to remember how far the doctor's office was from the elevator. Every few feet, dark corridors intersected the hallway. The beds and equipment parked against the wall looked ancient.

"It was down here," Will said.

"What are you doing?"

"Remembering."

The office was easy to find, about a hundred feet from the elevators and near two fire doors that could be shut, closing off the main corridor. The police seal was still on the door. The fluorescent lights were at least twenty feet away.

"He liked to strike in the dark," Will said. "He would unscrew porch lights so women couldn't see who was on the front step. He was thinking tactically."

"Are you nuts? The Mount Adams Slasher? Craig Factor was convicted righteously."

"Factor didn't do it."

"You and Dodds had him dead to rights. That was a totally clean case."

Now Mueller was really itching, left hand scratching the back of his right. Will studied the floor, wondering if any bloody footprints had been left. The Slasher had an amazing ability to avoid leaving shoeprints on a bloody crime scene.

"Dodds and the DA pushed the evidence. You know that."

"You can't argue with DNA."

A sudden rattle came from the hallway, as if a stretcher were being moved. Will strained to see, but nothing emerged into his line of sight and soon it was quiet again. He said, "Sure you can."

Mueller came around to face him, bent to his knees so their faces were on the same level. His cheeks were filling with blood.

"The Mount Adams Slasher terrorized this city for three months. Three women living alone were killed, including a cop's wife…"

"Ex-wife."

"There hasn't been a single case since you and Dodds arrested Factor."

Will pointed to the door, wincing as the pain coursed from his back to his upper arm. "Until last week."

Mueller laughed uncomfortably. "Come on, Borders. You want to go back and reopen the Cincinnati Strangler case, too?"

The Cincinnati Strangler had been in the mid-1960s. Homicide detectives still studied the case. Will wondered if Mueller was making fun of him. Mueller, who stood there, effortlessly shifting from one leg to the other in his impatience. Will was trapped in the wheelchair. He stared at his legs, useless in the sweatpants, feeling both heavy and light. He couldn't even stand. Not even for a moment.

"I'm not talking about ancient history, Steve. This is an open homicide. It happened right here. We owe it to that doctor and her family to pursue the truth."

"What are you saying?" Mueller's voice kicked up a notch. "Do you know what the chief would say if I even raised this? It had to be Factor. What other theory works?"

"Bud Chambers."

"No, don't. Don't you dare." Mueller backed away a step as if Will had pulled a knife on him.

"Damn it, Steve. Don't let Dodds piss this away. This homicide is the same MO as Mount Adams. It's him. Do they have a time of death?"

"No…I don't know. Look, Will, I don't know how to tell you this, but you're not going to be a cop now. Take the disability. You can get a good partial pension. My gosh, your wife must make a ton with the bank now. You don't need the money. Quit driving yourself nuts over this. Think of all the Reds games you can go to."

"You can break that seal and get in that office," Will said. "I want to look around. And I want to see the murder book. Nothing is right about this case."

"Stop."

"Just call security and let's look inside."

Mueller smiled and shook his head. "You were a good detective, Will, but never very smart about your career. I was worried about that when you transferred over. Big-time homicide copper having to lower himself to investigate chickenshit complaints against officers. I was afraid you'd always want to go for the big cases, even when you didn't belong there. You didn't disappoint me. The Reading incident, remember?"

"The city was in the wrong. I just went where the facts pointed."

"And you didn't mind pissing on a city council member to get there."

"Important people can still be asked questions. A good internal affairs investigator has to be able to do that. And he has to be able to disagree with his superiors."

"In your world, but it's not too smart. You can make enemies in high places. Most cases in our division involve pleasing our stakeholders."

"Our 'stakeholders,' as you call them, are the citizens of Cincinnati, not the brass."

"Sure," Mueller said. "That's what I meant. What I mean is you need to be smart this time, stop driving yourself nuts over some case that's just a lot of smoke."

"In the middle of the smoke lies the crime." Will wanted to slap himself. Now he was making up his own Muellerisms.

Mueller took on an uncharacteristically thoughtful expression. "You're not tracking, Will. I never wanted you on this detail. Homicide guys always think they're better. Never knew why you left a prestige detail like homicide to come here. But we had a new chief and I did what he told me."

"Does the chief know you're trying to retire me?"

Mueller gave an exasperated sigh. "Has the chief been to visit? It's time to take you back to your room."

Will felt enveloped in sudden exhaustion and pain. His back muscles rippled with spasms. He stared down the hallway, to where the floor and walls disappeared into the silent gloom. The black void seemed to erase any sense of the busy, noisy hospital above them. He imagined someone emerging from it any second, someone he and Dodds had missed before.

Chapter Five

The extra security guards lasted two days, then they were gone. Cheryl Beth was surprised they had lasted that long. The chaos that was Cincinnati Memorial Hospital was always overwhelmed by fresh chaos, fresh crisis, fresh calamity, like rolling waves. Usually she tap-danced her way through it. It was harder in the days after Dr. Christine Lustig's murder. The extra guards had been replaced, as if by memo, by holiday bunting hanging from the nurses' stations. Yet shock and dread were as present inside the hospital as the late autumn days outside, the cold December wind that whipped against her coat. The hospital held a memorial service for Christine Lustig in the cafeteria. The newspapers seemed to forget about the killing, too: fresh, terrible trouble in the ghetto just down the hill. Yet beyond that, the city was bundled up happy and waiting for Christmas. There had been no snow and little rain, allowing the magical heartland twilights that Cheryl Beth loved, where the black tree limbs stood out against the infinite cobalt blue horizon. This year she had barely noticed. She had barely slept.

Three days after finding the body, Cheryl Beth began her day as usual, in the tiny office she shared with two other nurses. Office space was always valuable, and this was the sixth shabby closet she had been crammed into in six years. Only the neurosurgery unit and administration had the nice offices. It was an unusual day, because there were no fires to put out, even after two days off. So she looked through the overnight referrals and quickly checked her e-mail. Today she wanted to get five patients off IVs and onto oral pain meds. She never stayed in the office long.

"I can't believe Lustig would be in that office at that time of night," Lisa said. Lisa was a nurse practitioner in charge of recruiting neuro-ICU nurses. She looked around thirty-five, but Cheryl Beth knew she was ten years older. She was slender with long, straight auburn hair, a pretty midwestern face, and the body of the high school cross-country runner she had been. Her husband worked for DHL at the airport but traded stocks online, convinced he would make a fortune from the Internet boom. Lisa was fascinated by the murder and kept up a running commentary, picking up the thread seamlessly the next day from where she had last left it.

"Have you been digging through my desk?" The drawers were unlocked—Cheryl Beth never left her desk unlocked. The files on top of the desk were out of order. The normally neat desk drawers had been pawed through, though nothing seemed to be missing.

"No."

"Somebody unlocked my desk."

"Maybe you forgot to lock it. Anyway, there's no way I would even go in that basement at that time of night without security with me. This place is nuts. We don't even know who's in these hallways half the time. Maybe it was Crazy Lennie who did it?"

Crazy Lennie was a homeless man who sometimes wandered the hospital. Security would throw him out. He would come back, sometimes when he was brought to the emergency department for his assorted ailments. Lennie was distinguished from the many lost souls that frequented the hospital by his passion to defecate in the hallways, and not in a corner but usually right in the middle of the floor. It had entered the hospital vocabulary: a pile in the hallway was a "Lennie" or, "Somebody Lennied outside the ICU."

"Lennie's harmless."

Lisa looked over her glasses. "Nobody's harmless, Cheryl Beth. Speaking of which, have you run into our newest urologist?"

"Oh, no."

Lisa was the keeper of the FDN List, as in Funny Doctors' Names List.

"Dr. Small! Get it?" She squealed with laughter. "He had a patient come into the ER with a hard-on he'd had for six hours. And the guy's name was Dick Wood!"

"He did not."

"Well, his name really is Dr. Small."

The FDN List, lovingly maintained over the years, included Dr. Aikenhead, Dr. Dingfelter, Dr. Buderlicker, Dr. Hyman Pleasure, Dr. Pine-Coffin (a pathologist), and Dr. Cutter (a surgeon). There was Dr. Payne, of course, and Dr. Hurt.

"So back to Christine. My God! How much had she bled out?"

"Lisa, my head is about to explode right this minute." The page from neuro-rehab rescued her. Everybody wanted to talk about the murder. Nobody else had been in that office, bloody and useless, as Christine lay dead.

"At least I may not have to go to any more of those goddamn SoftChartZ meetings," Lisa went on.

"Lisa!"

"You know how they spell it? SoftChartZ all run together, with a capital Z on the end. Isn't that cutting edge? Christine was really into it, but she could be such a pain in the ass. Well, she could! Gag, these endless meetings, and where's the 'totally digital work environment'? Lord knows how much we're paying these smart young things from Silicon Valley to do it. They look at me like I'm an idiot. The lead guy, Josh, he's twenty-six and rich—can you believe it? I think Christine's slept with him."

"I'm leaving…"

"You know how she was. And he's cute. Anyway, young and strong, go all night. Change your life, Cheryl Beth. You ought to get one of those."

Cheryl Beth heard the yelling, a man's voice spewing profanities. A cluster of nurses stood outside a door. As she approached, a compact young Indian doctor came into the hall, handing Cheryl Beth a patient chart.

"Maybe you can deal with him," she said. "He was in a motorcycle accident."

"Quad?" Cheryl Beth asked.

"His legs are probably lost to him," the doctor said.

She quickly scanned the chart amid the verbal barrage coming from the room. Then she carefully stepped inside.

"What the fuck do you want?" The first thing she noticed was the swastika tattoo that snaked around the man's neck. Involuntarily, she thought of the wound on Christine's neck. "Bitch!" His scream brought her back to reality. It came from a florid-faced young man encased in bushy red hair and beard.

"I'm hurting here, and nobody will help me."

"We're going to help you," Cheryl Beth said softly.

"I want it now!"

"Take it easy. My name is Cheryl Beth Wilson, and I'm a pain management nurse. Your doctor wanted me to see if we could control your pain better." She read the chart but already knew she was dealing with an addict. Even before his accident, he had likely been on high levels of OxyContin. So his body wasn't responding to the level of painkillers he was now receiving.

"Tell me what kinds of pain drugs you were on before the accident."

"Nothin'!" His eyes bulged.

"I'm not the cops. I'm the pain nurse. I need to see what kind of dosage…"

"Fuck you!"

She sighed. "Mr. Baker, tell me about your pain. Tell me how much it hurts, on a scale of one to ten, with ten being the…"

"Fuck you!" His head rocked violently around the pillows, his arms waving, tossing IV lines around like so much fishing tackle. The rest of his body lay like concrete.

"Stop!" Cheryl Beth yelled, dropping the chart on the bed and clenching her hands. The man was suddenly silent.

"You want to help us help you? Or you want trouble?" She waved her arm, beckoning him out of the bed. "You think you're such a bad-ass! Get out of that bed. I'm not afraid of you!"

The man looked at her with wide eyes.

"Come on. Let's get it on."

"I... I..."

"Get out of that bed. I'll fight you."

"It's okay, lady," he said. "Just take it easy."

The doctor was smiling when Cheryl Beth left, but just beyond the smile stood the black detective, Dodds. He intercepted her and they walked together toward the elevators.

"That's quite a bedside manner, Cheryl."

"Cheryl Beth," she corrected. "That was an exception. I prefer to make people laugh."

"Mmmm. So why do they call you the pain nurse, Cheryl Beth?"

"I'm the pain in the butt nurse, probably." She tried a smile, feeling so uncomfortable around him. His face was hard. "It's pain management nurse. That's my specialty."

"So you have easy access to drugs for yourself."

Cheryl Beth laughed at him. "Alcohol is my drug of choice."

He steered her into an empty section of the large waiting room. He sat heavily and she followed. "I want to go over your timetable Friday night again."

"We've done this twice before."

"Humor me," Dodds said, opening a notebook. "We have a killer at large." Again Cheryl Beth told how she had returned to the hospital for a patient and had then been summoned to Christine's office.

"And she called you?"

"She left a message at the nurses' station."

"Why do that? Why not page you?"

Cheryl Beth shrugged and shook her head.

"Did you keep the message?"

A flustered sigh escaped her mouth. "No."

She watched him closely but he said nothing. He regarded her with large brown eyes. Finally, "Why would you go into pain management? Do you have a drug problem? Does this make it easier to score?"

"No." She tried to keep her face calm. She knew he was trying to rattle her. "I have a great record. I've never had drugs go missing. You can check it."

After a long pause, Dodds said, "I have." He raised his head and studied her anew. "Why do you wear a lab coat?"

"I get cold, and I need all the pockets."

He fell silent for what seemed like an hour. Maybe it was five minutes. He just watched her, his eyes not quite kindly, not quite hostile. If he talked again it would seem as surprising and sudden as a stopped heart that suddenly began beating on its own.

Finally: "And it gets you more respect?"

"The coat? Maybe. I guess."

He made a humming sound, looking at her for a long time before returning to the notebook and leafing through it. She sat back in the seat, then squirmed forward again.

"Were you wearing a lab coat on Friday night?"

She nodded.

"Is this it?"

"No." She explained that lab coat had been smeared with blood and she threw it away in a hazmat container.

"Why would you do that?" His voice was even, but his eyes were large with suspicion. This was a man who did most of his talking through his eyes.

"It was ruined. What should I have done with it?"

"It was evidence. You should have given it to the police."

"It would have been nice if the police had told me that." She heard the defensiveness and stress in her voice.

He made notes—an impossibly long paragraph—and sat back studying her. He spoke after a long pause.

"So how long have you been seeing Dr. Nagle?"

"Damn it." She spoke quietly but vehemently. "Who told…?" She stopped herself, feeling small and off balance. "We saw each other for about a year."

"While he was married?"

"He was separated." She sighed. "Part of that time, but, shit, sure, he was married."

"Did Dr. Lustig know?"

She became only gradually aware of the avalanche bearing down on her. "Am I a suspect?"

Dodds pursed his lips. "I can declare you a person of interest. That's not quite a suspect."

"Holy crap," Cheryl Beth said. "You can't think I could…? I found her!"

"Dr. Nagle told us that you and he had an affair."

"Why isn't he a suspect? Because he's a hotshot neurosurgeon?"

"You might both be suspects," Dodds said.

"Look, Detective." Cheryl Beth touched his arm and drew back. "This isn't what you think…Hell, I know you hear that all the time. You're used to people lying to you. Me, too. It goes with my job. I broke it off with Gary three months ago. Christine probably knew about it for a long time. But we weren't enemies."

Dodds again let the conversation fall into another canyon of silence. He hadn't mentioned that Cheryl Beth and Christine had been at a bar together that night. That meant Gary hadn't told him, despite the threat he had made at her house. Why? She realized she didn't know Gary at all. Indeed, she was now afraid of him.

"How would you characterize your relationship with Dr. Lustig?"

Cheryl Beth was aware of how fast her breaths were coming. "Coworkers. Colleagues." She nervously added, "In another life maybe we could have been friends."

"Really?" Dodds' comeback was sudden. "Funny way to treat a friend."

Chapter Six

Dodds clapped his large hands on the tops of his thighs and stood, leaving the nurse sitting, staring at his back as he did his heavy stomp away. Then she put her head in her hands, just for a few seconds, before sweeping back her light-brown hair, adjusting her white coat, and at a brisk pace joining the flow of people headed into the main part of the hospital. She had large, attractive eyes and moved with an intuitive grace. Will watched from his wheelchair and turned to follow Dodds.

Two tough-looking, muscular black men stood outside one of the rooms, arguing with a uniformed officer. Leaving, they nearly ran into Dodds. They wore hoodies and very baggy pants, the mainstream gang attire that Will's own son favored. The shorter of the two chewed on a toothpick. They wore blue do-rags, signs that they were Mount Auburn Boyz, friends of the kid shot the night the doctor was murdered. Now he lay in that hospital room, three doors down from Will, unable to move his arms or legs. Dodds knew they were "representing" with hand signals and slang, but merely gave a look of bored contempt. They gave him the typical dead-eyes expression, before sidling down the hall in an oscillating pimp roll, sweeping past Will. "Monkey five-oh," one of the bangers said to the other.

"What's the deal?" Will asked the uniform, a petite young woman who recognized him. "I thought he tried to shoot a cop. Why isn't he in the jail unit?"

"They haven't charged him. He was just in the crossfire, and now maybe he'll tell us who the real bad guys were. I'm just here to make sure some of his buddies don't try to keep that from happening."

Will nodded and wheeled to watch Dodds. He knew that Dodds liked to walk a crime scene, sometimes repeatedly, always slowly. Now the big man moved leisurely down the neuro-rehab unit. It might make no sense to an outsider, even to many cops. But Dodds always had his way of things. They had made a good team once, Dodds seeming plodding and distracted, Will garrulous and focused. That was part of Dodds' camouflage and also how his mind worked. He would have done his slow move with the nurse, with everyone he interviewed for this case. The long pauses between questions, only to pause an even longer time after the subject had answered. What could his silence mean, they wondered? Dodds was a master. So, too, with his "homicide stroll," as Will called it. Dodds would walk a scene, keeping his opinions to himself until later. It was interesting he was working alone on this case.

Will could still see Dodds walking that day in Mount Adams. Theresa Chambers had been discovered murdered in her house. Borders and Dodds, the primaries. She had been splayed on the floor, totally nude, with vicious slash marks on her arms, legs, face, breasts. It didn't take the medical examiner to know she had died from a deep cut to the throat, but that had only come after the other wounds had been delivered. Her ring finger had been cut off, probably as she had been dying. Her clothes had been neatly folded and there was no sign of a break-in. Will had watched from the porch as Dodds had ambled down the street, into the little sidewalk between the houses, back to the alley. Theresa Chambers, who had been separated from her husband, Bud Chambers, a Cincinnati cop, who had no alibi for that night. Theresa Chambers, who was the first. But they couldn't know that then. All Will knew on that first spring morning was that Dodds' homicide stroll had been especially unhurried.

Now Will watched as he followed the wall with his hand, seemingly absent-minded. Dodds hadn't seen him. There were enough people, enough wheelchairs and food carts and pieces of obscure medical equipment to give Will some concealment. Dodds opened an exit door and looked inside. He walked more quickly to where the ward connected with the main part of the hospital and did the same thing. This time, he didn't emerge from the exit and the door closed behind him.

Will realized he was now one floor above the old basement, where Dr. Christine Lustig had been killed.

The elevator emptied out on the first floor and Will rolled himself in alone. When the car settled at the basement level and the big doors opened, he was uncomfortably aware of its heavy sound, the light spilling out into the dim corridor. He quickly crossed into a shadow behind a large, unused linen cart. He waited for the doors to close and the elevator to resume its return journey up into the tower. Once again he was in the darkened basement corridor, its silence still profound. His hands felt for the rim of the wheels and he cautiously moved out on the old tile floor.

Dodds was coming toward him, suddenly illuminated in one of the few light fixtures that was working. Will felt his heart rate explode and he quickly backed up behind the cart. He spun around, feeling a sharp eruption in his back, and pushed the chair into a side hallway. The pain consumed him, wrapped around his back and ribs, penetrating up into his chest. A phosphorescent glow came to the edge of his vision. He bit the fleshy part of his hand to keep from crying out, as the pain seared out from his middle back down to his hips. He was in complete darkness. This corridor might end suddenly or it might have held the entire membership of the Mount Auburn Boyz. The only sound was a distant mechanical throb. He felt ahead of him into black, empty air, then crept forward again. The cold, smooth wall gave way and he cautiously backed into yet another space. There was nothing to do but wait. Dodds' distinctive tread passed in the main hallway. The small beam of his flashlight played in front of Will's feet. Will hoped he couldn't find a way to turn on more lights. Another minute passed and he heard Dodds walking in the other direction.

Will slowly emerged into the main corridor and followed Dodds at a distance, making sure to stay short of the overhead light. The big man paused, suddenly hunching his back. He hummed an incomprehensible tune. It was amazing how little he had changed since they had worked together. Then Dodds walked more purposefully. At the door of Lustig's office, he produced a small knife and slit the evidence seal on the door. The door unlocked loudly and then light fell out onto the hallway tiles. Will rolled quickly through the brief lighted zone and returned to darkness. Just a few feet from the door, he pulled in behind another large cart, concealing himself in its shadow. The oppressive absence of sound settled over the hallway. He imagined Dodds standing in the doorway, then in a far corner, finally behind the desk, imagining what the killer and victim saw. Take your time, Will thought. He struggled to make his body relax enough that the hurting might ease.

Maybe ten minutes went by before Dodds' footsteps resumed. Will looked around his barricade and saw Dodds' massive back walking farther down the hall. It was the same direction Will had been wheeled that night, to his MRI. He made a quick, reckless calculus and wheeled himself into the office. The wide doorway opened in and easily accommodated the wheelchair. But inside, the office was just a confined box. This was a doctor's office? Who had she pissed off? Hearing Dodds returning, he tried to back himself behind the open door. The wheelchair pivoted awkwardly, too slowly. The noise of rubber wheels against the polished floor barked out too loudly. Then he was against the wall, trying to slow his breathing. He was sure those panicky breaths could be heard as far as downtown. Leaning forward, he saw that Dodds' notebook sat invitingly on the doctor's desk.

Will took a baby's breath when Dodds returned to the threshold, then stepped inside. Will sat up straighter, as if he could somehow reduce the profile of the wheelchair. Only the bulk of the open office door separated the two men. The sound of a chair. Dodds was sitting, probably making some notes. Will felt his bladder starting to grow full. How could Dodds not see him there, barely six feet away? The distinctive high-pitched wheeze of Dodds came from the desk. Will made himself look around. The office was square-shaped, with another door that probably held a closet. A metal desk cubicle faced the far wall. Was Christine Lustig facing away from the door when the attacker entered? Did the murderer even take her by surprise or somehow win her confidence?

Then the chair creaked and Dodds crossed the room, turned out the lights and closed the door. Will was in darkness again, realizing that he didn't even know if the door might have a deadbolt that could keep him from getting out again. Will had never been fearful or superstitious on murder scenes, but something about this was different. The darkness seemed almost to have mass and substance and to be narrowing in on him. He felt along the wall, and when it seemed safe, turned on the lights. Yet the sinister presence still weighed against him. He shook his head, adding to his pain, but somehow snapping the spell.

The room wasn't much. It looked as if it might have been an exam room once, and it still had a wall of white cabinets and shelves, a sink, and a red box on the wall labeled "biohazard," presumably for disposing of used needles. Otherwise, a desk, chair, and filing cabinet had been added. He looked more closely. The phone cord had been pulled from the wall. It now sat wound up on the top of the doctor's desk. The Slasher always disabled the phones. A Tiffany lamp sat unmolested on the desk. It would have seemed a natural casualty of a fight to the death, even by a woman who was paralyzed by fear. Indeed, the main evidence of trouble was dried blood on the Persian rug before the desk, the tile floor, the drawers of the desk, the wall.

That had been the case with every Slasher scene: the most violent crime, accompanied by little or no damage to the physical environment aside from the blood. The exception was Theresa Chambers, who was clutching a framed photograph of her daughter, the glass shattered into a spider's web. Had the Slasher taken his victims by such surprise, or had he somehow put them at ease? The arrest and conviction of Craig Factor had never really provided an answer. Aside from the semen evidence, they had found nothing linking him to the crime scenes, especially any of the missing ring fingers.

The walls told him that Christine Lustig was a graduate of Tufts Medical School and a fellow in the American College of Surgeons. The desk had a computer and beside it, thick note-books labeled Med-Interface and SoftChartZ. What was her job? Did she see patients? Will used a tissue to shield his hand as he opened desk drawers. Pens, pencils, more files with obscure names. There were no family photographs. He rolled around, seeing the office from the desk's perspective. How could you sit with your back to that empty hallway late at night? The news-paper story said a nurse had discovered the doctor's body, so the door might have been open. There was no sign of a broken lock. The Slasher never broke a lock, a door, or a window. Will pushed the drawer back in and by habit reached under it, sweeping the metal with his hand.

He felt duct tape and then the unmistakable outlines of a knife.

"Damn."

The doorknob shook. Will started and drew back from his discovery. He backed the wheelchair against the wall, hoping it would be in the safe place when the door opened. But no key was inserted into the lock. The knob rattled again and the door snapped against the frame from sudden pressure. Slap! The door was again pushed hard and the lock was rattled impatiently. Even when the sounds stopped, it was a long time before Will turned off the lights and ventured into the corridor.

Chapter Seven

Cheryl Beth answered the phone and could hear screaming in the background. It was the sound of the newest consult. It was going to be a bad day.

She had hurried to recovery, to a patient with pancreatic cancer who had undergone a Whipple Procedure. It basically involves lopping off part of the pancreas and rebuilding the digestive tract. It's difficult surgery, almost, but not quite, being made obsolete. The aftermath can be pain incarnate: evil, damnation, omnipotent. It reminded Cheryl Beth of the hell-fire Baptist sermons she had heard as a girl growing up in the little Kentucky railroad town of Corbin. This was pain as the Lake of Fire, and it was almost as hard to knock down as bargaining on judgment day.

It was engulfing a woman so small and eaten up that it seemed barely possible she had the organs remaining to destroy or the breath to scream so loudly.

"I didn't know what to do. I was afraid to violate the orders." A young nurse in purple scrubs spoke with a voice on the edge of panic.

"You're not violating anything, Megan," Cheryl Beth said, getting the woman's name off her name badge. Barely under her breath, she said, "I don't know why people want to cover their ass when a patient is suffering. And does the damned anesthesiologist care?" Megan stared at the floor.

Tamping down her fury, Cheryl Beth did a quick workup. The paperwork was a mess, as usual. It appeared that she had been undermedicated by one of the surgical residents. She touched the old woman, her skin like that covering a chicken wing after a week in the refrigerator. "I'm going to help you."

"I just want to die," she wailed.

Cheryl Beth's brain and hands were on automatic now, a coordination born from years of training and experience.

"What are you doing?" the young nurse asked.

"Rescue dose," Cheryl Beth said. She injected morphine and Ativan through a cap in the IV line. They rushed into the vein that would bear them like a liquid savior. She stroked the woman's hand and the screaming subsided. Her pager vibrated again, even as she wrote out extensive orders for the pain meds to follow. She looked at it and decided it could wait. Around her, the general surgery recovery room looked like much of Cincinnati Memorial, a surreal combination of modern medical technology haphazardly fitted into rooms that had been built during the Great Depression and left to slowly rot ever since. She noticed more than usual the attendant fleeting odors of disinfectant, feces, vomit, and various medicines. They seemed colored with a brooding, claustrophobic tint in the aftermath of Christine's murder.

She felt herself silently mouthing the word: Murder. She stopped when she was aware that Megan was hovering nearby. Cheryl Beth instructed her on monitoring and administering the morphine and the Ativan, an antianxiety drug, and regulating the PCA pump that would prevent an overdose.

"Thank you so much." She seemed so young. Was I ever that young? Cheryl Beth asked herself. She also knew how difficult it was to recruit nurses, especially at Memorial. She wrote out the new orders—she always covered her backside—and would get Dr. Ames to sign them.

"No worries," Cheryl Beth responded, smiling at her and handing back the chart.

"I just didn't know how her doc would react to changing her dose."

Well, thought Cheryl Beth, at least she was young enough to be honest. It was the usual chickenshit thing that left patients to suffer. Docs could be inattentive or stubborn, and nurses were afraid to challenge them. Cheryl Beth had never been that way. In this case, she had an added measure of protection because the patient's main surgeon was one of her fans.

"Do your thing and sign my name," the surgeon, Dr. Brice, had said years ago. "You know more about this than most docs."

Cheryl Beth was in the hallway outside recovery, slathering hand sanitizer into her palms, when the page repeated.

In five minutes she was in the spacious, wood-paneled administrative offices. The outer hallways were lined with oil paintings of eighty years of hospital presidents. Not surprisingly, Stephanie Ott made her wait twenty minutes in her outer office. She made conversation with Ott's secretary, Bridget, a compact, formidable woman with slate gray hair. She intimidated most of the staff, but Cheryl Beth got along fine with her. Halfway into a discussion about artificial Christmas trees, the door to Stephanie Ott's office swooshed open and a compact young man strode out. He couldn't have been more than thirty, with fashionably punked-up blond hair and a movie star tan on a face most women would have found cute. He wore black jeans and a French blue dress shirt, open at the collar. His fists were clenched and he stared straight ahead, his mouth set at an angry angle.

"Oh, joy," Cheryl Beth said. "I'm next."

"He's a prima donna," Bridget said after he had gone. "He's from California."

"He didn't look like he was from Cincinnati. I thought he might be Stephanie's son, he looks like such a kid."

Bridget looked over her reading glasses. "That kid is a multi-millionaire and the chief executive of a company in Silicon

Valley." The sarcasm in her voice was barely concealed. "He's twenty-six."

Cheryl Beth cocked her head in disbelief.

"Oh, yes. Mister Josh Barnett, the chief executive officer of SoftChartZ. He started the company when he was a graduate student at Stanford. Promises to take the entire health-care industry and 'digitalize it.'" She made mocking quotation marks in the air with her fingers. Bridget could be fun if you got to know her. She added, "We're paying him $10 million, you know. I haven't had a raise in three years."

Cheryl Beth thought about what Lisa had said, but couldn't believe Christine Lustig could have slept with the man. She said, "So he was working with Christine."

Bridget let the statement hang just long enough for Stephanie Ott to open her office door and beckon Cheryl Beth inside.

Chapter Eight

There are two kinds of nurses: scrubs and suits. Stephanie Ott, RN, MSN, emphatically fell into the latter category. Stephanie was even wearing a suit that day. Combined with her short dark hair and angular features, the suit's red coat and shoulder pads gave her the appearance of a toy soldier, or, Cheryl Beth thought, a nutcracker.

Suits and scrubs. The best nursing administrators maintained the fine balance. Stephanie Ott, RN, MSN, seemed to have little interest in such esoterica. After five years as vice president for nursing, she had yet to visit many of the wards and departments at Cincinnati Memorial. Most of the nursing staff had never seen her outside the large meetings or video-casts that usually announced an unpleasant new policy or staff cutback. She probably hadn't touched a patient in years, but her ability to reach out with vengeance was legend. One victim was Cheryl Beth's friend Denise, who had kicked an obnoxious film crew out of the ICU. Denise was one of the best ICU nurses Cheryl Beth had known, and she couldn't have cared less that the crew worked for an advertising agency owned by a member of the hospital's board. Stephanie Ott cared, and the next day Denise was banished to the overnight shift on a patient floor.

Now Ott was leaning against an L-shaped desk covered with thick reports constrained by colored binders, blue, taupe, yellow, orange, sage. A small Christmas tree anchored one corner of the desk. As Cheryl Beth entered, she stood, crossed the carpet and took both her hands, leading her to a nearby sofa.

"How are you holding up?"

"I'm okay. It's been a rough few days." She sat and relaxed a bit.

"I can only imagine." Ott sat precisely in a nearby armchair. "Finding her that way."

Cheryl Beth's native volubility deserted her. That had been happening a lot the past week.

"What in the world were you doing down there, at that time of night?"

The question was in the same conversational tone, but Cheryl Beth's initial caution returned. She explained about Christine's message, told more than was needed about the deserted hallway, the bloody body, the phone ripped from the wall and the inability of cell phone signals to escape that damned basement. Ott continued to look at her, but her attention shut off, as if on a timer. Cheryl Beth shut up.

"I got a call this morning from one of our board members. She told me that a friend of hers was brought here from an auto accident, and the emergency room had run out of stretchers." A harder tone slowly took over her voice. "Ran...out...of...stretchers. Can you believe it?" Cheryl Beth nodded sympathetically. The ER often ran out of stretchers. Memorial was the primary caregiver for thousands of low-income and indigent people. It also operated a Level One trauma center. The hospital had been through years of budget cuts that had not just made it hard to buy new equipment, but had even reduced the nursing staff. Cheryl Beth could see it on nearly every floor, the nurses overworked, understaffed. It was a wonder they did so well.

"This hospital is in trouble," Stephanie said. "I'm told this used to be the top hospital in the city, the place where the rich came for treatment. Now we have a great neuro-science unit. We're still a teaching hospital. Then, well, what's left is pretty much a welfare hospital." Her eyes narrowed. "There's talk of merging with University Hospital, if they would have us. Or simply shutting down. Do you know that?"

She didn't wait for an answer. Cheryl Beth, of course, had heard all the gossip. She also had been approached several times about joining University Hospital, which made her even less afraid of Stephanie Ott.

The suit kept talking. "It doesn't help that the black ministers have been holding a vigil outside every night this week, because of that boy, I mean, young man, whom the police shot. Do we need this kind of trouble? Why are they singling us out? I just don't understand this sense of grievance."

"Well, I'm not black," Cheryl Beth said. "So I can't see it through their eyes. There's a lot of hurt…" She stopped herself.

Ott looked at Cheryl Beth as if she should say something, to make sense of all this…to take the blame? She said, "Why are you telling me this, Stephanie?"

The woman stood and strode to her window, staring out at the black scrimshaw of winter trees. "I've always had my reservations about you. You like to make your own rules."

"I can play well with others," Cheryl Beth said lightly.

"You didn't want to stay on the pain management committee…"

"I just thought I could use those eight hours a week to be helping people."

"Yes, well. We'd all like to stay in our comfort zones." She turned back and stared at Cheryl Beth. "You do things you shouldn't. Doctors complain."

"Who? What?" Cheryl Beth demanded, unable to control her temper. "I work directly for Dr. Ames and Dr. Carpenter. I'm certified with advanced practice credentials." Just like her grandmother, she talked, shouted, with her hands. "Docs sign off on my orders. I work with them. My record is totally clean. The only ones who complain are the same bastards who say 'pain isn't an emergency' and let their patients hurt. They say, 'This namby-pamby patient's still moaning seven days after surgery and needs to get a grip.' And too many nurses are terrified to say anything about it. That's not me." She made herself calm down and put her hands obediently in her lap.

Ott was nearly shaking with anger. She took several deep breaths, sat at her desk, and rearranged a pile of papers. Her head shook fiercely. "My God, Cheryl Beth, what were you thinking?"

"What?"

"You're involved in a homicide investigation. You have involved this hospital in a homicide investigation."

"I found her," Cheryl Beth said heatedly. "She was murdered here."

"That's not what Detective Dodds tells me. They are looking at you, Cheryl Beth. You. And to have become romantically involved with Dr. Nagle. That's terribly unprofessional. Just… unconscionable."

Cheryl Beth felt a burning on her ears and cheeks. She said nothing.

"Why did you go to Dr. Lustig's office that night?"

"She left word for me. I told you. She asked me to come down."

"In the middle of the night?" Ott's voice rose. "So you were fighting with her over Dr. Nagle?"

"No. That was over a long time ago."

"So what did she want?"

Cheryl Beth shook her head. "I honestly don't know."

"Dr. Lustig was a key member of our technology committee. She was working directly with SoftChartZ to bring this hospital into the twenty-first century. Now she's gone."

Cheryl Beth made herself say nothing. Any words bubbling up inside her would only make things worse, especially the ones that were careening around in her head at that moment.

Stephanie stared at her. "You have charmed a lot of the physicians here. I don't get it, but that has given you tremendous freedom. But you have never charmed me. You're a bull in a china shop with some powerful protectors. I'm going to be watching you even more closely." Her shoulder pads quivered. "And if this matter is not resolved quickly… I will not tolerate this." She leaned forward. "You are not to discuss Dr. Lustig's murder with anyone: colleagues, patients, and absolutely not the press."

Stephanie Ott turned to her computer screen and began furiously typing. "You can leave now."

Cheryl Beth left the office and walked directly to the parking garage, barely containing her angry tears. God, she hated it when she cried. It made people think she was weak. Certain people. She had to get away from the hospital for a while. This, even though the work allowed her to momentarily forget Christine and the blood, that night in the basement, the yawning canyon in her life "before" and "after." When she was helping patients she could be herself again. She tried not to think how badly she wanted a glass of whiskey. Five minutes later, she was back home.

Cheryl Beth's small house backed up to a thick stand of trees. Beyond that, a park fell off toward Over-the-Rhine and downtown. But the incline began in her driveway. Her old, wooden garage was lower than the house, the result being that in the cold months she often parked nearer to the street, to keep from being stranded in the garage by an overnight ice or snowstorm. An oak stood in her small backyard, its branches overhanging the old garage. The location made her uneasy late at night. The park attracted unsavory characters, so even before Christine's murder Cheryl Beth had avoided the tree line after dark.

So it had been days since she had pulled down the driveway. She went all the way down today and walked back through the cold, crisp air. She looked back at the house and felt centered again. She would get through this, through the horrible discovery in the basement of the hospital, and through the debris of her breakup with Gary. She would live in this house, enjoy her music and her gardening, watch the tiny perfection of birds from her porch, forget about men. No more blind dates set up by friends. No more waiting for the phone to ring. No married men, ever.

She walked up the incline of the drive, admiring the flower beds that she had cleared of leaves. Even on her small city lot, she could fill dozens of bags with leaves every fall. The flower beds were the last touch. At least one thing in her life was neat, she thought, even as Stephanie Ott's words burned inside her head. Maybe next year she would plant gardenias.

The indentations on the ground. She noticed them only on a second look, the realization that comes when the brain processes a mundane scene, one noticed a thousand times before, but this time something is subtly different.

She walked slowly back to the flower beds that stood beside the house. It was unmistakable, two footprints dug deep into the soil, just behind the hedge that stood at the corner of the house. They might as well have been the first footprints on Mars for the primal force with which they hit her. They were large footprints, fresh since she had cleared out the leaves. Someone had been standing there, easily concealed by the hedge. Since Christine had been murdered. Standing there where he could look through the large bay window into her living room.

Chapter Nine

The city rolled out beneath his feet, the bare, black trees thick on hills tumbling down to the Ohio River, the sky a dirty white blanket. Landmarks sprouted comfortingly: Carew Tower, a baby Rockefeller Center, dominating the jewel box of downtown sky-scrapers, just as it had all of Will's life, all his parents' lives. The massive deco band-shell shape of Union Terminal stood against the Western Hills. The tower of St. Peter-in-Chains Cathedral. Closer in, the huge windows of the hospital solarium gave him a view of the crescent of tilting roofs of 150-year-old row houses, punctuated by all manner of church steeples. The vast rail yards connecting north and south ran along Mill Creek, and, beyond them, stood the old neighborhoods of the Germans and the Appalachian briars. All the green was drained out of the hills.

Down the hill was Over-the-Rhine, the old immigrant German neighborhood. The Germans were long gone and it was one of the toughest ghettos in the Midwest, a fact barely belied by its impressive architecture and dense, mystical streets. Many of the buildings had been left to rot and drug dealers ran the street corners. The mentally ill homeless roamed the sidewalks and camped in decaying Italianate landmarks. Years before, the city had stowed most of the social services in OTR. Tote up all the calls, all the cases, and Will had spent years of his career there. Main Street and a few other places were being gentrified and celebrated in the newspapers. Soon all those grand old row houses would be restored and gleaming, they said. But Will knew something the white chamber of commerce types didn't: OTR was defiantly black territory. Lots of hardcore Over-the-Rhine residents regarded the renovations and teardowns and Saturday night bar traffic by the westside white kids as an invasion. Cross Central Parkway south and you were in the white territory of downtown. But the north side of Central Parkway was an invisible boundary.

Cincinnati was good at boundaries. Interstate 75 was the Sauerkraut Curtain: to the west lay Price Hill and, beyond, the neat houses to which the German families had moved in the 1930s and 1940s as they grew more prosperous. East, beyond downtown, ranged the once-grand neighborhoods of Mount Auburn and Walnut Hills, now decrepit and dangerous. Once-grand estates had been subdivided into a dozen rat-infested apartments, and the teenagers carried guns like white kids carried cell phones. Then, another boundary, and you slipped into the leafy affluence of the old gentry in Hyde Park and Mount Lookout and Indian Hill. It was a nice polite midwestern city on the surface. Anybody who paid attention knew better. Neighborhood was identity, and some of the neighborhoods were lethal.

The leaves were all gone. Nothing could conceal Cincinnati: half its population decamped for the suburbs or the Sunbelt, leaving lovely old buildings and trees that had lost their leaves. His best friend from high school had left last year to sell houses in Arizona. The stubborn ones stayed and loved the city. Sometimes he felt that Cincinnati was a museum that was building new stadiums, a torn and wounded city without even knowing it, old money and denial being the camouflage, the best pain drug. Will knew better. Every place he looked he remembered trouble. It was the cop's lot. In college, he had taken a course on urban planning where the books would inevitably talk about this or that city as a "contradiction." Cincinnati was different. It was one reinforcement laid upon another, like the levees that held back the Ohio. Yet the great river still had its way.

Still, to Will's wonder Cincinnati looked luminous. Cindy looked luminous. *He was alive.* He had held her for long minutes.

She was still as slender as the first day he had met her, and he could still touch his elbows with his hands when he embraced her. She kept trying to pull away gently and he knew he must smell rank, but he just held on, feeling her sharp shoulder blades, the firm warmth of her breasts. For those minutes it all went away, the hospital, the killing, the pain.

She had pulled away before he could kiss her. Now he wheeled the chair around from the big windows and faced her. She wore her new charcoal gray suit. She had come straight from work. Her blue eyes that were startling in their intensity, and her chestnut hair looked the same color as when she was twenty-two, because or in spite of those expensive trips to the salon that they had once bickered over. So much money for such a severe hairstyle. He loved her hair natural, parted in the middle, and slightly wild as it hit her shoulders. She had said she couldn't look like a high school girl and be taken seriously at the bank. Just as she had said, after being promoted to senior vice president, that she would prefer to be known as Cynthia. He had squirmed when she wanted him to go with her to the symphony or the May Festival. Baseball bored her. It all seemed foolishly trivial now.

"You look beautiful."

She patted his knee. He couldn't really feel it.

"Cindy, you've got to get me out of here."

"What are you talking about?"

He knew he had blurted out the words with too much desperation. He looked down, slowed his breathing. He laughed and spoke in a slower voice.

"It's been nearly two weeks. Now-a-days they kick people out in two days after major surgery, but I'm stuck here." As he talked, he could hear the anxiety taking control again. "I feel like I'm in prison. I can't sleep. I can't get better."

He glanced up and she had an utterly foreign look on her face.

"Let me come home, please."

"You don't even like the house." She gave a light laugh. "'Out in Maineville, middle of nowhere.' That's what you used to say. What's the first thing you did when we separated? Moved back here to the city. Do you know how dangerous it is? A girl from our department had her purse snatched by a black kid just yesterday. I was walking down Court Street and there was this group of young, black men ahead of me. One of them bent down and a gun fell out of his pants! He just picked it up like nothing had happened. I dread the drive in here every day. But somehow you like it."

"I say a lot of silly things." Will smiled and looked down again, studying the bruises on his hands and forearms left by needles from IVs and blood tests. "My roommate needs constant care. Poor guy. They come in every hour to give him treatments. I can't sleep at night."

"Honey, I can't handle you. You can't even walk."

"I'm going to walk. I stood up today."

"That's wonderful!"

"They rolled me onto this platform with parallel bars, and one physical therapist on each end, and I was actually able to stand. I'd almost forgotten I was tall. I thought about the movie where the mad scientist says, *'It's alive!'*" She didn't laugh.

He sat there remembering the strange triumph, of doing something people do unthinkingly, the feeling of a stranger's legs lifting him, very tentatively, as if they could change their muscled minds at any moment and return to the stranger, leaving him with the dead weights attached to his torso and the long fall to the floor.

"You're doing great," she said, not meeting his eyes. Her smile didn't seem genuine. He used to kid her and call it her "sales smile" for the bank. Then even the sales smile vanished. "Julius came to see me today. At the bank. He said you're trying to investigate the murder of that doctor."

"Did Dodds tell you that he missed the knife that was hidden in her office? Some well-meaning, hospitalized cop guided him to it. He might have found it the first time if he'd looked a little harder."

She didn't meet his smile. Only he thought it was amusing that he had beaten the legendary J. J. Dodds at the game, and he was still a patient. He spoke in a serious voice.

"Cindy, the knife matters. That's the same MO as the Slasher. He would clean the weapon and hide it. We never told the media about that."

"Will…"

"This guy also cut off her ring finger, just like the Slasher. Nobody knew that but the killer and the cops. Don't you see, Cindy? It's the same guy."

"Will! This is not your problem!" She shouted a whisper, then looked around to see if anyone noticed. They were nearly alone. Across the room an old woman wheeled an old man. He had braces on his legs and looked miserable. He had once been young and virile. He had walked fast and made love to the young girl who was now old, too.

Will looked back over his shoulder at the dense cluster of buildings on Mount Adams, rising just east of downtown. Even from the solarium he could pick out the row house where Theresa Chambers had been slaughtered. When he turned back, Cindy had her arms crossed.

"I used to ask you not to tell me about your job." Her voice was severe, impersonal, as if she were talking to one of her employees.

"And I didn't." Will felt anger replacing his anxious fever to get out. He pushed it down, down into the seat of the cursed wheelchair. "I'm trying to make you understand that I'm not some hotdog trying to do Dodds' job. I just need him to understand what he's dealing with."

"Will, the Mount Adams Slasher died in prison! It makes my skin crawl just to say that name. You and Julius drove up to Lucasville to see the body, God knows why. This terrible thing that happened to this doctor, it can't be related. It's just another awful city crime. It's none of your concern."

"It's not that simple, Cindy. I'm the one who screwed up with Craig Factor, me and Dodds. We've got to put it right. He'll

kill again. He's got a taste for it. The next woman was killed
just a week after Theresa Chambers. All his victims looked like
Theresa, and so did this doctor! Now he's at work again. Don't
you see? He's going to kill again."

"No, no. Will, you're sick. You've been through a lot."

"I'm still a sworn officer. I have a duty..."

"Now stop." She shook her head adamantly. "Julius asked
me to talk to you. Stop this nonsense. Will, you're not the same.
You're going to be...handicapped."

The word fell on him heavily. *Handicapped.* That wasn't him.
That was the person in the wheelchair on the street corner, piti-
ful, avert the eyes... Will was still himself inside.

"I know that."

"Do you?" she asked harshly. "That means you won't be a
policeman anymore."

"I can use my brain. They need me."

"Is that what your commander is saying?"

Will didn't answer, recalling the conversation with Scaly
Mueller.

"I didn't think so. You're in denial, about a lot of things. That's
understandable, but I am not going to enable it."

"And I'm not going to argue with your self-help books."

Her eyes flashed, but then she just shook her head. "Will,
Will... I never understood your world. But it seemed to me that
within the police department you had a good job as a homicide
detective. I never understood why you left it to go to internal
affairs. The officers hate internal affairs."

"The chief asked me to do it."

"You went to the chief."

"It was a little bit of both." His back was starting to throb.
"I did it to make a better police department." He had explained
himself so many times.

"You did it," she said vehemently, "because of what happened
between you and Julius, over Bud Chambers."

"That was part of it." She was twisting time, twisting what
really happened. She seemed so strange to him now, but, in

reality, he knew that had been true for years. He fought those feelings. How did two people grow to be at such odds?

"This is what Julius was afraid of. Your going off half-cocked. He's really agitated about it. He was a good friend to you."

"I was his friend."

"Was." Cindy shook her head. "You don't make friends, Will. You don't know how. You didn't like my friends. I tried to open doors for you. You didn't have to work in the sewer every day, making no money. I introduced you to people, my friends. But you wouldn't even try."

Her words stung him into silence.

Her gaze roved past him. "Will, you need someone to talk to. Doesn't the hospital have…?"

"A shrink? Oh, there's one exclusively for neuro-rehab. Lauren something. She's been watching me, waiting for the big blowup. I don't feel that way. I just want to get my life back. Sometimes I wish I hadn't been wheeled down that hallway that night, hadn't seen it. But that woman's dead. And who will speak for her? J. J. Dodds? He just wants to be chief."

"That's a terrible thing to say."

"Who spoke for Theresa Chambers? Nobody. We messed up. Bud killed her. He got away with it because he was a cop."

"Theresa Chambers was killed by Craig Factor, Will. You know that."

"Bud Chambers had been separated from his wife. She had a restraining order against him. He had beaten her up once, and the patrol guys let it go. We fucked this one up, Cindy."

She winced from his profanity, or maybe because he called her Cindy. He couldn't tell which.

"I understand how strongly you feel." She touched his knee again. "But just because a cop is separated from his wife doesn't mean he should be a suspect. We've been separated for more than a year."

He realized she was making a joke. He forced himself to laugh even as his stomach dropped. It was time to shut up.

"I'll try to do better. I won't bother Dodds."

They sat quietly, more aware of the overhead lights as the city was overtaken by the early dusk.

"I talked to the woman in charge of rehab today," Will said. "She said you could talk to her about starting the process to get me out of here, bring me home." He laughed. "Everything's a 'process' now."

Cindy sighed and nervously tugged at her skirt.

"It would be nice to come home for Christmas."

"This is too soon," she said. "I see how you need help to even get into your wheelchair. We'd have to modify the house with ramps…"

"So I'll get a couple of big cops to wrestle me into a car."

"And what about when you're home? I can't even begin to…"

He reached over and took her hand. "You won't have to. I can be very self-sufficient. You'd be amazed at what I can accomplish just here in the hospital. I won't be trouble. Pretty soon I'll be walking."

Her gaze moved past him, again. "We haven't lived together in a long time."

He felt a paw grip his insides. He said quietly, "I know."

"Your doctors say you'll need a lot of physical therapy."

"I'll get it. I'll do a lot better on the outside. God, I can't even sleep. Can't you talk to them? Please, Cindy, get me out of this place." He knew he was pleading. He couldn't stop the urgent cadence of his voice.

"I brought your stuff."

He could tell she was managing him.

He was too tired to fight her. Too scared. After a moment, he looked through the bag she had brought. Another two pairs of sweatpants and some T-shirts, a CD player and CDs, small packets of Kleenex, his wallet with cash inside.

"Thanks. I haven't even been able to buy a Coke." He paused. "I feel bad that I wasn't able to get you a Christmas present. Remember, the doctors wouldn't let me drive once they found the tumor."

"It's okay." Her voice was barely audible. She was carrying the Coach handbag he had gotten her for Christmas two years before, meant as a peace offering as their marriage was coming apart, piece by piece. The room had emptied out completely. They were alone with the hospital smell and the Christmas garlands.

"Will, I can't…"

He suddenly felt such heaviness. She could have just stood and walked away, simple movements that were both miracles in his new life. But she sat there and spoke.

"I'm not like you," she said quietly. The harshness fell from her eyes, replaced by tears. "I'm not noble. I have a job. You have a…calling." She didn't speak the words like a compliment. He gripped her hand but she pulled it away. "I can't put my whole life on a shelf to, to…put it right for the dead. I'm not a damsel in distress anymore, so what am I to you? I'm not a murder victim."

"Cindy…"

"I can't…" She waved him away, pulled into herself. Her face became red and tears streaked her cheeks.

"It's okay."

"It's not!" Her eyes were red and fierce. "You're always so goddamned reasonable! It's not okay. None of it is. And you know it! You've never even forgiven me…"

"That's not true." He felt a sucking hole in his middle. He reached for her again, but she pushed away.

"Wait, Will. Please. I'm not…I can't. You and I, we're just too different. I can't do this."

"Can't do what?"

"I thought I could. I had thought it all through. I wanted to wait for all this to be over. I prayed you would be all right, and I'm so glad you came through the surgery. But this is never going to be over. Don't you get it? Will, I can't do this. I can't take care of you, be your nurse."

"I don't need a nurse!"

"I can't give up the rest of my life. I've given up so much already, for you, for Sam, and he won't even talk to us. I have a career. I'm still young. I'm entitled to a life, you know."

He had met her at a bank robbery. She was a teller and he was a young patrolman. Somehow he had found the courage to come back and ask for her phone number. She had been a young woman with a shy smile and a two-year-old baby. They had married six months later. It had all happened too fast. Eighteen years had happened too fast. He now recalled how, two days after his surgery, a nurse was helping him from the bathroom back to the bed. He had been constipated for a week, and suddenly he shit on the floor. Just shit on the floor. He couldn't move fast enough to get back to the toilet, or even take a step. He could just move enough to see, in the mirror, the horrible brown cord snake out of him onto the floor, and to see Cindy's expression of disgust. He knew she was thinking: *I had married this?*

Now he said nothing. The speakers called trauma team one to the emergency room, and then trauma team two. His mouth was too dry to speak, his lungs too tired to force out any words.

"I'll help you with money, Will. You won't have to worry."

"Just go."

"I've talked to your brother," she said.

He waved it away. "I asked you to bring me something else. Did you?"

"Damn you, Will." She reached into her purse and handed him the black leather case. Inside was his badge and identification card. "I shouldn't have done this. Julius will be…"

"Thanks." He spoke in a rough monotone. Then he violently wheeled around to face the city, provoking his back to spasm with pain, the one reliable in his new life. Night poured down on the city and lights pierced the puffy blackness. She spoke to his back. She had made plans for him. She was always good at planning. But Will wasn't really listening. For a long time after she left he just sat there, watching the city lights, knowing he was past due for his pain meds, not moving. He slid his wedding band off for the last time—Cindy had kept it during his surgery—and dropped it into his fanny pack. He thought about pawning it, or just walking out on the Roebling Bridge and letting the river take it away.

Chapter Ten

Cheryl Beth stood in the wide doorway into the solarium, watching the man. His back to her, he was framed by the darkness of the lonely broad windows, his posture rigid with pain. His shoulders heaved slightly. She knew he was crying and thought about checking on him. This was in character for her, checking on strangers, with or without a referral. She had the run of the hospital, something she thrived on. She loved to help people. Andy had said it was actually a character flaw, a selfish compulsion to be needed—those had been his words—not so much to help anyone as to feel secure herself. But he had only said that toward the end, as they were spiraling into the place where every sentence was an accusation, every phrase the quicksand of further estrangement. It was odd that the words still stung her, so many years later.

She watched the man in the wheelchair and almost went to him. He seemed too young and vital to be here, to be in that chair. But something in her hesitated. She hated that it was getting dark so early, that her home seemed almost violated by the footprints she had seen. She felt off her stride, Christine's bloody face and mutilated hand still hovering in her thoughts, deep footprints in her flower beds—she looked down at her own shoes as if to reassure herself that she wasn't standing in Christine's blood...*Ah!*

"I'm sorry. Everybody's jumpy right now, and you have the most right to be." The hand on her shoulder and the voice in her ear belonged to Dr. Jay Carpenter, the chief of general surgery. He was tall and rumpled, as usual the only neat thing on his body seemed to be the expertly knotted bowtie he wore. It was amazing how many docs still didn't realize their conventional ties could fall on a patient or a surface, picking up bacteria to be deposited elsewhere. Dr. Carpenter always wore a bowtie. Above it was a goatee of gray and brown, setting off a creased, craggy face, all topped by thinning white hair. His voice was always ready to assume its distinctive thundering tone. He was a notorious and highly successful ladies' man.

"Any Christmas plans?"

"I guess I'll go see my brothers in Kentucky."

"Walk with me, Cheryl Beth."

Visiting hours were coming to an end, so the halls were emptying out.

"Were you in the ER for the shooting du jour?"

She had been called in. The aftermath of gunshot wounds could be especially painful. The patient was a fifteen-year-old with a stomach wound. As usual, poor and black. As usual, from the violent ghettoes that separated downtown from the hospital district on Pill Hill.

"It's going to be a pain grenade," she said. "You know he's probably not opiate naïve."

"Not with all the addicts in that neighborhood." They knew the drill: a patient with a history of addiction didn't respond to doses of painkillers that would work in a normal, or "naïve," patient.

"So there's a good chance he won't be adequately medicated," she said. "I'm going to go back and check on him, post-surgery."

"That's good," he said, pausing to lean against a wall, his voice assuming its full freight-train tone. "If his doc isn't doing the right thing, you do what you need, and you have my verbal orders." He looked around and spoke more quietly. "The last thing we want is to have another African American kid screaming in pain in this hospital. Lord, this city is so tense. They won't admit it, of course. Everybody is so nice in Cincinnati." He paused. "They could have used you in peds today."

"I can't do peds." She spoke quickly.

"I know." He gave a gentle smile. "I've been worried about you."

"Me? I'm all right."

"I know, you're the tough one. But your job can get pretty lonely. Why don't you come up with me to the stroke floor? They're having their Christmas party tonight."

"Maybe I will, if I'm not persona non grata. Stephanie Ott is out to get me." Cheryl Beth said it lightly but the words still sounded dark. She sighed. "Things aren't right."

"With Stephanie?" He gave his trademark rumbling laugh. "Nothing is ever right with Stephanie. Don't worry about her. I've got your back."

"It's not just that. Someone was digging through my desk. The whole vibe here seems different. And I found footprints in my flower bed, right by my window."

"Maybe it was the meter reader?"

"No, the meter is in back. And they only appeared in the last couple of days."

"It wasn't me." He winked. "It's probably nothing, Cheryl Beth. Still, you ought to talk to the police."

"It was the first thing I did!" She heard her voice rising and slowed herself down. "They blew me off. They wouldn't even come out, just said call if I see a prowler. Damn it, they think I killed Christine."

"No."

"Pretty damned close." She slumped against the wall, suddenly exhausted. "They say I could be 'a person of interest.' Isn't that what it means? I always hear that on TV and those are the people who end up being the killers."

He patted her shoulder and spoke quietly. "Nobody thinks you would hurt Christine." He paused. "I do have to say, jeez, baby, Gary Nagle? If you were going to do that, I should have been hitting on you harder all these years."

"Yeah, yeah. Hell, does everybody in the hospital know about this?"

"Of course not." He waited a beat. "Of course."

She laughed with him but felt the rough stone of exposure pulling her down. What an insane thing, getting together with Gary, going for a drink with him that windy spring night, letting him kiss her underneath the streetlight. She tried to push the memory away.

"Maybe you need a vacation," he said. "I can't afford you to burn out."

Her immediate reaction was defensive, but she knew he meant her well. "Oh, Dr. Carpenter, you know how it is. Sometimes it's so sad. Sometimes something wonderful happens. A patient gets good news or makes you laugh. I always think, no matter how bad the news, at least I can control their pain."

They walked again, in the direction of the cafeteria, moving to the edge of the hallway as five people walked past, closely bunched together. It was obviously a family, three generations of women, the oldest looking a little older than Cheryl Beth. Eyes red with tears and faces stretched with fatigue, they bunched together in their thick winter coats as if any straggler would be pulled irretrievably into the deep space.

"Dr. Carpenter, who would want to hurt Christine?"

"Want me to make a list?"

"I'm serious."

He said nothing until they were in an empty hallway again. "Christine was a big personality, as you know. People loved her or hated her. Well, no, that's not true. People tolerated her or hated her. She didn't have many friends. You tangled with her, remember? When you were trying to get us away from using so much Demerol, using all your charm and all your data, she went ballistic. That was classic Christine."

"I'd actually forgotten that. There was another time, too. She told me her patient was being a problem, and I said, 'Dr. Lustig, the problem is how you're writing the orders.' She was way under-prescribing for this particular patient, who was just moaning, really hurting. The nurses were afraid to cross her. I wanted to say, 'You're killing people with these PCAs,' but I didn't. Great. These will be more reasons for the cops to suspect me."

He chuckled. "If arguing with Christine Lustig was a crime, I'd be under the jail. I knew her for fifteen years, and I can't think of one day when she wasn't after somebody. The truth is, she was brisk...well, beyond brisk, because usually she was right. I saw her stand toe-to-toe with the big guys many times, and that wasn't easy for a female doc of her generation. On top of all that, she was gorgeous and knew it. My God, those cheekbones..."

He stared wistfully. "She felt entitled and she was incredibly competitive. She and Gary were both that way. It's amazing they didn't kill each other. Guess I shouldn't say that. I thought she was a gifted surgeon, especially on gall bladders and GI stuff. But she was kind of a technician, if you know what I mean. Her people skills with patients sometimes left a lot to be desired. Let's just say she didn't have your emotional IQ. Not to speak ill of the dead."

"Is that why she was put on the computer project?"

"You mean to get away from patients for awhile? Maybe. She actually asked for the assignment, and she became a real advocate. I called her Tech Head, she became such a geek. She traveled to other hospitals and studied their systems. SoftChartZ is pioneering electronic patient records. Digital medicine. Christine was a believer. Don't kid yourself. This is what's got Stephanie's panties twisted, that the project might be delayed now. Not that she gives a damn about how much paperwork you do. But the docs in the neurosurgery practice are screaming for computerized records, and they're the ones who still bring real money into this benighted place."

"So who in this long list of enemies was capable of killing Christine?"

"Oh, Cheryl Beth. How would I know that?"

"Because you know everything, Dr. Carpenter."

"What, you're a detective now?"

"Someone has to be. This cop, Dodds—I have a really bad feeling about him. He just looks at me like he thinks I did it, like I'm hiding something."

"Are you?"

A shot of defensiveness stiffened her before he laughed.

"I'm serious, doctor. I feel like I need to do something, get him some information. And Stephanie, too. You should have seen how she went off on me."

"The detective talked to me. I told him you couldn't have done it."

"See! He has it in his head that I killed her!"

"Cheryl Beth, this is a big old urban hospital. And we have all the problems of an urban hospital. Yesterday, I saw a guy in a stairwell, dressed in rags, just walking up and down the stairs. He said his dead mother was chasing him, and didn't I see her? He was shaking and bawling. Scared the hell out of me. I called security, and it turned out he was just another street person who wandered in here for warmth. He was diagnosed paranoid schizophrenic, off his meds, hearing voices. Good Lord."

He stopped. Then, "Do you know how much of this hospital has been closed down the past decade? There are old, abandoned parts of this place that I've never even been to, that the security guards don't even know about."

"They're probably all my old shortcuts," she said.

"You know I studied here when I was a medical student? This was back in the Stone Age, when they had real wards, just long rows of beds separated by curtains. But it was great training. Young docs today, most of them don't really know how to listen to heart sounds. They don't get a chance. Hearts get fixed. People don't get rheumatic fever. Back then, we'd get lots of public health cases, lots of people with heart murmurs. It was great to be a student. The old basement, that's where the morgue was. It's so isolated. Why they would put offices down there, much less even put a woman alone in an office there…?" He shook his head. "It was just a horrible, random act."

That didn't make her feel better. She said, "So what about the footprints in my flower bed?"

He smiled, half to himself, staring at the floor. At first Cheryl Beth thought he was patronizing her and she grew angry. Then he spoke in a different voice. "The irony of the whole thing is that Christine was quite the sexual predator. She had cheated on Gary for years, and not with just one person. She was hardly the victim, however much I am baffled by your taste in men. I'll just leave it at that."

For a moment, Cheryl Beth was conscious of her every swallow and breath. She made herself smile and gently punch Dr. Carpenter in the arm. She said, "Don't tell me you and Christine…?"

"Not my taste," he said. "And my conquests are vastly over-imagined by some of my coworkers, not that I'm complaining… Cheryl Beth?"

She realized she had just been standing there silently staring at the wall.

"I was just thinking," she said. "The way Christine was cut. It was done with such rage. I've never seen anything…not in the ER…not anywhere. It could have been…"

He spoke quickly. "I probably said too much."

"It could have been a spurned lover."

"Cheryl Beth…"

"It could. My God, it could have been a lover's angry wife. A woman could be strong enough to do that…"

She stopped instinctively when his name came over the paging system.

"You." He put his arm around her. She didn't feel intimidated. It felt good, just to be touched. "You, my intense friend, need to go home and get some rest. But first, come with me to the party, get something in your stomach."

"Doctor's orders?"

"Absolutely." He took her arm and they walked.

Chapter Eleven

Gravity was his enemy. Anything dropped to the floor was lost. A pen, a book, a pill. A towel, a water cup, a dollar bill. He couldn't pick it up because he couldn't stand, much less bend down. His only recourse was to ask a nurse to retrieve it, or ask Cindy. But she wouldn't be coming back. He had lost her just as surely as if she had fallen out of his hands to earth, his useless legs unable to let him follow her. The morning had been slow and difficult, as he had pulled on his T-shirt and sweatpants, then, in greater agony, socks and shoes. Cindy had bought him workout shoes with Velcro snaps, to avoid the near impossibility of holding his legs in place long enough to tie shoes. Then he had angled the wheelchair close to the bed and locked each wheel in place, while he carefully pushed himself into a sitting position and maneuvered to the edge of the mattress.

Like so much, getting up had gone from an unthinking move of a normal human being to an act of significant physical effort. Using one hand to grip the bed railing, he would roll to his side. Then he could rise to his elbow and, again grabbing the bed, swing his body into a sitting position. He used his strong right leg, hooking his right foot into his left ankle to pull the weak leg along. It all took planning and care. He couldn't feel his bottom, so he had to be sure that he was actually sitting on the bed and not sliding to the floor. Then, relying on upper-body strength, he would lift himself across to the chair. It wasn't exactly kosher: he was supposed to wait for a nurse, but they were always busy. And no one seemed to notice or care when he just wheeled himself out of the room and down to the nurses' station.

There he would be given a multivitamin, stool softener, Vicodin for pain control. He was profoundly aware of the med times. He didn't need a watch. His body had betrayed him with the tumor, but its clockworks for pain were precise and as unforgiving as the enemy gravity. If he missed the pills by even a few minutes, the pain would break through again. It was a creature living inside him, pinned up in the fragile pharmaceutical cage. The pain frightened him.

After the morning physical therapy and lunch, he was on his own. No one told him how long he might be in the rehab unit. It was the way he imagined jail time. If he hadn't been free to roam the hospital he was sure he would go mad. But he could come and go as he pleased from the neuro-rehab ward and now, after so many days, had just become part of the landscape. Some people said hello. Most ignored him. So he wheeled himself through the halls, watching people, trying to keep dark thoughts outside. He ended up in the corridor leading to the old entrance to the hospital. It was a quiet place because the outside doors were sealed now, the main entrance moved. But the grand arched ceiling remained, along with a display of historic photographs from the hospital's history. The entrance to the hospital chapel was nearby, the chapel itself empty. Outside, the light was somber and wintry. A woman walked by, her hair bouncing on her shoulders at every step, reminding him of Cindy when he had first met her. He put the thought in a box, put the box on an imaginary shelf holding thoughts about his wife. He wouldn't be the first cop with a busted marriage.

He played a game of thinking about all the women he had crushes on or had lusted after while he had been married. One was a pretty young yellow-haired cadet with flawless fair skin. She had followed him around with a doe-eyed interest that was both innocent and knowing, and once, when he had seen her in a skirt, he had realized how attracted he was to her. Karen was his partner before Dodds, a woman going through a divorce, who said Will was her best friend. One night in the car they had started kissing, until he had stopped it. There was the assistant DA with the violet eyes, the writer who was working on a profile of the homicide detectives—in all those cases, he had felt the attraction, known it was mutual, and each time he had pushed it away. Only once did he slip, nothing compared with Cindy's serial infidelities. He pushed that thought away. He thought of the others. *Maybe now he would look up one of those women.* And do what? He hadn't had an erection since the surgery.

He had always known Cindy would leave him for good. He was such a fool. Last night he had cried for her, for what they briefly had, for what he briefly hoped they might have again, when she had flown to his side after the tumor had been diagnosed. One last time he had melted into his ideal of Cindy, rather than the frozen reality. When they had first met, she was a vulnerable young woman who had been left adrift by the father of her child, and Will had vowed that he would never abandon her. That vow, and the time when they had seemed to glow together, those fleeting, joyful moments early on, had kept him going so long. It was like an addiction.

But after the cry, he had returned to the odd mental box he had been in since surgery. One side of the box was his gratitude at being alive. Things had looked so grim when the tumor had first been diagnosed: it might be malignant; there might be more; he might never walk again. Another side was oddly calm, where he was a good, self-sufficient patient, working hard in rehab, foiling the dark expectations of Lauren the shrink. The third side was his periodic bouts of claustrophobia—he had to get out of this hospital, just to sleep for one night—this one he concealed, and then it receded. And the fourth was the doctor's murder, which brought it all back. That side was unfinished business, and, sure, he was also probably using it to distract himself from his life ahead: disabled, handicapped, crippled, dreading every new pain or change of feeling. Did the box hold anything?

"Pig."

The voice behind him made him start, but his adrenaline, didn't go down once the surprise was gone. He wheeled around, forcing himself to be calm. The man who stood before him was taller than Will; in fact, he knew that the man was exactly six feet five and, at one time, had weighed 250 pounds. Now he looked heavier, with a pronounced gut straining at his leather jacket. His face had always seemed ordinary except for the dramatic thick brown eyebrows that nearly met and the slight dimple in his chin that broke the monotony. Now, it looked puffy and his features seemed too small for that face. He had taken to shaving his head, which had long made Will imagine a malevolent Pillsbury doughboy.

"You're the only police officer I'd call pig," Bud Chambers said. "Or should I just say rat?"

Will said nothing. He had never felt more vulnerable. He vainly glanced at his lap for any weapon, seeing only the small fanny pack that held a few dollars, Kleenex, and his wallet.

"I've seen you look better, Borders," the man continued, pacing around him in a small arc. "Like when you got my badge."

"You did that to yourself," Will said. "You lied on your logs."

"Yeah," he said quietly. "Right." He folded his arms and looked down at Will. "So I hear you've been looking for me, so I thought I'd come looking for you."

"Where'd you hear that?" Will controlled his voice, used his calm peace officer voice.

"Oh, you know, the old cop grapevine. You know how that goes."

"Sure."

"Like I know your wife left you. Who couldn't a seen that coming from ten miles away? You know, I fucked her once…"

The atrium and two converging hallways were utterly empty save for the two men and the display boards with their historic photographs and newspaper clippings. Even the normal noise of the hospital didn't make it this far away. Will studied Chambers' hands, thick and pale, balled into heavy fists.

"Well," Will said, "at least you didn't murder her."

Chambers smirked with his thin, small mouth.

"Where were you on the night of December 6th?"

"What, aren't you going to Mirandize me? Oh, I forgot, you're not a cop anymore. You're just another jerkoff in the hospital." Chambers started to walk away but suddenly turned and came toward Will, moving his heavy body with quick strides. He grabbed the sides of the wheelchair and bent forward. His breath was foul.

"I didn't kill her! Got that? I didn't kill her or any of those girls. Craig Factor was convicted! The DNA was his!"

Will met the furious gaze, pushed all his fear down into his useless legs. At least they could be good for something. He said calmly, "DNA evidence can be tampered with."

Chambers pushed off the chair and stamped back. Will used his hands to brake the wheels, stopping himself from rolling backward.

"You couldn't prove a thing," Chambers said. "You wrecked your own career, trying to frame me. You left homicide to go to the rat squad."

"I want bad cops off the street."

"Fuck you. You know what that makes you in the eyes of every Cincinnati cop? The only thing you could do was run me out on some chickenshit thing. So fucking what? The brass still let me retire, take my pension." He stabbed his chest with his hand. "I'm doin' fine. Doin' private work now, corporate security. Consulting. It's easy money. I don't have to deal with the niggers and the bullshit and the rat-fuck cops like you, Borders. I'm doin' fine. Better than you."

It occurred to Will that the meds must help tamp down anger. They must even dampen thoughts and reactions, even ones that had taken millions of years to be stamped into the species: "danger" and "flee." It softened the fact that no other person was in the lobby or surrounding hallways. For the first time since his surgery he felt free of his body, projected instead into the charged space that separated him from Chambers. Will said, "You beat her, Marion, we know that."

His face reddened on hearing his given name. "I could beat you! God, I wish you could stand and fight like a man."

"She was afraid you would kill her."

Chambers' head dropped slightly as if a supporting cord in his neck had snapped. He looked at Will strangely. His tongue flicked out like a lizard's.

"Where'd you hear that?" Will said nothing. Chambers stuffed his hands into his coat pockets. "She had a lot of ideas." He stared past Will. "She was paranoid, fucking nuts. I put up with that for years. I wouldn't hurt her."

"You did hurt her. You beat her. The cops responded to a domestic at your house. They let you off. Then she got a restraining order against you."

"That was just being married, give me a break. Now all these bitches are counselors and lawyers and they tell gals to 'get a restraining order,' and the husband's always guilty. How many domestics did we respond to as uniforms that turned out to be nothing."

"How many where the husband came back and killed the woman."

Chambers leaned against the wall, pulled out a cigarette, and stuck it in his lips. He wanted to light up, but seeing a smoke detector overhead thought better of it. He stuck it back in the pack.

"We used to be friends, I thought," he said. "You were a righteous cop on the streets, Borders, back in the day, when we worked District One together. We'd all get together. We were all family. I was nothing but happy for you when you aced the sergeant's exam and then went to homicide. What'd I ever do to you?"

Will ignored him and wheeled six feet away and to the side, making Chambers turn to see him. Then he turned the chair toward him again and advanced. "I always wondered why you did it."

"I didn't."

"Not why you killed Theresa, because we knew about your temper." Chambers' left eyelid flickered when Will said the woman's name. "And motive. You had a girlfriend you wanted to be with. And Theresa had $500,000 in life insurance, still payable to you. I didn't even wonder about the knife. The more I learned about you, Chambers, the more it made sense. No quick gunshot for Bud Chambers. That would take away the fun, the fear. I just wondered why you killed those other women."

"I didn't!" His voice was a mechanical hiss.

"I guess you got scared when we looked at the logical suspect, the estranged husband. Pretty dumb for a cop, if you ask me, because we always look at the husband first."

"I was on duty…"

"That was your first lie to us."

"Well, shit, so I was with Darlene. It wouldn't be the first time a married cop saw his girlfriend on his dinner break. She told you I was there."

"Yeah. I'm sure your little white-trash girlfriend was as afraid of you as your wife was. Or was she an accomplice? But we caught you in a lie about where you were the day your wife was murdered. I hate cops that lie. If they lie about one thing they'll lie about the important things, too."

"I was a good cop." Chambers swallowed the words.

Will said, "I just never understood the others."

"What?"

"The other women. Jill Kelly. Lisa Schultz."

He moved up to Chambers, making him dance his toes away from the wheels, vaguely aware of his foolhardiness. "I mean, if you were going to tamper with the DNA and implicate Factor, why kill those other women? Why turn the beef with your wife into a serial killing that had the whole city terrified?"

"Factor raped her and killed her. He killed all those girls. It was his semen. A jury said so."

"It was his semen with Theresa. That's the only one he was convicted for. Craig Factor had a rap sheet as a Peeping Tom. He'd never even been arrested for a violent offense."

"Who the hell knows what makes a psycho snap."

"Yeah, you should know, Marion. Two other women all killed the same way. Their clothes neatly folded. Very violent knife attack. The knife wiped clean of prints and hidden in the same room. They had been raped, the same as Theresa. Only, the funny thing, there was no semen. You made them take showers before you killed them? And the mutilation. You especially liked that, right? Got your dick all hard, that sense of power."

"You say. Nobody believed that."

"Don't kid yourself. Who else could have done it? By the time the second murder happened, we were all over Mount Adams with stakeouts. Everybody was locked in their houses after dark. But the killings went on. Who else could do that but a cop, somebody who knew how we worked and could monitor our radio frequencies. Somebody who could get a woman to open her door."

"Get the fuck away from me." Chambers sidestepped him and stood at a distance.

"I'm just a guy in the hospital, remember? Just a curious guy. For awhile I wondered how you got Factor's semen. How'd you do that, Marion? Or did you get one of your corrupt buddies in the evidence room to tamper with the DNA?"

Chambers' eyes were bright with hate. His hands beat a silent tempo at his side. "You're out of your mind, Borders. This is over, done."

"No, Marion. We wish it were, but it just can't stop, can it? You can't stop. What was your connection to Dr. Lustig?"

"I don't know who the hell you're talking about now. All I know is I was exonerated. I always said a nigger broke in and raped her and killed her, and who'd it turn out to be? Nearly had a riot in Liberty Hill, I hear, when you and Dodds chased Craig Factor down in the street and arrested him. Somehow that wasn't good enough for you. But the killings stopped when Factor was busted." Chambers stepped aside and moved five paces away.

"I always wondered if you had a hard-on for me because I fucked your wife," he added. "But I didn't think you ever knew."

"We're talking about you. Why you killed those other women. Why you started again. You came down into the hospital basement on Friday night and did the same thing to Dr. Christine Lustig. Did you even know her name?"

"What are you talking about?" Chambers refused to look at him.

"Did you pick her like you picked the other ones? Remember, anything you say can and will be used against you. You also have the right to an attorney."

"Eat shit!"

"Christine Lustig. It was your style, Marion. The whole thing, right down to how the knife was stashed. It was you, all over again." Will studied his face for any telltales, seeing a moon of rage. But he was breathing deeply and sweating, even though the corridor was chill. It was just like those hours after the first homicide when Will and Dodds had tried to break him. Before command had told them to back off, and then the other killings had started. Will let silence fill the space between them for one minute, then two.

"She even looked like Theresa."

His eyelid. That involuntary flutter.

"You're done, Borders."

"Is that a threat?"

"It's reality, asshole. Look at yourself." He spat on the floor in front of the wheelchair.

"But we never answered that why. The criminal mind, you know? Why the other women, when you could have just tampered with Theresa's sample and gotten off."

"You tell me, Sherlock."

"I just figure you got a taste for it…Marion. That happens with some killers. Some are full of remorse the minute the killing is done. And some, well, they get a taste for it."

"Well you have all the answers." His voice was low and gravelly, yet it echoed strangely through the hallway.

"Wrong again," Will said, wheeling the chair again and moving so Chambers was forced to turn his head to follow him. "I don't even know what you did with those fingers you cut off, with the rings still on them. I think you've still got them."

"You…"

"Trophies. You still have them, don't you, Marion? You started out as a bad cop and you turned into a serial killer. Just another scumbag who could only get it up when he was hurting a woman, who can blame it all on his childhood and find Jesus before he gets the needle. And you will get the needle, Marion."

Chambers shook his head and laughed. Turning, he walked past Will. Suddenly Will was falling and the floor came up hard and cold, as the wheelchair clattered harshly against the tiles. His hips and ribs shuddered from the impact. A wildfire of pain broke out in his lower back. Chambers studied him from an even higher vantage, making a clucking sound with his tongue and teeth.

"I know about you, Borders. You don't have clean hands. And now look at yourself, cripple." He studied Will a moment longer, then walked away with a slow, confident saunter.

Chapter Twelve

Cheryl Beth rounded the corner into the old atrium and saw the man sprawled on the floor, his wheelchair on its side. One of the wheels was still turning. She ran to him and was relieved to see he was conscious.

"I'm all right."

"What happened?"

"Spill on aisle one."

She laughed loudly and told him to not move while she checked for any possible broken bones. Fortunately, he looked to be about her age, a dark-haired tall man. He wasn't one of the elderly patients that seemed to find every opportunity to get over the railings of their beds or lose hold of their walkers. The nurses called them falling stars. He had sutures in the middle of his back, an incision about nine inches long, but they were in good shape, probably overdue to come out. It looked like the handiwork of Dr. Goldstein. A spinal cord tumor, she guessed.

"I told you I was okay." He pulled down the sweatshirt that had ridden up on his back and belly.

"We need to get you up. Can you stand?"

He shook his head. He was on his side with his legs still drawn up against one arm of the upset wheelchair. He raised himself to an elbow but couldn't get any higher. She would need help. She glanced into the chapel but it was empty. No one was coming toward her from the main part of the hospital.

Suddenly she smelled it. He must have lost control when he fell from the wheelchair. The noxious, all-encompassing odor of feces seemed at odds with the man's handsome, lived-in face and his full head of lush wavy hair. Her well-trained gag reflex didn't react. He started coughing and stared over her shoulder. She turned and saw Lennie.

He must have just stepped out of the stairwell. His gray pants and blue workshirt were smeared with shit. An old green parka looked little better, turned brown with age and dirt. As always, Lennie greeted her with a rotten-toothed smile beneath the large crimson nose and its ever-expanding map of broken veins. His hair was long and wild, spiked out like the images she had seen of Medusa. It was just Lennie. His eyes were different, though. His stare was fixed and uncomprehending, looking into a dimension that existed only in his mind.

"Lennie, what are you doing?"

He didn't immediately respond. Then, "Gotta, gotta, gotta, stop. No. Fuck, fuck, fuck…why are you doin' this to me? Why are you doin' this? No! No! Fuck! Fuck!" His voice rose with every word. He stared back at the fire door, then over his head.

"Get out of here, Lennie or I'm going to have to call security. And no crapping in the hallway!" She said the last with a laugh in her voice, but he screamed at her.

"Don't you see him! He's right there!"

He seemed to be looking in the direction of the patient on the floor.

"He's right there, the devil!" Lennie's eyes were huge and puffy as he stared first at the fallen man, then at her. His eyes changed with a fresh thought, as if a new reel of his private movie had been started. He licked his lips with a fat, dark tongue. "I get it, you're one of his demon-angels. You want to confuse me!"

"Nobody's the devil or an angel, Lennie. You know me." This was new. She had never seen him like this before.

"I know! I know! Oww!" He snapped his head around, first to the right, then straight up. "Ayyyyyyyy! I hear. Yes! Yes!" His eyes focused on her anew, something primal in them. "Can't fool

Lennie, no you can't…" His voice trailed off in a mumble. "I saw the devil kill right here…right here…" Then, "Kill the devil!"

He said it with such a drawn-out shriek that Cheryl Beth felt a chill spread with infinite slowness across the back of her neck.

"It's the devil from hell, he's coming out of the floor! Fuck fuck fuck fuck! I hear! I hear!"

He reached into the parka and his filthy hand returned with a knife. The handle itself seemed huge and the blade was longer and black. Lennie held it out like a cross to ward off vampires, then started jabbing and swinging it against unseen phantoms. He flapped the sleeves of the parka, the movement sending out fresh waves of foul odors.

Her feet felt like the cement of dreams and from her stomach came a nauseous lurch she hadn't felt since she had seen her first autopsy as a nursing student. She fumbled to pull the cell phone out of her lab coat, nearly dropping it. All she could see was the long thick dark blade.

"Lennie," she said in as calm a voice as she could manage, "Lennie, put down the knife. You're going to hurt…"

"He's right there behind you!" he bellowed. "The devil from hell. He's come up from hell to get me. But nobody's gonna get Lennie. No fucking devil's gonna get Lennie."

Cheryl Beth's fingers felt numb and huge as she tried to punch in the keys to hospital security. Where was everybody? She looked around for help, found none. Then he was there, a blur of dark color, a heavy mass rushing toward her. Her hand exploded in pain and the cell phone flew into the wall, smashing into several pieces. Time moved fast and slow. She was conscious of every part of the phone clacking down to the floor, her stethoscope, pens, and Starbucks card flying out of her lab coat, as if each was taking days to reenter the atmosphere. But he had gotten to her so fast, faster than her brain could even send a signal to step back or block his swing. He pushed her roughly and her left ankle gave way, then she was flying and sliding backward on the waxed floor. Somehow her head didn't hit the tiles. She turned to see him rush toward the patient, the knife held high as he screamed in a language she couldn't comprehend. Now it would happen, just like it had with Christine, and then he would come for her. This was how it had happened. Oh, God.

Suddenly he seemed to hit a wall and collapse. His bulky form abruptly turned horizontal and crashed. She realized the man on the floor had shoved the wheelchair forward, tripping Lennie, who now fell forward across the chair.

"No, devil!" He landed at the patient's legs and was flailing. The knife was still in his hand. She heard the blade strike the floor, a hard, off-key sound. She remembered a game her brother had played as a teenager, poking a hunting knife as fast as he could into a table between his outstretched fingers. Was it called mumblypeg? Cheryl Beth could never bear to watch and she thought it made him seem like a redneck. Now she heard the same chilling sound: bak, bak, bak, bak.

Lennie pulled himself up over the man, climbing and slithering up his body, swinging the knife. But the man grabbed his wrist with one hand, then two, while Lennie screamed, spat, and thrashed atop him. The man's face was red and he grunted with effort, twisting his torso. God, the sutures would come out. She pulled herself to her knees with difficulty, as if she were willing some other body to move. Her hands wouldn't stop shaking. She grabbed Lennie from behind and pulled on him, feeling the parka rip. Then it gave way entirely and she fell backward again, landing painfully on her butt, half a filthy jacket in her hands. Just then the patient bucked his head, crashing his forehead into Lennie's nose. He screamed and the knife slipped from his hand, hitting the floor loudly. Lennie tried to roll toward the knife but the man grabbed his shoulder and Lennie fell back. He was again on top but this time facing the ceiling, being restrained by the patient. He kept flailing his hand toward the knife. Cheryl Beth ran and kicked it away. By the time she turned around, the man had his arms locked around Lennie's neck in what looked like an odd wrestling hold. Lennie struggled with renewed fury but only for a few seconds. Then his eyes rolled back and his body went limp.

"Oh my God, are you okay?" Cheryl Beth pulled Lennie off the man. "Is he okay?"

"Probably," the man said, lying on his back, his chest heaving to get breath.

"You're sure you're all right? Can you feel your toes?" The man nodded. "Your right leg's doing well. That was quite a trick, pushing the wheelchair under him. Probably saved us. I used to think I was a good woman in a crisis."

"You are."

She looked back at Lennie. "I thought he was harmless."

"Nobody's harmless." The man smiled and held out his hand. "Will."

"Cheryl Beth." His hand felt warm in hers.

"That's a pretty name."

Just then she heard Lennie moan, but Will almost involuntarily kicked his right leg. His foot connected sharply with Lennie's skull and this time the man lay still.

Chapter Thirteen

The security men came and handcuffed the derelict. Will was into his wheelchair and Cheryl Beth brought his two p.m. meds. She checked the sutures on his back, which somehow had survived intact. He had slathered hand sanitizer on his hands, arms, and face. The adrenaline from the fight was still fueling him. He was high on it, even if his muscles were starting to ache and he could still smell the man's odor on him. Then the uniforms arrived and led the suspect off to a squad car. He was mumbling to himself but looked no worse for the choke hold Will had administered. He had seen cases where the hold could kill a suspect and hated to use it. But it had been a few years since he had been in a fight like that, and back then he could walk and run. He had needed every advantage he could get.

Now he sat in a small conference room with Dodds and the head of hospital security. He was a former cop named Stan Berkowitz. Will never knew him well. He was always in patrol and had risen to sergeant. He had retired at fifty, but he looked ten years younger, right down to his fine suit, sculpted chin, and perfect haircut. He looked like a congressman.

Dodds said, "Stan 'Don't Call Me David' Berkowitz." Will chuckled, knowing Berkowitz hated the nickname.

"I made ninety-five thousand last year," he said. "So screw you both." He still talked like a cop. "Why are you still putting up with the shit out there when you could retire, get a pension, then start to make real money. Private sector loves retired cops for security gigs. They give you respect, too."

Dodds said, "So how'd this guy get in the hospital with a knife, now that you got respect and all."

"Welcome to my world." Berkowitz opened his hands and smiled gently. "We do a lot of Medicaid cases here. This isn't Indian Hill. We knew about Lennie, of course. Leonard Snowden Williams Jr.—he sounds like chairman of Procter and Gamble, huh? He had been a patient. He was homeless. He would sometimes get inside. That's not uncommon, especially in the wintertime. We have to run them out of the old boiler room, the closed wings. We do what we can, what with budget cuts and all. We had to lay off nine security officers last year. There's no money for screening devices at the doors. That wouldn't be practical anyway. There's always risks. We have a risk-management officer, know that? Some things fall between the cracks."

"Like security for the basement wing where Dr. Lustig was killed," Will said.

Berkowitz shifted his jawline to Will. "What the hell happened to you, Borders?"

"Bad back," Dodds said, studying the knife through the plastic of a large evidence bag. Will stared at it, guessing it was a Ka-Bar brand, carbon steel blade, maybe seven inches long. It looked smaller in the bag than when it was being thrust over his head. He realized he hadn't exhaled.

"We thought Lennie was harmless..." Berkowitz started.

"Did you know Christine Lustig?" Will asked.

Berkowitz paused, seemed thrown off stride. "Sure. They wrote her up in last month's newsletter, the big computer project she was doing. She was a surgeon. So I saw her around. And, well. She was...well, hell, she was an attractive woman. You know how it is. I noticed her."

"Did she know Lennie?"

Berkowitz pushed out his chest, knocking his tie aside. "What the hell, Borders, you're a patient. Why are you asking questions?"

"Indulge us," Dodds said.

"Oh, I get it, the great salt-and-pepper homicide team, back together again. How would I know if she knew him?"

"Maybe," Will said, "you could check his records here, see if she ever treated him. Maybe there was a connection." Will was surprised Dodds was letting him talk. He already knew there was no chance Lennie had killed Christine Lustig. He said, "Did you investigate any threats against Dr. Lustig in the months before she was murdered?"

"I thought the hospital president himself had already talked to the police. He came down here the night Dr. Lustig was, well, killed."

"I didn't see you that night," Dodds said.

"The president talked to me. We thought everything that could be done was being done. I didn't need to be in the way... You wouldn't believe the bureaucratic crap we have here. Just like being with the cops, only more meetings. Anyway, I thought this was already resolved. You've got the man. It was obviously Lennie." Berkowitz shifted imperceptibly, pushing back the chair slightly and running a hand across his congressional hair. Will had learned how cops showed discomfort during interviews.

"So what about it, Stan? Had she?" Dodds' large almond eyes were innocent with inquiry. Suddenly it felt to Will like the old days, where they would double-team a suspect.

"Well, I'd have to check the records."

"Didn't you do that after the murder?" Will asked.

The sweat appeared on the sides of Berkowitz's neck, an odd place. But it was definitely sweat. "Damn, do you have any idea? Can we go off the record here?"

Neither Will nor Dodds spoke, but just as they knew he would, Berkowitz filled the gap of silence. "There's a huge issue of liability for the hospital here. Do you have any idea how much we could be sued for if it came out that Lustig had been threatened and the hospital didn't do enough to protect her? You know how lawyers twist everything." He swiveled toward Will and his mouth crooked down. "You know, you got kicked

out of homicide and ended up on the rat squad. You twist cops'
words all the time. Why am I even talking to you?" By now he
was sweating enough that it had broken through the light-blue
dress shirt.

Will said, "So she had been threatened?"

"Phone calls, all right. Somebody was calling her office line.
Mostly hang-ups."

Dodds said, "Mostly?"

Berkowitz leaned forward, his face pinched. "We're off the
record, remember? Right? I've got a good thing here."

"What is mostly?" Will demanded. Berkowitz's youthful face
started dissolving into wrinkles.

"I don't even know if it was real, understand? She came to
me about a month ago and said she was getting calls, down in
her office. The phone would ring and she'd answer and nobody
would be on the line. I mean, nobody talked. But she was convinced they were there, just listening to her. She was a babe,
okay? So what babe hasn't gotten a breather at some point in
her life? Anyway, talked to the telecom people, and we ran the
times of the calls. They weren't coming from inside the hospital.
So all we could do was complain to the phone company and
change her extension. We had a work order for that when she
was killed."

"That doesn't sound like something a homeless guy would
do," Will said.

Dodds said, "Go back, Stan. You said 'mostly.'"

He was hunched forward, his hands clenched together.

"About three days before she was killed, she came back to
me and said there had been a call. Started out same as the rest.
She answers and it's dead air. Then she hears a whisper. Says
she's going to die. Hangs up. She was shaken up. I offered to
call the police for her. But then she just changes, gets really icy.
Says to forget it."

"And you did."

He nodded.

"I don't know what it all means." He sat back up and fanned his coat jacket. "It's not going to be a problem, right? You'll test the blade of Lennie's knife. You'll find Dr. Lustig's blood on it. Look, I've got a meeting." He stood. "What I told you was all off the record. I'll deny it if you try to screw me, and you can just deal with the hospital's lawyers."

The door closed and Dodds shook his head. "Stan 'Don't Call Me David' Berkowitz. The assholes always land well. It's a shame he wasn't good enough to get into homicide. Would have loved to have a homicide cop named after a serial killer." Dodds folded Lennie's weapon inside the evidence bag and yawned.

Will said quietly, "That's not the knife."

Dodds' artillery shell of a head swiveled. "What are you talking about?"

"It's not the knife. Did you really check her office? Like under the desk?"

Dodds stared at him. He'd seen the look before. Then Dodds stood, like a redwood suddenly appearing full-grown, and roughly grabbing the handles of Will's wheelchair, rushing him out of the room, nearly banging his feet on the doorjamb. They burst into the hallway, nearly T-boning a patient bed being wheeled by, then almost running down two nurses who jumped aside. Dodds pushed the wheelchair fast while he bent down to Will's ear.

"You fucker, you cocksucker, damn you all to hell, you'd better be pulling my chain. You'd better be in some drug-induced hallucination…"

"You know better. Slow down."

"God damn you to hell, Borders."

Dodds flashed his badge at the elevator bank, people cleared out, and they got a down-bound car all to themselves. "I ought to bring you up on charges, if you've been meddling in a crime scene. Bastard, bastard, bastard…" The doors opened into the darkness and Dodds sped them toward Lustig's office, past the single bank of overhead lights. He stopped the wheelchair so hard Will was thrown forward.

"Don't apply to be an orderly," he said.

"Fuck you, fuck, fuck you," Dodds mumbled. "Crime scene seal broken. Son of a bitch. There's no chain of custody now, whatever the hell we find. This is worse than a rookie mistake. Without the seal on the door, any defense lawyer can say we just planted the evidence. We can't prove chain of custody. The DA would have our jobs—what the hell am I saying: my job. I ought to use this Ka-Bar on you myself."

"Calm down. Don't open the door yet." Will pointed to a strip of medical tape across the yellow seal. It had his initials written on it. "That's me. Nobody's been inside since."

"You put that on there?"

Will nodded.

"After you broke the seal to go inside."

"No. Actually, I followed you inside. You left and I was still in there."

"Sneaky, fucking, cripple bastard."

"So when I left I wanted to make sure the chain of custody was clean. So I got the tape, wrote my initials, taped it across where the seal was split. You see it."

"I'm gonna arrest your ass right now."

"I'm still a sworn officer."

"Damn you to hell." He slit the tape with a pocketknife, fumbled with a key, and swung open the door.

"It's under the desk drawer, taped there with duct tape."

Dodds moved to the desk, looking back angrily. "Did you take it out, touch it?"

"Sure. I also wiped it clean of prints."

"Bastard. Asshole."

Will thought about what Scaly Mueller had said about two old married people fighting, but it didn't make him smile. He had a fleeting image of Cindy to add to the constant reminder of her leaving. Somehow he was lousy with partners.

Dodds produced a pair of latex gloves from his jacket pocket. He felt carefully under the center drawer of the desk. In a moment he pulled out a dark rectangle cradled in the duct tape that had held it to the bottom of the center desk drawer. He put it on top of the desk and carefully unwrapped the knife. Using an evidence envelope from another coat pocket, he meticulously slid the duct tape inside and sealed it. Then he opened the knife. It clicked into place with a sharp metal sound.

Unfolded, it looked like the skeleton of a prehistoric predator. The handle was thick and black. The blade was stainless steel, with a sharp leading edge that turned into a nasty looking saw-like serration as it got closer to the handle. There was a hole in the upper part of the blade, as if in dinosaur days it had been an eye socket.

"That would scare the hell out of anybody who saw it coming."

"Fuck you."

"It will also be common enough that we can't trace, and it won't have prints."

"Fuck you."

Dodds studied it under the light, his mouth turning deeper and deeper into an inverted U. He slid it into another evidence envelope and sealed it. He swung around in the chair and sighed.

"When were you going to tell me about this?"

"I assumed you had found it by now. Anyway, I was going to check on the seal today and if it hadn't been broken, I was going to call you. I didn't expect a hero's welcome for what I was going to tell you."

"That's sure as hell right."

"Let me ask you something. That day when you came down here, when I snuck in behind you. Did you come back in a few minutes and try the door?"

"No."

"Somebody did."

"Maybe it was a security guard."

"This was different. Somebody tried the door several times."

Dodds murmured something and shook his head. "Well, I guess our shit-stained boy didn't kill her. That may not work out for your Florence Nightingale."

"Cheryl Beth?"

"Cheryl Beth Wilson, RN." He drew out each syllable. "I consider her a person of interest."

"Come on…"

"She found her, you know."

Now Will remembered that night, when he had been groggy on drugs, terrified of the late-night trip to the MRI. He had seen her there, outside the office, her white lab coat stained with blood.

Dodds went on. "It gets better. She was banging Lustig's husband. I call that motive."

Will was starting to hurt again, but he had to hang on. He had gotten this far. He said, "Yeah, you should have seen how effectively she fought against this guy in the hall. No way. Why aren't you looking at the husband?"

"Fuck you."

"Because you know it's the Slasher. It takes you awhile to come around sometimes, if you didn't think of something in the first place. But you know, Dodds. You know who did this."

Will moved his wheelchair closer. "You know why I was in that old atrium today, on my ass, on the floor, when the homeless guy attacked me?"

Dodds opened his hands as if a bird would appear and fly away.

"Bud Chambers dumped me there on the floor. It's probably a miracle he didn't do worse."

"What the hell are you talking about?"

Will told him about the confrontation. "Thanks for spreading the word about me," he added.

"It wasn't me, but believe what you want," Dodds said. "Look, I get where you're coming from with Chambers. I didn't just like him for Theresa, I loved him. But we couldn't make the case.

Remember how much time we spent on him and that skank girlfriend, what the hell was her name?"

"Darlene."

"We couldn't build a case. Hunches aren't evidence. And command didn't want another scandal. So they eased him out. Okay, they eased him out after you pushed for it. But we never could find a connection between Chambers and the other killings. Then we got Factor. A jury agreed. How the hell do you explain the DNA?"

"That was only on Theresa."

"So?"

"So, Factor was technically only convicted on that crime. It was just assumed he did the other two. Anyway, you're the one who always says young detectives depend too much on DNA, that they've lost the ability to do old-fashioned police work. We screwed up. He's killing again. This one," he indicated the doctor's office, "has all the marks of the Slasher, right down to the hidden knife. Nobody knew about the hidden knife except us and the killer. He just loves to mind-fuck us."

"Okay, assuming Bud was good for the three women. And don't go nuts, because that's a big leap. I'm not there with you. But assuming… Why would he kill Christine Lustig?"

"I don't know. Let me see the murder book."

"You're unbelievable." Dodds gave a petulant laugh. "Take my word for it. There was no link. The doctor didn't know this guy. Why would he come for her? Even if he's a serial killer, why her?"

"Have you questioned Chambers? Until you do, you won't know." Will suddenly felt a crushing exhaustion, as if a wave had hit him. He pushed on. Even the words hurt to say. "Maybe she was his type, the one that makes his fucked-up mind want to kill again. He just sees her once and this nut-job gene goes off in his brain. She looked like Theresa. See if he's been around the hospital. He knew his way well enough to find me."

Dodds stared into his lap. "Maybe. But we never heard about hang-up calls with the three."

"They were dead by the time we could ask, and they were all single women living alone."

"We ran the LUDs on every one. We only saw Chambers' number on Theresa's phone, which is explainable. And we found…"

"I know," Will interrupted, "what we found. Killers can buy disposable cell phones, use pay phones. Hell, we see that every day with drug dealers. He was a cop, for God's sake."

"Maybe."

"Let me see the murder book."

"I'll think about it. In the meantime, you'd better watch your ass. You have a gift for making enemies, and let's just say you're not in fighting trim."

Will wasn't listening. He was so tired. He managed, "He's going to kill again. Soon."

Chapter Fourteen

The guard walked Cheryl Beth to her car that night, as he had since the killing. His name was Don and he was a tall, lanky black man whose stride she had difficulty matching. Still, she had grown to enjoy his company. He talked about his children and his car, comforting subjects. He had never asked her about finding Christine—he seemed like the only person at the hospital who didn't want to know all the details. Tonight, he was out of character.

"You must feel relieved they got him," Don said. "Ol' Lennie. You just never know…"

"You never do." She added, "Scared the crap out of me," and Don laughed. It was a nice sound. She knew she should be relieved. Her body didn't feel it. Her legs were tense and exhausted from the confrontation. She kept those words *lucky to be alive* at a distance, still marveling at how the patient had wrestled Lennie into submission. She had learned that Will Borders was a police detective, and he was in the hospital for a spinal cord tumor. He had saved her when she, a caregiver, should have been saving him. That was her mother's voice, which could adapt to so many useless occasions. She shoved it aside.

She was alive and didn't begrudge the long day that resulted from the time giving the police a statement. Still, she had to complete her new consults, check on a dozen other patients, write out new order sheets, and end the day in her office, doing paperwork. Not even Lisa was left to regale her with hospital gossip or hear about her adventure. She hadn't gotten out until nine. Now her hand and back ached from where Lennie had knocked the cell away and roughly pushed her down. The knife had appeared so suddenly. Had it been so sudden for Christine? How could it have been that way, if she was already naked? It must have gone on much longer. He must have planned it. She thought about all the times she had seen Lennie and had dismissed him as another hospital eccentric, one more poor soul that fell through the cracks. She had been alone with him in an elevator once. She shivered inside her coat as they walked in silence. She would be okay now, she told herself, looking forward to getting home and having a drink.

They walked through several sets of automatic doors to reach the parking garage, going from the old building, through a newer wing, up and down the ramps made to allow beds and wheelchairs to transit buildings that didn't exactly match, and finally down a long, brightly lit tube of glass that crossed the street and emptied into the parking area. It was a ten-minute fast walk and tonight she walked slower, aching. Don would just have to wait. She hated to inconvenience him but she was still grateful for his presence. If Christine's killer really were in jail, soon she would have to give up her escorts from Don. Growing up in Corbin, she would have been terrified to be alone with a black man in a parking garage. She was sure her relatives still felt that way. *Thank God I got out of there*, she silently mouthed.

"Everybody must be clearing out for the holidays," Don was saying, surveying the nearly empty floor of the garage. The concrete surface, walls, and pillars all glowed gray-orange under the halogen lights. The relative shelter against the cold provided by the crossover was gone and the garage was freezing. Their breath made foggy clouds ahead of them. Several blue emergency stations were visible, where people could call for help in emergencies. "Always makes me sad, Christmas," Don said. "Especially for the people who are stuck here."

The man stood framed in a stairwell, at the opposite corner of the garage. He was maybe fifty yards away. A white man, he wore black jeans, a Reds cap, a brown leather jacket. He just stood there. He hadn't bounded up the stairs and was walking to his car. There were only about five cars left on the floor. He just stood there, watching them. Cheryl Beth felt her heart start racing.

"Don…"

"I see him."

Her red Saturn was comfortingly close.

"Probably nothing, but I'm gonna talk to him," Don said. "Once you're safe and sound."

"I can take it from here," she said, patting his arm.

"You sure?"

She nodded. "I'll feel better to have you between me and him anyway. He's probably just looking for his car, but…"

"Don't you worry, Cheryl Beth." Don peeled off and walked toward the man. Cheryl Beth made her aching legs cross the last twenty feet to the Saturn. By habit, she already had her key out. She stepped between her car and the black Accord parked next to her.

Something in the Accord made her look. It was white, on the front passenger seat. An envelope. Then it all happened at once: the name *Dr. Christine Lustig* written in a neat script in blue ink. Cheryl Beth hadn't been snooping, she would later tell herself. She just saw the name—she had always had twenty-twenty vision—and at first couldn't believe it. That made her look closer, until she was leaning against the Honda. The envelope was addressed to Christine. It was on a pile of files and a portfolio sitting in the gray passenger seat. She glanced toward Don and saw that both he and the man in the Reds cap had disappeared. She lingered at the window, knowing she was being nosy, feeling a terrible dread from such an ordinary piece of paper. The envelope addressed to Christine had been opened; the top of it was torn and ragged as if it had been unsealed with fingers, not a letter opener. It was just sitting there. She strained to see the return address, but couldn't. She pulled out her penlight and shone it inside.

The rest of the car looked neat. The outside had been recently washed and glowed under the lights. The backseat was empty, the front seats clean…no spent Starbucks cups in the cup holders like in her car. Just a pile of files and a portfolio, maybe three inches thick, and on top of it a No. 10 envelope addressed in blue ink to Dr. Christine Lustig. A folded letter was visible at the edge of the serration. It wasn't addressed to her office at the hospital. Cheryl Beth could make out her home address in Hyde Park. The return address, damn, just too small…

"May I help you?"

She gasped in a second of hysteria, then recovered. She slipped the penlight in her pocket. A man had appeared on the driver's side of the car. He was wearing green scrubs and had a striking face: pale skin, prominent dark eyebrows, small eyes, intense stare. His dark hair was close-cropped and was creeping well back from his prominent, pasty forehead. She guessed he was in his early thirties. And he was wearing only green scrubs in this cold. His upper arms had sharply defined muscles.

"I…dropped my keys. Oh, here they are." She bent down and scraped her keychain on the concrete. When she stood again, he was still on the driver's side, staring at her. She was too overcome at being discovered to feel scared. Anyway, he had a hospital identification clipped to his shirt pocket. It read: Judd Mason, RN. She didn't know him.

"It's freezing out here." She forced a smile. "Aren't you cold?"

"No."

"Well, have a nice evening." She turned, unlocked her car, slid down into the seat, and relocked it. Her hands were shaking as she pushed the key into the ignition. Her breath was already fogging up the windows. She didn't dare look at the Accord again. She turned the key. The engine started.

As she drove away, she looked in the rearview mirror. He was still standing beside his car, watching her go.

Chapter Fifteen

Will watched Cheryl Beth walk through the automatic doors toward the parking garage. He was relieved that she had a guard, even though he thought most security guards would be worthless in a confrontation. Dodds' talk about her as a person of interest, a potential suspect—he wouldn't have bought it even if Christine Lustig's murder didn't have all the signs of the Slasher. He guessed that Cheryl Beth was about Cindy's height, five-five, and she had a small-to-medium build: not someone with the strength or reach to kill with a knife with repeated, almost teasing slashes, followed by deeper wounds and a coup de grâce to the throat. The only case he could remember of a woman slashing a person's throat had been years ago in Price Hill. A drunken husband sleeping it off, he'd beaten his wife once too often. She had taken a kitchen knife and had driven it into the side of his neck. When Will and Dodds had arrived, she was still hysterical about the copious blood from the wound—and she had looked like a tough biker chick. No, Lustig had not been killed by a woman.

Why wasn't Dodds going after her husband? Will had learned he was a doctor, a surgeon, named Gary Nagle. Neither he nor Dodds had ever been shy about investigating powerful people. A husband playing around had a powerful motive, even if he could hire expensive lawyers or call friends at City Hall. Will knew Dodds didn't have any real theory of the crime other than the Slasher. Dodds just didn't want to admit it. If Will had been running the investigation, he would have done anything to get Chambers back in an interrogation room, find probable cause to execute a search warrant. But when Dodds had asked if Will wanted to press charges for the assault, Will had said no. A chickenshit beef where Chambers could make bail, if he were even charged, would just make him more cautious. Or it might make him more dangerous.

All this was on his mind as he watched Cheryl Beth and the guard pass through the last set of automatic doors into the garage. Will had wheeled himself up the ramp into the glassed-in bridge that connected the hospital to the parking garage. He was alone in the long, glassy, carpeted expanse. It looked like a part to a space station in an old science fiction movie. He spent a long time just watching the empty winter street below, watching the traffic in the distance, where healthy people were living their lives on the outside. He held his hand against the glass and let the cold move from his fingers up his wrist and arm. The feeling was good.

The sound behind him caught him daydreaming. His fright seemed to expand every blood vessel. Chambers. Damn. But, no, it was just a doctor or hospital worker striding past toward the parking area. He wore only green hospital garb, no coat. An iron man. At first Will wondered if the man might challenge him, sitting alone out there. It was past visiting hours, past time for him to return to the neuro-rehab ward. He wondered if they would even miss him if he just took an elevator down to the lobby and wheeled himself out into the big world.

With his chilled hands back on the rims of the wheelchair, he reluctantly turned himself around and rolled back inside the hospital. The usually bustling offices on these floors were closed and the hallways empty. Oncology. Diabetes Center. Endocrinology. Blood Services. The signs neatly denoted doorways or directed people down hallways. The signs pointed to dread and pain and suffering, but maybe that was just the mood he was in tonight.

He turned the corner as he heard the voices, a man and a woman arguing. They were standing maybe fifteen feet ahead of him, facing each other but with their sides to Will. They were holding each other's hands, but the body language was tense, as if the connection could quickly be broken. Will immediately retreated back behind the wall. Her voice was young and emotional, his older, rich-timbred, slightly condescending, words with extra enunciation. He was trying to get her to do something, or calm her down, and she was having none of it. Will knew the woman. It was one of the physical therapists that worked with the neuro-rehab patients in the gym each morning. Her name was Amy and she was cute and kind. The other man was tall and lanky, with a neat beard and wearing a white lab coat over well-pressed slacks, white shirt, tie—a doctor. He couldn't make out the words, just the mood, stormy, until he very clearly heard the words from the man: "Cheryl Beth" and, a few beats later, "police."

"Police?" Amy nearly shrieked before bringing her voice down and then Will was back to hearing angry gibberish. He didn't dare show himself. He strained to hear more.

Then there was silence, too long a pause, followed by footsteps coming toward him. Will hunched forward and fired his arms to get the wheelchair moving. He slid into a deserted waiting area. Muzak piped annoyingly from the overhead speakers, made louder by the emptiness of the room. It was just rows of chairs, tables with sticky magazines, a couple of sickly plants, and windows looking into blackness. Will put his head down and his hands together.

"Hey, Will, are you all right?"

Will raised his head. Amy was bent down on her haunches to be on his level, a position you'd use to speak to a child. He pushed the thought aside and said, "Long day."

"I bet." She forced a smile and gave a long sniffle. "Allergies," she said. Her eyes were red and swollen. Will fished in his little pack and produced a small packet of tissues. She pulled one out and wiped her nose and eyes.

"Thank you. I heard about your fight with Crazy Lennie at the old entrance today. Wow, all those lat pulls you've been doing must have paid off!"

She was so young and pretty it almost made him ache, but it also made him sad for her. She spoke with the voice of the young and pretty and innocent. "You know, I was taking a shortcut from neuro-rehab to the cafeteria the other day, and I turned the corner and there was Lennie. I will still shaken up by what happened to Dr. Lustig, but I didn't put two and two together. It was just Lennie."

Just part of the furniture here, Will thought, like me.

"He did seem more agitated than I had ever seen him. Said something about seeing the devil, and then he ran to the stairwell. Anyway, I'm really glad you're okay. You shouldn't seem down."

Will watched her face. It was like a dam ready to burst. He lowered his head and shook it.

"My wife told me she's leaving me."

"Oh, my god! Oh, Will, I'm so sorry." She took his hands. He kept his head down.

"I'm not surprised. I can't really say I blame her."

"Don't say that!" Amy started sobbing. "That's not true. I'm sure you're a wonderful man. You've got…you're going to come back. How could anybody do that to another human being…"

"She deserves someone who's not crippled."

"Don't say that! She's a fool…"

He held her hands and let her cry. Back in the old days, this is when Dodds would have given him the look known only to the two of them; it said, *you manipulative bastard.*

"She's a fool," she repeated. "You seem like a nice man."

"Why don't you pull over a chair." She did.

She sat next to him and he put an arm around her slender shoulders as she sobbed. "This is so unprofessional," she softly wailed but didn't stop crying. Nobody else was around.

"The first bad call I ever went on when I got out of the academy was a multiple shooting. It was really bad, but we didn't know what it was. Just an unknown trouble call. I'd been on the job for maybe two months. I knocked on the door and a woman throws the door open. She's got a little girl in her arms and her expression is…I'd never seen anything like it. She knew she was dying but she's staring intensely at me. And then she falls forward into my arms and it's me and her and the little girl in between us. I eased them both down and when I take the girl, I see the woman's been shot. It's like she has on a red blouse it's so bad. The little girl is alive, not a scratch, but she's completely silent. You'd better believe I cried after all that." It was true. His training officer had berated him for months as "Weepy Borders."

This only made Amy's shoulders heave more until she said, in a very clear voice, "Why are people so cruel to each other?"

"I don't know." That they were was the policeman's paycheck.

"I bet you've seen some pretty bad things," she said.

Will said he had.

"Did you ever play around on your wife?"

"No," he lied. The dynamic was going his way and he didn't dare any diversions that might keep him from the chance to find out why she had been talking to the doctor about police and Cheryl Beth. He gently moved his arm from her shoulders, resting his hand on her arm.

"I didn't think so. You're a good man. I always fall for the bad boys." She gave a teary sniffle-laugh.

"Well, he's a fool if he doesn't appreciate you. You've got way too much going for you to put up with that."

"He's married."

"I figured that," Will said. "It doesn't make you a bad person. Stuff happens."

"He said he'd leave his wife. God, I sound like such a dummy."

Will didn't say anything. He could hear a siren in the far distance, through the very quiet hum contained in the hospital walls.

"He was having an affair with someone else, too. He didn't leave his wife for her, but I thought it would be different with me. He probably told her the same lines. He's a doctor, of course. They think they're gods. Such a sense of entitlement."

"You deserve better," Will said.

"Oh, god, I don't know what I deserve. This has gone so bad."

"So kick him to the curb. If I wasn't crippled, I'd be chasing you around the room."

She laughed and put her hand on top of his. "It's really bad. I'm really afraid."

After she fell silent for several minutes, he coaxed her. Why was she afraid?

"You're a cop, right? Police officer, I mean."

"That's right."

"What happens if someone lies to the police?"

His side was killing him from being twisted in her direction. The muscles were twitching like little earthquakes. He didn't dare move. "It's not good. It could make someone an accessory to a crime." It could also be just giving a false statement, but why tell her that? She gave a sharp intake of breath. Her head was down and all he could see of her eyes were long blond lashes.

"He was her husband, you know. The man I've been involved with."

"Whose husband?"

"Dr. Lustig. Gary is her husband. It happened so fast between us. We've been seeing each other only about two months. He said they were getting a divorce."

"It's okay, Amy. Have you lied to the police?"

She nodded once, half an inch up and down.

"Are you going to have me arrested?"

"No. But you have to make it right."

"I'm afraid. I could lose my job. He could blackball me."

"You're not that way, Amy," Will said. "I've seen the way you work with the quads. You're no quitter. You won't let any of us quit. Right?"

The pretty head nodded, more adamantly this time.

"Who asked you to lie to the police?"

"Gary."

"This was Dr. Lustig's husband, Gary Nagle?"

"Yes."

"What did he ask you to tell the police?"

Amy looked him straight on. "He wanted me to say that we were together the night she was murdered."

Chapter Sixteen

Dr. Gary Nagle was a man with a secret and he wanted his girlfriend to lie for him. It didn't matter much to Will, unless it would help focus Dodds' mind, get him off his theory that Cheryl Beth had anything to do with the murder. Knowing Dodds, however, he realized this new information might cause him to wonder if Cheryl Beth and Nagle had acted together to eliminate a wife that was in the way. He would have thought the same, if all the evidence hadn't pointed to the real killer. Nagle's secret was a distraction. Any other explanation was too fantastic: that Nagle himself was the Slasher. And what? He killed the other women to throw the police off, in preparation for killing Christine Lustig? Will chuckled to himself as he wheeled down the empty hallway, back to another dreary night trapped in neuro-rehab. He didn't even have a shower to look forward to—that wasn't until tomorrow night. And he wouldn't be expecting a morning visit from Cindy, ever again.

He rolled down the slight incline through another set of automatic doors and then he was in the old hospital tower, with its narrower hallways and drab, fading walls. He passed a waiting area that was empty except for one young man, wearing jeans, a black T-shirt, and a jacket. He was tapping into one of those personal data assistants—is that what they called them?—while he had an agitated conversation on the cell phone. He lowered his voice as he saw Will roll past. So many sad stories in the hospital.

In a minute he would reach the main elevator bank then take the elevator down to his "home." But he had to pee like a sonofabitch. The feeling had come upon him suddenly, as it always did now. It was as if he were inhabiting someone else's body and starting all over learning about it, and it sure as hell didn't work as well as his old body, the one lost to the tumor. The hallway ahead of him mostly consisted of long, empty walls, white with pastel stripes, as if you followed them long enough they might lead to Oz or someplace wonderful. The one thing lacking was any sign of a restroom. But he reached a narrow corridor leading to the right with a restroom sign and an arrow. This passage was unlighted and he depended on the light coming in off the main hall to guide him. He glided in ten feet and touched the door. It opened and he turned on the lights. He desperately didn't want to urinate on himself.

Now it was the tricky part. There had never been a graduation ceremony where he could get to the toilet by himself. It had just happened, with him on his own and the nurses so distracted with the worse-off patients. He couldn't stand, of course. He angled the wheelchair by the toilet seat and locked the wheels into place. Next he kicked up the footrests—this took more doing with the one for his weak left leg—and slid himself to the edge of the seat. With one fluid motion he used the railing on the wall by the toilet to pull himself over. Then he took down his sweatpants and relieved himself. The bathroom lacked the usual call button with a long string, in case a patient fell and needed help. It was also ancient, with tile so old it was mottled with decades of dirt and efforts to remove it. Tile pieces were coming apart where they had retrofitted the handicapped railing into the wall. When he was done, he repeated the moves in reverse. One bad move and he would have been helplessly on the floor.

Ready...flex...shift. He was back in the chair. He washed his hands and used the hand sanitizer he had become obsessive about, knowing he was surrounded by germs and illness. When he backed the wheelchair out of the restroom he saw it. At the end of the short, dim corridor was an elevator door. He had been all over this part of the old tower but he never knew there was another elevator outside the big bank of six elevators at the center of the building. Now here was this: a small set of unmistakable elevator doors. The buttons were black and stuck out half an inch, something from the fifties maybe. This whole end of the corridor smelled like dust. He wheeled his way there and pressed the down button. He was surprised to hear a distant motor whirring.

The car arrived and the doors pulled back, revealing a long, narrow space. Unlike the spacious cars at the main elevators, this could fit at best one bed, maybe not even that. Whatever the small, rogue elevator's purpose, it didn't look as if it had been used much for years. Unlike the hospital, it had a distinct sour smell. A single fixture in the center of the ceiling provided light; it held a hundred dead bugs. The floor was broken linoleum, the color of dying winter lawn. The walls were linoleum bracketed by long metal strips. Once the walls must have been as white as an old nurse's cap, but now they were fading, too. A dozen prominent scars told of years of banging carts and beds against them. Will wheeled the chair in and turned around. Down the hallway the main corridor of the hospital was known and safe. He looked at it a long time, keeping the doors open with his hand. Finally, he let them close with a creaky bang. He pressed the old black button that read B, and the car lurched, making a deep, echoing clang, then found its footing and began a smooth descent.

The door opened on the blackest dark he had ever experienced. The little overhead light of the elevator barely penetrated past the threshold. A musty smell assaulted his nose. The door started to close as if it didn't want to linger in such blackness. Will dug into his fanny pack and pulled out the small flashlight he had kept in it since long before it became his bag of provisions in the hospital. Powered by two C-cell batteries, it was enough to illuminate a few feet in front of him. Still, he hesitated and stayed in the elevator car, keeping the door open. Ahead of him was a ten-foot-deep space with scuffed gray walls and rubber mats over a broken gray linoleum floor. No light switch was visible. Then the space made an abrupt right turn.

Will hadn't been afraid of the dark since he was six years old. He had to banish that fear to take care of his younger brother, who had night terrors. It was a good attribute for a policeman, who might be alone in the empty night inside one of the abandoned industrial cathedrals of Cincinnati. But he still hesitated, studying the utilitarian walls ahead of him, somehow comforted by the fragile light of the elevator car. But there were questions. Questions he and Dodds had never answered. It had been that kind of case. The door banged against his hand and the car started buzzing. Will clenched the small flashlight in his teeth and wheeled himself out onto the rubber mat. The elevator closed behind him and he was alone, armed with the small cone of light.

His hands pushed lightly, moving the well-machined wheels of the wheelchair forward. He stopped at the angle and took the flashlight in his hand to play across the next space. A nearby wall held an old time clock. Like so many antiques, it had a black metal plaque with the manufacturer's name and "Cincinnati, Ohio." So many things used to be made in this city. The clock was broken at 12:13 and covered with dust. He made a quick sweep with the light and at first thought this might have been an old kitchen. It was a large room with tile walls, metal shelves, large sinks, and what looked like freezer doors. Water and rust stains marked the walls. A rickety wooden ladder sat askew against one. The silence wrapped around him.

But it was no kitchen. It was a morgue.

A shiver slithered up his left shoulder blade to his neck. It was a silly thing. He had been in countless morgues. Here, the distinctive porcelain autopsy tables were still in place. In new postmortem labs they tended to be stainless steel and fancy. This place was old and probably hadn't been used in years. The old elevator must have been used to bring down the dead, out of the sight of families and patients. Still, the smell of decaying flesh lingered. Will gave it a once-over with the flashlight and rolled toward a set of double doors.

He knew he was on borrowed time. The pain meds Cheryl Beth had given him would soon wear off and he was far from the nurses' station in neuro-rehab. He pushed the chair to the double doors. They were secure, but he noticed the remains of a push bar. The bar was gone but the lever was still in place. He leaned against it and the doors gave way. Now he was in a long, wide, dark corridor, but a bank of fluorescent lights was visible maybe a hundred feet away. And suddenly he knew exactly where he was.

Christine Lustig's office was a hundred and twenty feet straight ahead. Cheryl Beth had walked down this hallway alone that night, finding a nude body with dozens of slash marks. She might have seen the doctor's clothes folded neatly on a desk or a shelf. Did she scream that night, out into the empty dark hallway? Did the killer know Cheryl Beth was going to be there?

Will turned back to the doors to the old morgue. They were tightly locked and the buttons on the latches refused to budge. But when he trained the beam of the flashlight on where the doors joined, he saw how the lock could easily be picked. He was playing a hunch, a long shot. But it might not only answer a question about the night Lustig was killed, but also one of the most puzzling issues about the Mount Adams Slasher. He fished in the fanny pack and pulled out a slender black-and-silver object. He pressed his thumb against the button and a blade flashed out and locked into place. It was a switchblade he had taken off a suspect years ago and he had kept it. It was illegal and useful in tough situations. Will slipped the blade between the doors and easily released the latch. He pulled the door open and wheeled himself back inside. He discovered the lights and, using the knife instead of his fingers, turned them on. Gradually the old fluorescents came alive, giving the spacious room a yellow-green tint. He carefully studied his surroundings.

A newer plastic wastebasket sat by one shelf. Inside were torn condom wrappers and used condoms. Some of the living had been having fun down here. He wheeled himself to the dozen freezer drawers, lined in two rows one on top of the other. He pulled down his sleeve to cover his hand to keep his fingerprints off the handles and began opening the doors. The refrigerator hadn't been on in years and the decaying flesh smell worsened. Meanwhile, pain was starting to radiate out of the middle of his back like mercury rising in a thermometer on a summer day. It scared him more than the old morgue around him.

Just a little more time. A little more...

It was the drawer on the lower tier, one drawer in from the left. Will slowly pulled out the body tray, making a loud metal-on-metal racket. Just inside was a black trash bag. He carefully folded back the bag and saw the bloody clothes. Using the switchblade, he poked through the fabric until he found something solid. The knife hooked into it and Will pulled. The blade had caught on a lanyard used to hold an ID card. It was the kind of hospital identification Will had seen on every employee at Cincinnati Memorial. This one was caked with dried, dark blood, but not so much that Will couldn't see the photo of a beautiful, auburn-haired woman and the lettering. It said Christine D. Lustig, MD.

Chapter Seventeen

She wanted nothing more than a long, hot shower and a Bushmills on the rocks. She could almost feel the softness of the robe against her as she waited to take her first sip. She would make it downstairs, bring the drink up to her bedroom, and lock herself in with her music and a book. With the commotion and arrest today, there was no reason she couldn't get back to her old habits and just enjoy the downstairs. But not tonight. The day had been too intense. In addition to Lennie, she had been overloaded with patients. Just as she had been leaving, she had been paged to the emergency room with Trauma Team One. An ambulance had brought in a burn patient.

He should have gone straight to the burn center at University Hospital, but there had been a mix-up. Now they had to stabilize him. A twenty-three-year-old kid who had been using gasoline to set a building on fire. He had deep, thick burns on both legs and the smell of burned flesh filled the exam room. The usual morphine dose didn't work, of course—too many years using narcotics on the street. He moaned and screamed like a child. Just seeing the team set up made him more agitated. Cheryl Beth pushed as far as she could to ramp up the IV morphine dose, but he never really settled down. She could still smell the burned flesh.

A hot shower and a Bushmills would settle her down. She might even smile recalling how the cop in the wheelchair had taken Lennie down. But after she left the parking garage, she pulled into the valet parking lane at the hospital and watched the garage behind her. Soon the Honda Accord emerged. She couldn't explain why she did what she did next. It just happened. She let the car reach the end of the block, where the long red light annoyed drivers, and she pulled out behind him. It was as simple and foolhardy as lingering beside that car, which had caused her to see the letter inside, addressed to Christine Lustig.

She was only half a block along when he turned right on Madison and disappeared. She gunned the little Saturn engine to keep up and made a rolling stop at the light. He was already several blocks down the avenue. Traffic was light and the asphalt was dry. Would he keep going straight into Walnut Hills, Mount Lookout, and Hyde Park? No. He turned onto Interstate 71 and headed north. She felt her stomach in a vise, but pushed to make it through the light so she could follow him. Soon they were both going seventy. Cheryl Beth had never tailed anyone in her life. She had only seen it done on television. It was an odd guilty, exhilarating feeling. She hung back several car lengths, trying to keep herself from being distracted by other taillights.

The Accord took the Galbraith Road exit, shining silver under the streetlights as it exited the freeway. Cheryl Beth followed, slowing to let another car get between them. They took the green light and drove past the deserted Kenwood Towne Center and its vast parking lot. The normally crowded suburban roads were placid. The business signs glowed merrily. She was so far behind on her Christmas shopping. That all seemed a grotesque joke now. All the Santa Claus red only reminded her of Christine on the floor, awash in her own blood. She nervously started checking the gas tank: the gauge showed a quarter of a tank.

They went more than a mile on Galbraith and turned into a residential street, then followed a spaghetti of streets past cul-de-sacs and look-alike houses with big garage doors. This part of town had a mix of houses, older subdivisions with ranches and tri-levels from the 1950s and 1960s, some very old surviving farmhouses, and the newer, large houses that had been built as the mall expanded. She couldn't believe how much it had grown since she had first moved to Cincinnati to go to nursing school. These houses looked only a few years old. The trash hampers were all neatly moved to the curb for tomorrow's pickup. Cheryl Beth hated it out here. She imagined Andy was now living in a house just like these somewhere on the outskirts of Corbin, with his new wife and children. New wife! Cheryl Beth and Andy had been divorced for more than fifteen years. She laughed at herself, hanging as far back as she could without losing the red taillight beacons ahead. The Accord suddenly slowed and swung into a driveway, as a garage door opened and the garage light flooded into the cold night.

"Just act like you belong," she said out loud, pulling to the curb three houses down. Suddenly a pair of headlights appeared behind her and swept across the dashboard. She was clammy with guilt. *What if they live here?* She slid down in the seat, trying to let the headrest conceal her. But the black sedan drove on by and turned into a cul-de-sac farther on. Only after it passed did she think to turn off the engine so the fog from the tailpipe was not visible. She had never been a sneak. It felt strange.

At the house, the garage door stayed open as long minutes passed. Then she saw Judd Mason emerge on the driveway, still wearing only his scrubs. He stood at the top of the long driveway, seeming to survey the street. She unconsciously slid down further in her seat. He walked down the driveway. In his hand he held a plastic bag. He looked around again, then deposited the bag in the trash hamper sitting by the curb. With quick, long strides he walked back to the garage and the door closed behind him. She tracked him through the house as lights came on in the front room, then went off, followed by the lights turning on in the second story.

Cheryl Beth sat in the car as the cold infiltrated the windshield, came through the door, took control of her feet. She tried not to breathe so deeply. The windshield was starting to fog up. She could hear herself lightly wheezing and she took a puff of the Combivent. Cincinnati was hell on asthma. Sinus Valley. Anxiety was hell on asthma, too. She pulled out the bright red Tylenol lanyard that

held her ID and her yellow pain card and started fiddling with it.
She had been a nail-biter in high school. Now she pried at the
lamination on the yellow card showing the Wong-Baker faces
pain rating system. It started with a circle with bright eyes and
a smile and moved up the scale to a circle with tears and an
inverted U as a mouth. She had felt that way lately.

What happened next was pure impulsiveness. She started the
car and crept down the road with the headlights off until she
was in front of Judd Mason's house. His upstairs lights went out.
She took a quick look around—all the houses on the street were
asleep—and opened the door, stepping out into the chill. She
counted the steps to keep herself calm: eleven. Then she was in
front of the heavy plastic trash hamper. The lid came up easily
and the plastic bag was right on top of a pile of white, tied trash
bags. She grabbed it, set the lid down carefully, and walked back
to the car, only ten steps this time, her throat tight with tension.
Then she was safe in the car and moving. She didn't turn on the
headlights until she was another block away.

She came out on Galbraith Road alone. Or she thought she
was, until she saw headlights appear out of the same side street.
Her stomach tightened. Surely Mason couldn't have seen her and
given chase. She accelerated and left the headlights far behind her,
then she was around more cars as she neared the freeway. At the
red light, she turned and picked through the trash. There it was:
the white envelope with Christine's name written on it. She had
stolen it. Was it stealing if something had already been thrown
away? Was it stealing something that had already been stolen?
What was this nurse doing with an opened envelope belonging
to Christine?

She turned back toward the city and merged into the fast lane,
exhaustion starting to make her body feel heavy. Now she was
really looking forward to home, and hoping that everybody could
make it through the night without a page to return to the hospital.
The heater was a relief after sitting so long in the cold.

The rearview mirror was irresistible. Was that the same pair
of headlights that had followed her out onto Galbraith? Now

she was just tired and guilty and paranoid. She would decide tomorrow what to do about the letter. She would read it tonight, though. She plucked it out of the trash and slipped it in the lab coat pocket that held her other notes from the day. Then she settled in the seat and drove as the freeway made its gentle descent toward downtown and the Ohio River.

She eased off the interstate and turned onto Taft, the one-way that would take her home. She crossed Reading and it turned into Calhoun. The bundle of buildings of Pill Hill blazed with lights, dominated by the vast University Hospital complex. Farther to the east was the imposing deco tower of Cincinnati Memorial. Soon she would be passing the University of Cincinnati on the right, as she did every night. But her stomach was folded in on itself. She was sure the same car had followed her off the freeway and was just a few blocks behind her. She cursed each red light, but it gave her a chance to look back. The car was right behind her at Vine. It wasn't the Accord. But it might be the black sedan that had passed her back in Kenwood. There was only one occupant, but she couldn't see more because of the glare of the headlights. When she looked forward again the light was green.

She was overreacting, she just knew it. The car would pass on when she turned left on Clifton Avenue to head home. But it didn't. Both her hands clamped the steering wheel until they ached. The driver was brazen now, right behind her. It was the black sedan. Panic flooded her limbs. Now she was in her neighborhood of old bungalows and century-old trees, but he was right behind her. She couldn't let herself be trapped on her dead-end street. So she turned on Warner, doubled back north on Ohio and turned right on McMillan. Traffic was light and all the businesses that catered to the university were closed. Only a couple of bars were open. The black car stayed with her. She accelerated and turned south on Vine, not yet sure what to do. Her right hand fished out her cell phone. Should she call the police? Maybe it was all a mistake.

The skyscrapers of downtown shimmered ahead as Vine dropped down through the dreary blocks of the ghetto. She raced past the dark, abandoned buildings toward Central Parkway. She hit sixty. She never drove this fast in the city. The sedan paced her. The light at Central Parkway was green and she turned onto the wide boulevard. It had once been a canal, and the decaying, unfinished subway was underneath it. But tonight it was just a wide, desolate expanse. The Kroger building looked like a silver shoebox set on its side. The needle on the gas gauge was below an eighth of a tank.

"Damn!" Her voice sounded as if it were coming from far away.

Then she saw salvation in the squat, plain building that was Cincinnati police headquarters. She swung onto Ezzard Charles Drive and stopped directly behind a police car where the officer was getting out. She slammed the gearshift into park and leapt from the car.

"Help me!" Cheryl Beth ran to the cop. "I'm being followed."

She saw in terror that the black sedan had stopped right behind her.

"That's the car."

The cop was an overweight man in his forties in a dark uniform jacket and the white peaked cap that always made her think of an ice-cream man. She pointed again, seeing that the car had turned off its headlights. She could see one silhouette behind the wheel. She looked at the gun in the officer's belt for comfort.

He arched his black flashlight against his shoulder and pointed at the car.

"I can understand, ma'am," he said. "Black male. Menacing behavior. He's been a problem before."

She was about to speak but then saw he was smiling at her. Then she saw Detective Dodds emerge from the sedan.

"What's the matter with you!" She had stomped over to him and was yelling before any prudent centers of her brain could take hold. "Are you crazy? What were you trying to do?"

The big man adjusted the collar on his camel hair coat and arched his eyebrows.

"You took quite a way home, Cheryl Beth. And why were you digging in other people's trash?"

"Damn you! Why were you spying on me, following me!"

"Since you left the hospital." He looked at her with easy suspicion.

She could feel herself close to crying, which she did when she was really mad. She hated it because it made her seem weak. She shook her head vigorously to stop it and let herself feel the cold. Her foggy breath was coming out in quick, angry bursts.

"I'm sure you won't mind if I search your car."

She stared at him, suddenly afraid, feeling naked. "I sure as hell might mind." She struggled to keep her voice calm. She settled herself down with an effort, like riding a bicycle uphill. "What's going on?"

He was about to speak when his cell phone rang. He held out a finger and answered it.

"What do you want? What the hell?" This was followed by worse profanities, his face pinched with rage. He put away the phone and rested his hands on his hips, looking uncertain. Then he gave her arm a light but firm pull.

"Come with me."

She felt her pager buzz and pulled back, studying the number on the readout.

"Sorry, I've got to go back to the hospital."

He took her arm again, gripping more tightly this time. "That's fine. I do, too."

Chapter Eighteen

"So what does a pain nurse do? I've never heard of a pain nurse."

"Maybe that's a good thing."

"Never spent a day of my life in the hospital."

Cheryl Beth glanced across the seat at Detective Dodds. He stared ahead, one big hand on the steering wheel. He drove across Central Parkway and through the dense, narrow streets of Over-the-Rhine.

"Then it's your good luck," she said.

"So what does a pain nurse do?"

"You keep asking that question." Cheryl Beth stared ahead, too. She made herself put her hands flat on the tops of her thighs. It was a posture she had learned to keep calm.

"I'm just curious," he said. "My daughter has talked about going to nursing school."

"Well, we need good nurses. Now pain management is a recognized specialty. You have nurse practitioners doing it, too. She could look at the American Society for Pain Management Nursing…"

"Is that what you studied in school?"

"No. It took a long time for pain management to get respect. A lot of doctors didn't think pain was a critical issue. But I scrubbed in with a fabulous surgeon. What a character! He was a tyrant. Every day he would scream at me, 'Had enough?!' I would scream back, 'I like you!'" She looked at Dodds to see if he was capable of a smile. His face stared ahead like the bow of a battleship. "But he was a big patient advocate and really cared about pain. I would check on his patients the day after surgery. He taught me a lot. I worked in the OR for eight years. Then I worked in a hospice for three years. They were doing cutting-edge stuff. Eventually, I ended up doing pain management seminars and Memorial hired me."

"But why pain?"

"It really matters. I hate to see people suffer."

"So this is personal. You had some experience with this in your life?"

"Yes," she said, her mouth dry. "Someone I loved."

They rode several minutes in silence before he spoke again. She didn't like being alone with her thoughts and the silence.

"Where do you work?"

She looked at him quizzically.

"Do you work in a ward, in the recovery room?"

"I work all over."

"So you have the run of the hospital. Interesting."

The way he said it made her uncomfortable again. He wasn't just making conversation.

"Detective…"

Just then something dark raced across the windshield and shattered on the roof of the car. She visibly jumped. Around them were lovely derelict buildings and an empty street, no sign of an assailant.

"Just the neighborhood knuckleheads." Dodds drove on at the same steady pace. "I don't have time to go start a riot tonight."

He wasn't smiling. He looked as if he never smiled. She looked back to see several silhouettes emerge into the street behind them. He drove two blocks over to Main Street and turned north. It was a cold night but people were on the sidewalks, nicely dressed and holding hands, going from bar to bar. The restored old storefronts glittered, a startling difference from the disrepair and neglect of even three blocks away. She looked the other way when they passed the bar where she had met Christine that night. They sat in a rear booth and drank. Christine had a martini, and Cheryl Beth ordered her usual Bushmills on the rocks. One was enough. Two was probably more than she could handle. She had drunk two. Christine had downed three martinis. A pair of handsome young men had actually hit on them. Cheryl Beth pulled her coat tighter against her.

"Detective." She recovered her voice. "Why are you taking me to the hospital? Why were you following me tonight? I thought you had arrested the man who…"

"I still consider it an open case." He spoke calmly, no malice in his voice, but Cheryl Beth felt her limbs go cold.

"That nutball didn't do it," he went on. "You might have. You have motive, because you were sleeping with her husband. You have opportunity: you have the run of the hospital. You can be anywhere, any time. Apparently you met with her the night she was killed. Maybe you two fought, and you followed her back to the hospital…"

"Wait a minute!"

"I haven't read you your rights," he said—same calm but domineering voice. "So if I were you, I'd just listen. Now it turns out that your lover lied about where he was that night. He has no alibi. So tonight I ask myself, what happens when Cheryl Beth Wilson leaves work? As it turns out, she drives out to Kenwood and trash picks. I find that very interesting."

"I can explain." She had no idea what she would say next.

Dodds ignored her. "Now maybe on television, something like this happens and the story makes it out to be some boogeyman, some serial killer. In the real world, it's almost always somebody who knows 'em. Estranged spouses and romantic triangles. It's usually that simple."

"You're wrong."

"I'm warning you…"

"No." Cheryl Beth could hear the sharpness in her voice. "You're telling me you didn't arrest the killer today? It's not Lennie?"

Dodds was silent. She felt a sudden wave of nausea knock through her.

"You're wrong about me. And there's still a killer out there and somebody was standing in my damned flower beds looking into my house—after Christine was killed!" She knew she was over the top. She didn't care. "Now, you either arrest me, or let me out at the hospital, because a patient needs me."

They were pulling into the ER parking lot. "Don't go far," he said. "I know how to find you. When you're done, come down to the basement. You know where."

Cheryl Beth padded along on the new, heavy-duty carpet of the hallway into Four-East. It was already looking ratty. She was surprised to see Denise there, away from her usual floor.

"Angela was sick, so they moved me over at the last minute," Denise said. "I'm sorry to get you up here, baby girl. I called his doc and he said to call you. It's a compliment, really."

"Right." Cheryl Beth looked around the chart caddy for the paperwork. As often happened, the chart was missing. She squinted at the white board, which gave a basic rundown of the patient and his meds.

"Sorry," Denise said. "This station is a mess. Blunt chest trauma as a result of an auto accident. Chest tube. It's been in for a week and he's really hurting. Why are your hands shaking?"

Cheryl Beth stripped off her coat and sat heavily, studying her hands. They never shook. But a tremble ran through both. She knotted them into fists and it stopped. "The cops don't think Lennie is the killer," she said.

"What?"

"That's what I said. But it gets worse. This one detective, he's acting like I'm a suspect. Denise, I could get fired and blackballed. Stephanie Ott already hates me. I don't know what to do." She folded her arms across her chest, feeling her breasts through the soft fabric of her scrubs. They were softer now. Her body was becoming a stranger in middle age. She looked up at Denise. "It looks bad on the surface. The thing with Gary…"

"I know." She said it low and sympathetically, but Cheryl Beth angrily waved her hands.

"Everybody in this fucking hospital knows!" She brought her voice down. "Sorry. Sorry." She held her hands out and they were steady. "Let's get to work."

"Baby girl, nobody could think you had anything to do with it. That's crazy. I was with you that night. I gave you the message to go down there."

"That would play well before a jury," Cheryl Beth said, laughing ruefully. "Did you take Christine's call that night?"

"No," Denise said. "The ward clerk handed it to me. It must have come in when we were working on poor Mrs. Dahl."

So Christine might have called just before she was killed. Why did she call when she could have paged her? Why did she want to talk at all—what more was there to say? The details of the night came rushing back upon her.

"So you came on duty at eleven?"

Denise nodded. "And that poor old lady was hurting so bad. I say, 'enough of this, I'm calling Cheryl Beth.' So I paged you."

"Had you seen Lustig that night?"

"On that floor? No way. Anyway, she wasn't even cutting any more."

"So I came in around eleven-twenty, say? We worked with Mrs. Dahl for maybe half an hour and I spent another half an hour writing the new orders."

"Makes sense."

"So it was nearly twelve-thirty and I was about to leave when you saw the message?"

"Right. It must have come in while we were in the room with Mrs. Dahl. It definitely wasn't there when I came on duty."

Cheryl Beth made herself stand and they walked toward the patient's room. She could hear moaning in the distance. She stopped and faced Denise. "Ever run into a nurse named Judd Mason?"

"Creepy dude, huh?" Denise said. "No bedside manner at all. You know he used to be an OR nurse for Lustig?"

Cheryl Beth stopped and held Denise's shoulder. "What?"

"He scrubbed in with her for years," Denise said. They stood in the dim hallway next to the code cart, speaking in low voices. Except for the moans coming from the next door, the only sound was loud snoring. "He was good in the operating room, I hear. Lot of those nurses love the teamwork, the stress, the autonomy. They don't have to be great with direct patient contact."

"So were they still together?"

"Nope, they had a falling out. This was before Lustig went on leave to do the computer project."

"What do you mean, 'falling out'?" Cheryl Beth felt revived by an adrenaline shot through her system.

Denise shrugged. "That gossip never made it to the graveyard shift. Maybe he was another one of Lustig's conquests gone wrong. They want to know who killed her, they ought to look at the list of her old boyfriends. I think it's called the Cincinnati phone book. There's one other thing."

Cheryl Beth waited, watching Denise swallow conspicuously.

"I had to stop by employee benefits today," she said. "So I'm in street clothes, in the upscale part of this dump. Out in the hallway I see Stephanie Ott talking to Dr. Carpenter, and I distinctly hear your name."

"He said he'd have my back," Cheryl Beth said.

"Hmmm." Denise closed her eyes for a second and shrugged. "He told me he'd have my back, too, and next thing I knew I was kicked out of ICU. Today they looked pretty chummy, his arm on her shoulder. And I heard your name and Lustig's name more than once." She stroked her cheek in thought. "Something I've thought about…"

After a pause, Cheryl Beth asked her to continue.

"Oh, you know, after being done in by Ott once before I believe in conspiracies. But think about this. Lustig is working on the digital medicine project—every patient record will be online, every order or change of treatment entered instantly. Think what that would do to docs who screw up."

"They couldn't blame the nurses anymore."

"Right," Denise said. "Old Doc Palmer? He's got lawsuits against him. He's way past his prime. Dr. Stewart—I watch his stuff like a hawk. I've seen major screwups from residents that were quietly ignored. How many times have the doctors closed ranks to protect one another? The new computer system, if it worked, would make that a lot harder. They couldn't bury their mistakes anymore."

"You're saying there are powerful docs who wouldn't have wanted the project to succeed. Who might have wanted Christine… God, if Christine was really pushing the project, it could have threatened a lot of people."

Denise laughed. "Oh, forget it. I'm just scaring you when you're already scared. I'm probably being paranoid. But I did see Carpenter talking to Ott about you. Watch out, baby girl. Hospital politics can be murder."

Cheryl Beth stared at Denise, then found her bearings and walked through the wide doorway. In the first bed was a gaunt young man with skin nearly the color of white paper. He implored her with wide, scared eyes. Faces told so much.

"I'm a pain management nurse," she began. "One of your doctors wanted me to see if we could make you feel better…"

Forty-five minutes later, she took the elevator down to the basement. Her feet felt like lead, making this familiar trip. She never used the basement shortcut now. She had already decided that if the hallway were deserted when the doors opened, she would immediately close the door and go back to the first floor. The car was cold but she was burning up. She should have asked a guard to come down with her.

But when the doors opened, the hallway was brightly lit and she heard voices. She followed them toward the doors that led to the old morgue. The voices were loud and angry.

"We always assumed that he forced those women to take their clothes off, fold them neatly, and be carved up. Don't you get it? He didn't, maybe not even with Theresa. He cut them to pieces, then took off their clothes and put them in a garbage bag. Then he folded up clean clothes from their closet, or maybe he even brought some."

"How do we know any of that?" That was Dodds' voice. She recognized it instantly.

"How do we not know it? We didn't know what we were missing. Are you going to call crime scene or not?"

It was Will. She had not heard his voice when it was agitated.

"Why would he do this?" Dodds demanded. Cheryl Beth stood against the wall listening, ten feet from the door.

"He wants to show he's all-powerful. He can make a woman disrobe for him, make her welcome death."

"So why would he, or she, leave them here?"

Cheryl Beth shuddered when she heard the pronoun. Leave what?

Will answered, "He must have been interrupted. Maybe he was going to come back for them. Put in a video cam and a transmitter and leave them here once crime scene's gone over it."

"Maybe your pain nurse did it."

Cheryl Beth leaned back against the wall. Somehow just him saying it made her feel guilty. It was like a cop pulling into traffic behind you. It was way worse than that.

"You know she didn't," Will said. "Quit being such an asshole."

"You always had a weakness for the pretty girls, Borders. I think she's lying. You'll see."

"You're wasting time."

"Quit trying to tell me how to do my job!" He bellowed it.

Will yelled, too. "Then *do* your job."

"What am I going to have to do to make you stop meddling in a homicide investigation? I will arrest your ass if you don't stop."

"This isn't about me or you. This is what a psycho cop would do."

"Oh, hell, Borders."

"This is the best breakthrough we've ever had in this case," Will said. "I'm asking you as a friend."

"No," Dodds cut him off harshly. "We're not friends. You make up any story you want about going to Internal Investigations, but you know. I fired your ass as a partner because you lied to me."

There was a long silence with only the background noise of a distant generator. Cheryl Beth walked in as if she had just arrived.

"You. What took you so long?" Dodds glared at her with hostile eyes. Will looked as if he were about to crumple and fall out of the wheelchair.

"We need to get you upstairs," Cheryl Beth said.

"That can wait." Dodds opened a leather portfolio with a legal pad in it, then picked through several pages of dense handwritten notes and diagrams. He was leaning against one of the old autopsy tables.

"Why are you in here?" she asked.

"Maybe I should ask you that. Come in here often?"

Cheryl Beth felt instantly defensive. "I've never been in here. I knew it was here, but they stopped using it before I was even hired."

Dodds slid a pair of reading glasses over his nose. He silently paged through the notes. "We're going to do this again, Ms. Wilson. The night you say you discovered the body of Dr. Lustig. I want to hear your story. All over again, from the top. Then I want you to walk me through it, from where you started down here, to when you claim you found her, to what you did next." He looked over the glasses at Will. "You can leave."

Will wheeled himself out the double doors, and Cheryl Beth told her story in a hoarse voice. Then she took him out to the main elevator bank, walking down past the shadows of old carts to Christine's office, then showing him the path she had taken to the stairwell that brought her back to the first floor to get help. It all looked benignly alien with the full lights on. Will trailed well behind them in his wheelchair, saying nothing. His face was a mask of pain and exhaustion. Dodds ignored him.

"So you get off the elevator, walk down the hall, see the light coming out of her office…"

"That's right."

"What else?"

"What do you mean, 'what else?' There's no more else. I walked down the hall…" And she remembered. Dodds could see it in her face but he said nothing.

"I heard a sound. It was like metal on metal. I just remembered…"

"From where?"

She took her time, but she was sure. "From that direction." She pointed toward the old morgue. Will, who had rolled closer, looked sharply at Dodds.

"What kind of keys do you have to the hospital?" Dodds asked.

"Oh, come on," Will said.

"Shut the fuck up," Dodds snarled at him, then turned again, looming over her.

"Keys? I don't have any keys."

"Could you get into that morgue? Maybe after you killed the doctor, you ran down here and opened these doors and took the old elevator up and out? It would be a clever way to avoid being seen. Now you don't have to talk because you have a right to remain silent."

"Are you crazy?" Cheryl Beth heard her accent become more pronounced. It happened when she was mad. She thrust her keychain out to him. "See this? Car, house, desk, bicycle lock!"

Dodds reached out and delicately took her lanyard. "Tylenol, huh?" He pulled it out from her lab coat and examined it. "Partners Against Pain…NAPI scale…" He let it go and it draped back against her. "That card looks pretty ratty on the edges. Like you used it to pick a lock. Mind if I keep it?"

Cheryl Beth looked at him coldly. In a soft voice she said, "As a matter of fact, I do."

"Get the hell out of here, both of you." Dodds turned and walked back toward the morgue. Cheryl Beth wheeled Will toward the elevators in silence. Only when the doors closed and the car began to move did she speak.

"I didn't mean to eavesdrop, but what did he mean back there, about him firing you?"

Will was staring straight ahead and didn't answer. It took a moment before she realized he was asleep.

Chapter Nineteen

Will was so exhausted that he slept deeply for three hours. It was the longest uninterrupted sleep he had enjoyed since coming to the neuro-rehab unit. At five-thirty, a nurse woke him for his meds. Then he dozed fitfully as his roommate, Steve, received a breathing treatment, the technician working hard to get the poor man to cough. His muscle control for even this simple act of living was gone with the spinal cord injury. Will had learned about the "quad cough," where the nurse or technician used his hand to thrust up in the patient's abdomen, all the while coaching: "cough…cough…cough." It sounded like torture. In Will's mind the thought of "that could have been me" was ever present, yet the sessions behind the curtain a few feet away had also just become part of the background noise. The man never seemed to have visitors. Will didn't have visitors. Brother officers always deluged cops in the hospital with visits. Not Internal Investigations cops, not the rat squad. *Were we all just abandoned here?* Will wondered in hazy half sleep, and then he lost the thought, his mind orbiting between the noisy morning coming to life of the hospital and his body's desperate hunger for sleep.

He dreamed of old arguments with Cindy. Not really dreamed: he wasn't that far under. His mind, half asleep, reprocessed the same disagreements. They always said the same lines, like veteran actors in a long-running play. Then he fell under enough for dreams and she was there that spring day when the rain came down hard and straight. She was telling him her decision, a decision she had made on her own. It wasn't fair or right but she had done it. He had been on a big case, working nights, not there. It was done. He was pleading with her and crying, in his dreams at least. It was too late, too late.

His next vision: Cheryl Beth Wilson was sitting in the chair beside his bed. She was in her usual white lab coat and green scrubs, just watching him. The small-boned features of her face were beautiful when it was watchful. It was a warm dream. No, he was awake. He was aware of a wetness at the edges of his eyes. There was so much suffering around him, and he had been so fortunate, so spared, that he couldn't dwell on old griefs. That would be yet another sin.

"Hi."

"Hi," she said. "How are you sleeping?"

"Barely. At least they took the sutures out last night. I got back in the middle of the night, and one of the night nurses took them out. I felt like I was an old suit being let out."

Cheryl Beth gave her musical laugh. "That's good."

"What time is it? How long have you been sitting there?" He felt oddly shy around her, pulling the sheet over his flimsy patient gown. He thought he had grown accustomed to the hospital's relentless lack of privacy.

"It's seven-thiry. I just wanted to check on you. How are you feeling?"

Will could already feel a monumental soreness, running from his right shoulder down into his thigh. He pushed the button to raise the head of his bed. It complied slowly with a hum and cranking sound. The movement helped set off the burning ache in his left side. It was the wages of being dumped out of his wheelchair and onto the floor, then getting into a fight with a knife-wielding scumbag. Just another day at the office.

"I can feel yesterday, believe me."

She bit her lip and looked down. "Could I talk to you sometime today?"

"How about now?" Of course, she could talk to him. He was grateful for the company. But as he came more awake, all the events of the previous day filled his head like a flood of foul water. They needed to talk. He asked her to give him a minute to get dressed and they could get out of the stifling room.

"Can I help you with anything?"

"No," Will said, feeling that shyness. "I'll be out in a minute."

"Want me to call one of your nurses?"

"No, they have enough to do."

She walked out, closing the curtain around his bed. Fifteen minutes later he had gone through the morning agony, made more difficult by his body's memory of the physical exertion of yesterday. He knew he was sweating and looking grim when he wheeled the chair out the door. They moved silently through the busy hallway. He stopped at the nurses' station to get a cup of new pills. Then he felt her pushing him up the ramp into the main hospital. He sat back and let her do it. His Quickie moved easily and they didn't talk.

They found a deserted spot in the huge cafeteria near a heavily decorated Christmas tree. It was a reminder that he would likely spend Christmas in neuro-rehab, in this hospital prison. For the moment, he could keep those feelings in check. He watched as Cheryl Beth brought them both bagels. She walked fast and lithely. The bagels were a relief from the daily routine of a cup of scrambled eggs, a slice of bacon, and toast. Will knew that his breakfast tray was sitting inside the big cart back in the ward, an aide wondering where he was. His orderly mind worried about it for fifteen seconds, no more.

"Detective Dodds implied that Lennie didn't kill Dr. Lustig," Cheryl Beth began, putting the bagel on its plate after taking a single bite. "It's hard to get anything straight out of him. He's so eager to arrest me…" She stopped and ran her fingers through her hair, which fell back like strands of light-brown silk against her shoulders. When she spoke again, some of her previous intensity had dialed down. "I'm sorry. I haven't slept much, and I should leave you alone to get better. I just don't know where else to turn."

He watched her face redden as she spoke. "That means the murderer is still out there." Her voice was drained of its music. "Somehow I knew it. I knew there was more to this than Crazy Lennie."

"How did you know it?"

"My gut. I'm very intuitive." She gave a slight smile. "My mother saw ghosts. I'm not that intuitive."

"Lennie didn't do it. We have other evidence." He watched her carefully. She was pulled into herself, as if expecting a blow. He went on, "Why were you down in the basement that night?"

"She left a message at the nurses' station, up at Seven-North, saying she was in her office and I should stop by."

"This was when?"

"I don't exactly recall. I've tried to put a timeline together, though, with the supervising nurse on that floor. I had been called in for a consult. The message came in while I was with the patient. So I went down probably around twelve-thirty."

"Why would you do that?"

Cheryl Beth pulled back and sighed. Will knew he had made a misstep. He spoke gently.

"I'm just curious. I mean, it's the middle of the night. That's a very deserted part of the hospital."

"Oh, I feel like I've told this story so many times. Sorry, it's not you. I'm here at all hours, especially after dark. That's when people hurt. It isn't unusual to see docs here, either, especially surgeons checking on their patients." That much was true. Will's surgeon might routinely cruise through at one or two in the morning. It seemed like cops' hours, with better pay.

Cheryl Beth continued, "After she took a special assignment to work on the digital project—help us get this paperwork on computers—she was working in the admin wing. At some point, she took an office in the basement."

"Why?"

"I don't know. Wouldn't have been my choice. Maybe it was odd she was working so late, but she was a workaholic. I didn't really think about it. I take shortcuts all the time. I used to, at least. And that corridor through the basement is a great way around some of the logjams in the main hallways. It just didn't seem odd until later."

Her bagel remained untouched. Will had eaten his quickly, appreciating the taste and texture as never before. Now he was drinking a Diet Coke, all these things precious in his hospital jail. He asked more questions. The hallway had been deserted when she got off the elevator. It was only later, when the cops had sealed off the main first-floor hallway because of the gang shooting, that traffic would pick up in the basement, the time when he had been wheeled by, only hours out of surgery. When she had first got there, only the usual bank of lights was on, leaving most of the length of the corridor in darkness. As she had walked to Dr. Lustig's office, she did hear a metallic sound. She didn't think much about it at the time.

"It didn't scare you to be down there?"

"It sure does now. I hate that. I used to love being in the old parts of the hospital, thinking about the history of this place." She lowered her head slightly. "Will, there's something you need to know." He waited with a neutral face. His old detective face.

"I had an affair with Dr. Lustig's husband." She spoke the words slowly, in a hard, low voice. Will imagined her teeth grinding at the thought. This was not a happy memory. Yet she looked at him straight on. "It had been over for a long time. For several months. It was really bad judgment on my part."

"This is Gary Nagle?" Will smiled gently. "I know about it."

She shook her head. "You must think I'm a really stupid person."

"No."

"Your friend Detective Dodds thinks I killed Christine!" Her eyes were wide with apprehension.

"I wouldn't worry," Will said.

"You believe me? I had nothing to do with this."

He nodded. Still, she didn't look reassured. For a long time she just stared into the tabletop. "I think he's going to arrest me."

"If he really thought you had done it, he would have executed a search warrant long before now."

"Why can't they catch this person then?"

Will wanted to say, *because it's not TV.* He had heard these questions so many times, often from grieving family members desperate for news, any news. "I'm out of the loop, believe me. Dodds doesn't want my help. I'll tell you this much: the first forty-eight hours after a homicide are the most important. It's been more than two weeks now.

"Every day that passes after that makes it less likely that the case will be solved. That's when the real drudgework of homicide begins—don't believe all the crap you see on TV about the miraculous forensic breakthrough. Usually it's just grueling footwork. But there are a lot of cases that are never solved."

"But this was a doctor, at the hospital," she blurted. "It's not like some drug killing down in Over-the-Rhine." She stopped herself with a sharp intake of breath. "Oh, God, that sounded awful. I'm sorry."

"I've heard worse," Will said. "To be honest, I don't know why they don't have somebody in custody." He was conscious of the alien word *they* instead of the familiar *we.* "I know there was another high-profile killing. The city's on track for a record number of homicides this year. The detail is short-handed. There have been budget cuts." He shook his head. "Excuses. Bullshit."

She reached out for his hand. "Do you believe me, as a police officer, when I tell you I had nothing to do with this?"

Her hand felt warm and fragile inside his. He squeezed it. "I do."

She drew it back and pulled a white envelope from her coat. "I've been feeling that if I didn't try to play amateur detective, they were going to try to make me the bad guy. Maybe I went too far." She handed him the letter. By habit he took it lightly by the edges, holding it as if between the calipers of his fingers. It was addressed to Christine Lustig and the stamps had been canceled.

"I need latex gloves," he said.

"Oh, hell, I touched it. I am truly a stupid person." She buried her head in her hands momentarily, then reached into a coat pocket and pulled out a whitish bundle. He rested the letter on the table and slid his fingers into the gloves, as he had done so many times before. Cheryl Beth quietly cursed as he pulled out a sheet of white stationery and read the neat script in black-ink handwriting:

Chris,

You've betrayed me for the last time. I'm going to put a stop to you.

There was no signature. "Where did you get this?" Will asked, and she told him the story of seeing the envelope on the front seat of Judd Mason's car, and how she fished it out of his trash.

"I was really dumb to do this, wasn't I?"

Will thought about it, the layers of what had seemed like a simple case getting deeper. "Maybe not. Dodds said he saw you picking in the trash." He thought it through for a moment as she watched expectantly. "I want you to take this to Dodds. Don't tell him you showed it to me."

She nodded, hesitantly. Will could imagine the hell Dodds would raise. He asked, "Who wrote this note?"

Cheryl Beth pursed her lips. "I think Mason did, then tried to get it back after she was killed. Which might mean he killed her. How about this, I can find out where Mason works, get one of his charts, check his handwriting."

"Don't," Will said, a little too hard. He softened his voice. "Don't do that. He's already seen you."

"So you think he might have…"

They both let it hang between them. Finally, Cheryl Beth said, "She didn't like to be called Chris. The only other person who did that was Gary, and he did it because he knew it bugged her."

"Just tell Dodds the truth. Don't jump to conclusions." Will studied the letter one more time and then leaned over and slid it into her coat pocket. No Slasher case had involved a threatening letter. Suddenly the pain returned, emerging from his back and wrapping around his ribs in a pincer movement. He couldn't stop himself from visibly wincing.

"You're still hurting," she said. "I'm going to talk to your doctor. And I want you to take what I give you. Don't worry about becoming a drug addict. That's not going to happen."

He smiled in spite of the sharp stabs he was enduring. Finally, he made his face relax, got his breathing down.

"What were you guys doing in the morgue last night?"

He hesitated for only a moment. "I'll tell you, but don't tell Dodds. First I need you to answer a few more questions about that night." He went through it with her and the answers were chillingly reassuring. He had seen it before. The doctor had been on the floor, naked and bloody, knife wounds on her arms and torso—slashes—and the deep cut to her throat. Her ring finger was gone, chopped off. Her clothes had been neatly folded on top of a small filing cabinet, as if she had undressed for a lover. Cheryl Beth began shaking her right leg as she recounted the details. By the end, she was sniffling and teary, reaching for hospital paper napkins to dab her eyes and nose.

"Those might not have even been her real clothes," Will said. "I found bloody clothes in the old morgue last night and her ID card was pinned to them. Jeans, a blue wool top, a black leather jacket. Would she have worn something like that?"

"Yes…" Cheryl Beth was almost whispering. "If she had come in late, she wouldn't wear something fancy. She owned a black leather jacket."

"That means you may have just missed seeing the killer," Will said. "He killed her, planted the folded clothes, gathered up her real clothes and went down the hallway to the morgue, where he stashed them. Then he took an old elevator up and out."

"Oh, shit." She seemed stricken, her body slumping back, seeming to lose five pounds in front of his eyes. This was not the body language of a killer.

"Are you sure the hall was deserted? Think back."

"I'm sure." She reached for her bagel but her hand shook.

"What?"

"A couple of days after the killing," she said, "I noticed footprints in the flower bed by my window at home. I had only cleared the leaves out the day Christine was killed, and those footprints weren't there."

"Is there any chance…?"

"No," she cut him off. "I don't have a gardener. It's not near the meters. It wasn't the cable guy. I told all this to Detective Dodds. He didn't care. He said call nine-one-one if I see a prowler." She furrowed her brow. "There's something else. I forgot about this. A couple of days after Christine was killed, I saw my desk had been opened. Somebody had gone through it. I'm scared."

Will reached across and took her hand and held it a long time. She didn't resist. They sat that way as Will conducted a silent debate with himself. But in the end, there was only one thing to do, only one right thing. He had drunk nearly the entire Diet Coke and yet his mouth was suddenly dry.

"Cheryl Beth, do you remember the killings in Mount Adams two years ago?"

Chapter Twenty

Cheryl Beth walked down the middle of the busy hallway, dazed, barely acknowledging the nurses and docs that said hello. She had three new consults and half a dozen follow-ups. She wanted to get as many of her patients over from IVs to oral pain drugs as soon as possible. People were hurting: stabbings, shootings, chest tubes, every kind of mayhem in the belly. Will was hurting, the pain etching deep ravines around his eyes. He was a young man, her age. She had to argue with one of the surgeons about continuing to use Demerol—it was a crappy pain drug, even if it gave the patient a buzz. Slow drip Dilaudid, that was a wonderful drug. How many years had she spent teaching them about it? The patients had to be watched closely for side effects or irritation to the vein, but most of the time it was very effective. Then the afternoon would get really busy with new consults, as people came out into the recovery room. Some of them would come out of surgery, wake up, and hurt so much they'd rather be dead. Did some of the anesthesiologists care?

Her feet kept moving, but dizziness was coming in and out, her pager feeling like ten pounds on the drawstring belt of her scrub bottoms. She made a sudden turn, cutting through a throng carrying flowers, and pushed through two double doors. It was the back way into the emergency department.

She cut down a narrow hallway and opened the door into a large supply closet. Her hands found the cool wall and she just stood there, slowing her breathing, trying not to throw up. She had gotten used to every hospital smell: feces, urine, decaying flesh, vomit, the peculiar odor of disinfectant and putrification that attended many cancer patients. She never flinched. Right at that moment, she didn't trust herself to move. She wasn't thinking about the probable explosive reaction from Detective Dodds when she showed him the letter. Her hands splayed against the wall, she read the labels on the nearby drawer, silently moving her lips as she had in grade school until her teachers had stopped her.

The Mount Adams Slasher. She wasn't even sure she had heard everything Will had told her after hearing those words. An avid newspaper reader, Cheryl Beth remembered the crimes vividly. All the nurses had been terrified. One of them lived a block away from one of the killings. Women had bought guns and big dogs. For three months, the city had seemed transformed into a terrifying stranger, familiar on the surface but with a sinister current running beneath it like a poisoned underground river.

Will Borders had worked on that case with Dodds—they were the "primaries," he said; every profession had its jargon— and now he was telling her that the same killer had murdered Christine Lustig. And he might have seen Cheryl Beth as she walked out of the elevator into the darkened corridor that night. She knew a man had been arrested for the murders, but Will had been adamant. He hadn't done it. The Slasher was killing again. Now, with the note she picked from Judd Mason's trash, she knew who might have really done it. Her breathing was so shallow she was barely conscious of it. The nurse in her imagined how little of her lung capacity she was using, even worried she might be on the verge of hyperventilating.

That was when she caught sight of the large black shoes and white pants.

"Sorry," she started, then raised her head to see that Judd Mason was standing there, just inside the doorway. It had been a long time since she had seen a nurse wearing whites at Memorial. His face showed that he knew she recognized him.

"You're an open book," her mother had always said, derisively. Her mother didn't know her.

Cheryl Beth stood straight up and walked toward the doorway but he didn't move. "Excuse me," she said. He just stood there. In the bright light of the supply room, she was more aware of the pallor of his skin, with a dark stubborn beard fighting to come out. His hair was nearly black and close-cropped, revealing a wide forehead. He just stared at her, his mouth compact and his lips nearly bloodless. His eyes were small, intense, and blue. She looked again briefly at his large shoes and imagined matching them to the imprints in her flower beds.

"Excuse me." She said it louder this time, imagining how she might try to kick him in the groin and run past, or at least scream like hell. Inside she was shaking. He raised his right arm and leaned a hand against the doorjamb, further blocking her exit.

"You're the one who discovered her body." He looked her over. He displayed no sympathy or even the expression of a man who was attracted to her. His features were flat and immobile. "Had she suffered?"

She spoke quietly. "I'm going to go now."

"You were spying on my car last night," he said, his voice even and calm. "At first, I didn't know who you were."

"I wasn't spying on anything," Cheryl Beth said, using her best tough voice for standing up to a blockheaded doc or nurse. The problem was that she might be standing up to a killer.

"What were you looking for?"

"I wasn't looking for anything." She studied his face, reading nothing. "You worked with Dr. Lustig, didn't you?"

"Are you the police?" The same steady voice, neither angry nor friendly.

She wanted to say, no, but the police will want to see you very soon. That was, if she could get out of this room with the purloined letter that was in the bottom left pocket of her lab coat. She looked past him into the corridor. Deserted. Not a sound. Only fifteen feet away was the busiest trauma center in southwestern Ohio. If only she could walk through walls.

He raised his arm and stepped aside. She walked past him, making herself move at a normal pace.

"You didn't know her." She heard his voice behind her. "I did."

She turned and faced him. He was leaning against the wall, still staring at her.

"What is that supposed to mean?"

His lips turned up. "You were sleeping with her husband, but I guess all's fair."

"You don't know what the hell you're talking about." Cheryl Beth braced her shoulders as a sudden rage overcame her. No—she made herself cool down. She had the entire hallway behind her now, the entire hospital. He was more than an arm's length away. She tried to take stock. He had obviously seen her looking into his car. He might even have surmised that she saw the letter—but maybe not. He didn't realize she had it. "I'm sorry," she said. "We should talk. If you'd write down your number and a good time to call you, we can sort this out."

"Hmmpf." He shook his head. "You can find me. I'm in the directory."

"I hear you used to work in the OR with Christine. What was that like?"

He studied her again. She imagined he was measuring the distance between them, but she refused to move. She folded her arms and stared back.

"You don't know me. You didn't know her. Let's say we saw the world differently and leave it at that. When she was assigned to go to the SoftChartZ project, I wasn't surprised."

Now it was Cheryl Beth's turn to just watch him. She felt strangely brave.

"Whatever you think you know is wrong." His small eyes became smaller, darker.

"What do I know?" Cheryl Beth made herself laugh. "I'm just a small-town girl from Kentucky. Just the pain nurse."

"She was a good doctor. She didn't want to be in that basement office, you know. They moved her down there."

"Why?"

He shrugged. "By that time she'd broken it off with me. So I never found out." It was said in the same flat, easy voice. He took a step toward her and Cheryl Beth retreated two steps. "You're afraid, aren't you?"

"What doctor are you talking about?" Cheryl Beth tried to draw him out, her gambit to see his handwriting having failed. *Say "Chris,"* she thought, just like the salutation on the note.

Mason gave a tight smile. "Just a small-town girl who likes to play games. By the way, I thought you had been instructed to not discuss Dr. Lustig's murder with anyone: colleagues, patients, and absolutely not the press."

With that, he turned and walked away, striding through the double doors and out into the hospital.

Chapter Twenty-one

For days, Will had eyed the closet in the big rehab workout room with lust: it held walkers, crutches, four-footed canes and regular canes. He would walk again. He would make himself walk again, whatever noodles he now possessed in place of legs. This spinal cord, it was such a creation. His legs still had the same strong muscles that had existed before the tumor, before the surgery. But the signals couldn't get through to them. Slowly, some were starting to come back. He did his usual walk up and down the wooden walkway, holding the parallel bars, as Amy guided him from the front and another physical therapist followed them with his wheelchair, in case he needed to suddenly sit. He wouldn't consider such a defeat. His legs moved more easily, even if they still seemed almost detached from his torso. Amy held the multicolored gait belt she had cinched around his waist—he didn't know how she could even slow his two hundred pounds if it started down, much less stop it, but the rules were the rules. Back and forth he walked, standing erect. It reminded him that he was a tall person.

Finally, after letting him rest, Amy unfolded a walker. It was scuffed and old, but it would do. They locked the wheels of his chair and he kicked back the footrests. She had him by the gait belt as he hoisted himself up and nearly fell. But then he was up, standing, holding the arms of the walker. "Easy... take your time... you're doing great..." He heard the words and moved slowly, his mind focused solely on not falling. For those moments, he couldn't stew about Judd Mason and the letter to Christine Lustig. Could he have been wrong all these years about Bud Chambers and the Slasher case? He couldn't worry about Cheryl Beth, who might be in danger. He could only try to… walk. His body was now an awkward, dangerous contraption liable to go down at any second. *Don't fall…don't fall…* every brain impulse was focused on one command. But his feet moved. His legs pushed forward. He was using the walker. Five feet. Ten feet. Turn. He was grateful to ease himself back down into the seat of the wheelchair. Amy patted him on the shoulder.

"Great job today," she said. "You're just doing great." When the other therapist left to deal with a different patient, she whispered. "Thank you for talking to me the other night. I feel better telling the truth."

"I know."

It was nearly three p.m. when he wheeled himself into the newest wing of the hospital and through the highly polished wooden doors that led to the administrative offices. Stan Berkowitz didn't just have his own office, he also had a secretary, a petite young woman who seemed shocked to see a patient in a wheelchair in a hospital. She gave him the brush-off, but then he showed his badge and told her he and Stan were old friends. Her manner instantly changed from brusque to cooperative. The old cop who had broken Will in on the homicide detail had told him that a good detective rarely needed to show his badge, that he should be able to get answers just by the way he handled himself. It was true—real detectives didn't flash badges with the repetition of their counterparts on television. But now Will needed any edge he could get. The woman reappeared and said Stan would be happy to see him.

Berkowitz didn't look that way.

"Just when I start thinking happy thoughts, Mister Internal Affairs shows up again." Berkowitz was sitting on a round, cherry wood conference table dangling his legs over the edge like a child. He looked like a man with too much time on his hands. It wasn't as if a doctor had recently been murdered in his hospital. He wore a dark blue suit and a red paisley tie. Will wore his usual sweatpants and T-shirt, hating them. He had always worn suits on the job. A suit said serious detective.

While much of the hospital looked threadbare, Berkowitz's office was comfortably outfitted with an L-shaped desk, leather sofa, and the conference table flanked by three chairs, all of it new. His old CPD badge was mounted on a plaque behind his desk, along with several framed community awards. A large trifold of family photos sat on his desk.

"My sons," he said, pointing to the photos, showing two teenage versions of himself. "At Country Day. Never could have afforded that on a cop's salary. What part of town you grow up in, Borders?"

"Oakley."

"Getting kind of fou-fou now," he said.

"It wasn't back then." Will rolled up to the table and faced Berkowitz, who continued to swing his legs playfully, a man without a care in the world. Will was sore and constipated. He fought to keep it off his face.

"Don't you have a son? How's he doing?"

"Fine," Will said. There was nothing more to say, certainly not to Stan Berkowitz.

"So what, aren't they treating you right down in rehab?"

"I just have a few questions…"

Berkowitz laughed, showing bright white teeth, looking relaxed and congressional again. "Wish I could help, a former brother officer and all that, but Dodds told me not to talk to you."

"Huh." Now it was Will's turn to laugh. He started to wheel around but Berkowitz's voice stopped him.

"What the hell is that for?" A cop harshness crept in.

"I'm just surprised you'd listen to Dodds, considering what he's said about you and all, David."

"Don't fucking call me David!" he sputtered. "What are you talking about? What about Dodds?"

"I've said too much."

"Hell, no. Tell me."

Will turned back to face him, looking him in the eye, then looking away and sighing. "Oh, hell, Stan, not your fault you washed out of homicide. It's a shit job anyway. Look where you are now. Better than any of us." Berkowitz had stopped swinging his legs and now had his hands flat on the tops of his thighs, his suit jacket open wide, exposing a little .38 Smith & Wesson in his belt. Will went on, "Let's just say Dodds wasn't your friend when you were on loan to the detail…"

"Goddamn it!" Berkowitz slapped the table, slid down, and walked heavily over to his desk, seeming to seek safe harbor. "I always knew it, always knew it. Shit, he wouldn't even have that job if the department wasn't under pressure to hire people of a Nubian persuasion, if you get my drift. All the shit we used to take from the Sentinels—hell, they have their own organization! They won't even support the FOP! I always knew Dodds did me in. I was a good detective."

Will didn't bother to correct him: black officers were members of the Fraternal Order of Police, too. The right hot button had been pushed, and how. Will hadn't exactly lied: Berkowitz had failed to make it in homicide and Dodds had thought he was a lightweight. When the shouting stopped, Will spoke again.

"So tell me about Judd Mason."

"Yeah, screw Dodds." Berkowitz flopped into his chair. "Judd Mason. I know him. He's a circulating nurse. Used to work in the OR."

"He worked in the operating room with Dr. Lustig."

"That's right, now that you mention it." He rubbed his chin and stared down at the neat piles of papers on his desk. "I always wondered about him. We had a nurse here a couple of years ago, said he was a stalker. I guess they had a thing going and she tried to break it off. We try not to get involved in these kinds of things—hell, there's more screwing going on around here than you'd believe. But she filed a complaint and I talked to him."

"Is she…?"

"She left. Moved to Columbus. He left her alone after I talked to him. But he kind of seemed to have a screw loose."

"How so?" Will asked.

Berkowitz shrugged. "Just something about the guy. Something quiet and strange. I guess he's an okay nurse. Strange to me to see guys as nurses anyway. What's their thing unless they're homos, right?"

"So did you think about Mason when Dr. Lustig was killed?"

"Not really," he said, crooking his mouth into a downward U. Will looked at him long enough for him to exclaim, "What?"

"Just seems kind of strange," Will said. "He was stalking a nurse. He had worked with Lustig. She received telephone threats."

"Didn't seem connected to me." Berkowitz held out his hands guilelessly.

"Did this Mason have any cop connections?"

"Huh? Cop connections?"

"Did he have cop friends? Drop any names when you talked to him about stalking?"

He waved it away. "Hey, I'd love to visit all day, but I've got a meeting. Off-site, as they say. I'll let you in on a little secret, Borders. I'm about to leave this dump and take a job as head of security at University Hospital."

"Congratulations."

"Hell, yes. Thanks. This place…who knows what's going to happen. Those neuro docs wanted all the paperwork put on computers. I heard they were going to pull out their practice if it didn't happen. So they bring in these kids from Silicon Valley, get a big federal grant, and a year later, nothing. Your Dr. Lustig was part of this. Now that she's dead it'll be delayed even longer. This place can't survive on just treating the ghetto. Neuro's good, though. You were lucky. Lucky to have that city insurance, too.

Anyway, University is where this old cop is headed. No more budget cuts. No more worrying about gangbangers coming in to finish off some schmuck they shot down in the 'hood."

"Why is the hospital covering up this murder?" Will tossed it gently, just as Berkowitz took a breath to continue speaking.

"What are you talking about?"

"A doctor murdered at a city hospital. When I was on homicide that would have been a red ball. Unless somebody had the juice to make it go away."

Berkowitz sprang up—that effortless move to his feet seemed like a miracle—and started for the door.

"Buddy, I got no comment on any of that. Get my drift? You need to get feeling better."

"Do the bigs at University know about Robert Cecil?"

Berkowitz stopped midway to the door, his skin suddenly drained of color.

◇◇◇

It was difficult to explain cops and race to civilians. When Will and Dodds had caught up with Craig Factor, crashing at a crack house on the edge of Liberty Hill, he had sprinted outside and down the street. As usual, it had been left to Will to lead the chase. He knew Dodds would come huffing behind, but he had the speed. He had gotten close enough to grab Factor's shoulders and wrestle him down to the pavement. They were in the middle of the street. Factor was a big guy, at least two hundred and fifty pounds, and wrestled and swung punches. By the time Dodds had arrived, the two of them were able to get Factor under control, face down, Will's knee in his back, as they cuffed him. The schools were on spring break, and at least two dozen young black men with nothing to do had gathered on the sidewalk, watching, then catcalling. Then one threw a bottle. It might have gotten uglier if a lot of backup hadn't arrived quickly. But, Will knew, if a news crew had been filming the arrest, many civilians might have assumed that there was no more to the story than the image of a big white cop abusing a handcuffed black man.

Most cops weren't racist, but in a city like Cincinnati, with a huge underclass, the police spent most of their time dealing with crime and trouble in black neighborhoods. You could become jaundiced after one shift. You had to fight to remember, most of the people in those neighborhoods were law-abiding, trying to get by. They were under siege. Drugs and guns and too many unemployed young men were a lethal combination. Will had taken the classes, heard the sociology, back when he thought he might get a master's degree. On the streets, it was a scary reality not covered in the studies and the textbooks. Being a solitary cop at night in a hostile neighborhood.

Too many black men were being shot by the police. Will had investigated some of the shootings; some were righteous, some there was a question. He always tried to do those cases by the book. He knew that he hadn't been there in that moment of terror, when a life-and-death decision had to be made. When he had been fighting with Craig Factor, before Dodds got there, Factor had been wildly reaching for Will's gun. Another cop might have just shot the son of a bitch. Will might have, too. Then the first thing the media would have reported was that Will Borders was "a white police officer." Nothing else would matter but race.

But some cops were racists, and Cincinnati was in many ways a Southern city, right across the river from Kentucky. The color line was hard, reinforced by the city's makeup of Germans and briars, fierce loyalties and old grudges, built up over time like geologic sediments. Ten years ago, Robert Cecil might or might not have been aware of this history when he pulled off the interstate to eat at a White Castle. He was driving a new BMW, went through the drive-thru, and pulled into the parking lot. It was a warm May night, a little before midnight, so he rolled the driver's side window down. That was when a white man came up behind him, produced a gun, and ordered him to get out of the car. Cecil instead dropped the car into reverse and tried to get away. The white man fired eight shots through the open window and every one connected. Robert Cecil was black and the white man was an undercover police officer named Berkowitz.

Will and Dodds had rolled in as the primary homicide team. Berkowitz claimed Cecil had been reaching for a gun even as he tried to drive away. No gun was found in the car. A witness said Berkowitz had never identified himself as a cop. Berkowitz claimed he had. Why had he approached the BMW? Berkowitz said it was suspicious. Will knew what that meant: a black man in a fancy new car. Cecil was a lawyer from Cleveland, and the city ended up paying a big settlement to his family. But somehow Berkowitz got out of it. Command wanted the problem to go away. Internal Investigations took over the case. Stan stayed on the force another three years before retiring. In a city of such long memories, some things could be easily shoved in a closet. But Will knew the Robert Cecil story wouldn't go over well with the bosses at University Hospital, who were putting a premium on community outreach, doing the right thing. The philanthropist hospital board ladies, married to big shots at Procter, American Financial, Kroger, and Federated, might wonder about the cop who killed Robert Cecil. So might the hospital's CEO, a black woman. Berkowitz knew it, too. He delayed his meeting "off-site" and talked to Will for another thirty minutes.

Chapter Twenty-two

Cheryl Beth stood in the doorway, watching as Will slowly stood and stepped into the walker. Every move looked painful, but he took one step forward, then another. It made her smile when the hospital actually helped people. Then she felt her pager vibrating.

It was a new consult on the fourth floor. The nurses' station didn't have the chart, which wasn't unusual, so she walked down to the room. She remembered a meeting in the fall, when the hospital brass and the people from SoftChartZ had talked about the progress on the computer project. All medical records would be on PC workstations, which would be available to nurses and doctors all over the hospital. A patient's history, medications, and orders would be available at the touch of a key. It seemed almost too good to be true. Cheryl Beth didn't remember the boyish CEO from SoftChartZ being at this meeting. Christine had led it and taken questions. She had worn a very attractive blue suit that day—she always wore a skirt at work, unless she was in scrubs. And she had spoken with more passion, more compassion for what this might mean for patients, than Cheryl Beth had ever seen from her. She knew Christine as prickly, icy, tightly wound, businesslike. Never caring. Cheryl Beth had broken off the affair with Gary that night.

The room was at the end of the hallway, where it ended in the fire stairwell, and the door was closed. As she had so many times before, she knocked twice, then opened the door and stepped inside. The nearest bed was empty and neatly made up. The bed by the window was concealed by a curtain.

"Hello?"

She felt the air rush of the heavy door being closed behind her even before she heard it slam shut.

Gary Nagle stood behind the door, wearing nothing but a fierce erection. He leered at her. "Hey, baby."

She instantly grabbed the doorknob, but he was stronger and kept the door shut.

"You used to like this…"

She was momentarily in a coma of surprise and shock. His eyes were an animal's. Beneath her animal fear, her mind began processing: this is it…*this is what the moment before being raped feels like.* She vowed to herself she wouldn't go down without a fight.

"Gary." She tried to keep her voice calm, but heard it waver. "You're not yourself. Your wife died…"

"Ex!" He shouted it and made a flourish with one hand. "Yeah, poor Chris. Poor, poor Chris…the whore!" His eyes narrowed and he thrust his right hand out toward her in a half-fist.

"Slash! Slash! Slash!" He made violent cuts back and forth with an invisible knife, crouching down like a street fighter. His hard penis shook like a diving board. "You know I can use a knife! Chris, you whore. For what you did to me…"

He stepped toward Cheryl Beth, but his effort to hold the door kept him just enough off balance.

Springing to the foot of the first bed, she slid the rolling table that usually held a patient's dinner tray between them.

"Gary, I swear to God I'm going to start screaming."

"You used to like this, Cheryl Beth." He stroked himself. He had always been irrepressibly proud of his endowment, bragging about how difficult it was to find size thirteen shoes. Now the memory made her shudder.

"You're acting like some kid resident, not a seasoned physician," she said, making her voice sound a haughtiness she didn't feel. "And I'm sure not a nurse looking for a doctor husband."

"Oh, Cheryl Beth, we had such fun…"

There he was with his finely toned physique, but she felt nothing. It was just a body. Another fragile container of bone and muscle and tissue in the hospital. Nursing aides giving sponge baths often caused male patients to have erections. It wasn't sexy. It was kind of sad. She felt all this, but only below the incoming waves of fear.

He could see her take a deep breath to call for help and began speaking rapidly.

"You've got to help me, Cheryl. The cops came to my apartment this morning, with a search warrant. That big black detective." He held his hands in a pleading position. "He thinks I killed Chris. They took away things. Evidence. Please, please…" His chiseled, confident face dissolved into tears and he slid down against the wall sobbing. "Please, I need you."

"Put your pants on or I'm out of here." She squared her shoulders and gave him her nastiest look. She wouldn't let herself show fear. "And step away from the door."

"You'll talk?"

"If you step away from the door."

He pulled himself up and walked slowly to a chair that held his clothes. She saw the clothes only now—they might have been a clue to stay out if she had seen them earlier. As he moved, she kept the rolling table between them. With the door unguarded, she made two wide strides to it, threw it open, and started out.

"Please!"

She turned to face him. "I'll stay for the moment, if you don't piss me off or get weird. But get dressed. And don't call me Cheryl. You know what my name is."

"Sure, sure." He was half mumbling as he slid into his boxers and his slacks. She dropped down the doorstop so the door was half open, and she leaned against the wall by the jamb.

"God, I need to fuck right now."

It was true: he used sex to relieve stress. It took her awhile to realize that he was most aroused when he was under the greatest pressure. Soon after that, she came to understand that she might just as well not have been there. She was just a female body to him. A way to work off stress. Another conquest.

"Talk to your pal, Amy." Cheryl Beth folded her arms, half feeling sorry for him, but still drunk with adrenaline fear.

"That bitch." He slipped on his dress shirt and quickly buttoned it. His face was a caricature of little-boy petulance. She half expected to see him use his sleeve to wipe his runny nose. "She sold me out."

"Sold you out?"

"The cops said she didn't back up my story that we were together that night, the night that Chris was killed."

"So she told the truth." She was comforted by the sounds of a housekeeping crew working in the hallway close by.

"Do you know how much money I bring into this hospital as a neurosurgeon?" His adult voice was back, but with an angry edge.

"I know, you're the famous two-million-dollar man."

"They told me this would go away. They said it would not touch me!"

"Who told you? What are you talking about?"

"The hospital! Jim Bryant!" The CEO of Memorial. Cheryl Beth had a hard time believing such a thing. Gary's eyes were still wild.

"Gary, I told you that night you should immediately go to the police and tell them the truth."

"Bryant said he'd shut it down. No one would even talk about it."

Cheryl Beth took that in but kept her face as expressionless as possible. *You're an open book.*

"You've got to help me," he said, adding, "Cheryl Beth."

"I've done all I can do, Gary."

"Damn you!" He shook his fist at her. "You're such a cold bitch. It's all because your mother never loved you. I get you."

She pushed her anger down into her shoes and quietly said, "Gary, you never knew anything important about me. What matters to me. You weren't man enough to ask or to understand. We just fucked. It was nothing special." The cold harshness of her voice surprised her. His eyes widened and he actually twitched, jerking his head to the left, the veins standing out in his neck.

"Please, I'm sorry."

She just watched him.

"You saw me at the bar that night on Main Street…"

"No, I didn't. You just said you were there."

He stood, but didn't move toward her once he realized she would walk out the door. "You're not playing well with others. I was there, you saw me."

"I did not."

"Don't you understand the favor I did for you? When I first talked to the police…"

"You said I was your lover. We hadn't been together for months. That was no favor."

"I didn't tell them you were with Christine that night, on Main Street, before she came back to the hospital."

"So? I told them. They already know." She was amazed at the effortless way she lied. He started to talk, but she was already out the door, walking fast to the elevators.

Chapter Twenty-three

The next morning Will wheeled himself out to the busy main lobby and lined up at the Starbucks. It was one piece of the normal, outside world in the dreary daily hospital routine. His brother had brought him some money and fresh underwear, and then gone off to his shift as a firefighter. They were not close, and he could sense the discomfort from Mark, that he and his family might end up having to care for an invalid. Will vowed that wouldn't happen. He would find a way to be self-sufficient. People worse off than him could do it. Cindy—he didn't know when he would see her again, and didn't want to care. Their marriage was just a scar now, not a wound. He couldn't fix it, never could. His physical pain was less—it was noticeable, now more an anxiety he might miss his next dose than the constant vicious companion of recent weeks. Don't worry about becoming an addict, Cheryl Beth had said. So he wouldn't worry. He ordered his coffee, got it and rolled over to a table, then he saw the front page of that day's *Enquirer*.

"Nurse charged in doctor's murder," a large headline said. A smaller one added: "Police suspect a romantic triangle led to killing." He set the coffee down and read:

    Police on Wednesday arrested a 35-year-old
    nurse in the Dec. 6 murder of Dr. Christine
    Lustig at Cincinnati Memorial Hospital.

Judd Mason, who also worked at the hospital, faces one charge of aggravated murder, according to Cincinnati homicide Det. J. J. Dodds.

Mason, of Deer Park, was arrested at his home around 4 p.m. Tuesday without incident. He is being held in the Hamilton County Jail on $1 million bond. Dr. Lustig, 41, was found dead in her basement office. According to the medical examiner, she died from repeated stab wounds.

Police say Mason was having an affair with Dr. Lustig, the ex-wife of prominent neurosurgeon Dr. Gary Nagle. Lustig broke off the affair and an enraged Mason sought revenge, police allege.

Officials at Memorial said they were relieved that "this horrible chapter has been closed," according to a spokesman.

Relieved. Will lingered on the word. *Closed.* He read the story to the end, letting the coffee scald the roof of his mouth, but he really wasn't comprehending the other words. It was the boiler-plate of a hundred news stories about murders, usually telling little, often telling outright lies. Something went out of him and he just sat there staring at the table. Maybe he had been wrong. Maybe it had been this simple, all along. He suddenly felt so tired, so sad beyond the words even to express it, much less to examine its headwaters. And Will wasn't that kind of man.

Homicide is not that hard. That's what the old detective who had broken him in—the man's name had been Charlie Brill, but everyone called him Bull—had told him when he had joined the detail. Most homicides are simple. Family fights, drug deals gone wrong, disputes over money. Young men with guns and no control over their impulses. Jealousy. Lovers killed each other. Most murder victims knew their killers. Most killers eventually screwed up. Gather evidence. Make an arrest. Take it to the DA. Testify. Simple.

Sometimes one good case solved many others. As a young detective, Bull had worked the Cincinnati Strangler case. Seven women had been raped and strangled in 1965 and 1966. The swirling, lethal dangers of the sixties had come down on never-changing Cincinnati. Will had been in grade school, but he remembered it. The cops had eventually arrested a cab driver after a woman had been found beaten and stabbed in his abandoned cab. The MO hadn't been the same as the others, who had been strangled. But each murder had been slightly different. One woman had been strangled with a necktie in a park. Others had died thanks to plastic clothesline. Two had been exact copies: women beaten badly and strangled with electrical cord. Bull had said they had a theory, played a hunch: that the cabbie was the strangler. He was convicted on only one murder, but after his arrest, the strangler killings had stopped. One veteran newspaper columnist later compared the case to the Slasher attacks: only one conviction, but no more killings.

Except that the Mount Adams killings hadn't been simple. Theresa Chambers' body had been found on an April afternoon when a coworker had become concerned and stopped by to check on her. She had looked through the kitchen window and seen a naked leg and a lot of blood. Inside the one-hundred-and-twenty-year-old restored house, the scene had been surreally calm, neat—no broken dishes or overturned tables or chairs. A set of women's clothes had been neatly folded on a chair, with black panties on top. The body had almost been arranged: completely nude, legs open, arms and hands holding a framed photo of her daughter, who was away at college. Yet all was not calm: the body had been nearly flayed in some places by a very sharp knife, then her throat had been slashed. Blood pooled darkly on the floor. She had been sexually assaulted and semen had been recovered by the medical examiner. And her ring finger had been cut off and taken.

Will and Dodds had immediately looked at her estranged husband, Bud. The spouse almost always was the killer. Simple, remember? Their marriage had been marked by physical abuse and she had a restraining order against him. He was also a

Cincinnati cop who had faced more than his share of brutality complaints. Theresa's time of death had been estimated at around three a.m. the day her body had been discovered. Bud had an alibi—he had been on duty on the overnight shift. But that broke down within a day when it turned out that he had gone off his beat early, his shift commander agreeing to cover for him, thinking he needed to run an errand. Day after day, Will and Dodds had interrogated Chambers in one of the dismal little rooms at headquarters. A cop with a bad temper and a history of threats against his wife had finally killed her. Where had he been that day? Chambers had said he hadn't been feeling well, so he went home to his apartment and took a nap. No alibi. Lots of motive.

But it hadn't been a simple case. No witnesses could place Chambers at the scene anytime near the murder. He had claimed he hadn't seen Theresa for two weeks before the murder. The kitchen had lacked Chambers' fingerprints. He had said it was because he hadn't lived there for a month, but Will thought Chambers had wiped it down. Other evidence—bloody shoeprints, fibers, skin under the fingernails—was missing. A search warrant executed at Chambers' apartment turned up nothing. The knife was missing from the scene, and wouldn't turn up for days, when Dodds went back to Theresa's house, did his homicide stroll, and finally found it in the back of the freezer. It had no trace evidence.

On the fifth day of interrogation, Chambers had seemed to crack. He changed his story, said he had left patrol to visit his girlfriend. She would back him up. Her name was Darlene Corley, a white-trash woman living down in the flood zone of the Columbia neighborhood. They had found her in an ancient, paint-peeled duplex that seemed like the moon compared to the Victorians being restored a block or two away. They had stood on the porch talking to her, and she had said that she had been with Chambers early that morning. He had pulled his patrol car right up to the curb there, and come inside and they had made love. The two detectives were about to invite themselves inside when the call came: another homicide in Mount Adams, same MO.

Jill Kelly was a thirty-eight-year-old single woman, an assistant professor at Xavier University. Her fiancé had found her inside her apartment at seven p.m., exactly two weeks after the murder of Theresa Chambers. The apartment was two blocks away from the location of the first killing. Like Theresa, Jill had a petite build and shoulder-length auburn hair. The scene had almost been a carbon copy, right down to the folded clothes and missing ring finger—with her engagement ring on it. This time, however, the medical examiner found evidence of sexual assault but no semen. The assailant had worn a condom. Will had found the knife on the first sweep, buried in the cat box. Like the weapon that had been used on Theresa, it was a folding combat knife.

Mount Adams is a sky island of a neighborhood perched over downtown and the Ohio River, on the leafy edge of Eden Park. Sit in one of the bars and restaurants with a view, and you're eye level with the top of the imposing cluster of skyscrapers. On clear summer nights it's as if you can reach across and touch their necklaces of light. Mount Adams had long since been reclaimed by gentrification and its narrow streets were home to galleries, restaurants, townhouses, and expensive homes, mostly in closely-spaced, restored nineteenth-century buildings. Although it sat in the midst of the city, its height and affluence seemed to offer an illusion of safety. Trouble was down the hill—not there. When the media learned of the Jill Kelly homicide coming just fourteen days after the killing of Theresa Chambers, they thought: serial killer in paradise. They called him "the Mount Adams Slasher." That was fine with Dodds and Will, who also adopted the term. The most horrific, distinctive fact of the two crimes had been concealed from the media: the amputation of the ring fingers. Between themselves, the cops called the killer something altogether different.

They called him the Ring Bearer.

And two weeks later, he struck again, four blocks away, when Lisa Schultz had come home late from work to a house that was supposed to be empty. Her husband had been on a business trip to London. Instead, the Slasher had been waiting for her. His method was identical to the Kelly murder. And then the city had gone into near panic. Police patrols had been increased yet again. Two nights later, a unit responding to a prowler call had chased a black male from beside a house on St. Gregory Street. He had run through Longworth's, out the kitchen and gotten away, but one of the patrolmen knew the suspect. He was a small-time burglar and sometime Peeping Tom named Craig Factor.

Will had always known they had the wrong man, despite the fact that the semen matched. Departments made mistakes with DNA every day. Chambers had seemed right for many reasons. But one was especially powerful: what woman would automatically open her door at night for a stranger, particularly after an unsolved murder had happened nearby? A woman who was reacting to a police officer, standing there under the "burned out" porch light, showing his badge. But they had never run across the tracks of a male nurse named Judd Mason, not once. Maybe he had been so wrong because he had never seen the case objectively. But right at that moment, burning his mouth with expensive coffee, it was a thought through whose threshold he didn't dare pass. He pulled out his cell phone to call Dodds. Then he put it away. What was the point?

He raised his head just in time to see Cheryl Beth walking purposefully toward him. She was wearing street clothes, jeans, a turtleneck and carrying a heavy coat. He couldn't help noticing how nicely she filled out those clothes. He managed a smile— she had to be relieved at the news. But she had a look of wild fear in her eyes.

"I've got to talk to you." She pulled a chair close.

"Did you see?" Will indicated the newspaper.

"It's not right. Mason may be a little creep, but he didn't kill Christine."

"How…?" Will barely got the word out before she continued in an agitated voice.

"Somebody broke into my house last night. I've stayed the last couple of nights with my friend Lisa. I was just too creeped out to stay at home. Yesterday afternoon, around six, I stopped off at home to get some clothes. Everything was fine. Today I drove by just to check on things and my front door was open. I called the police. Somebody had broken in." She leaned in close. "My bed, the comforter and the pillows, had been sliced up. Somebody went up to my bedroom and did that. There was a computer and a stereo and a TV, and they're all fine. But somebody sliced up my bed, and they threw everything out of my desk drawers."

"Mason would have already been in jail."

"Exactly." She bit her lip. "There's something else." She hesitated then recounted her ambush by Gary Nagle of the day before. Will listened carefully, listened as a simple case fell apart.

"Could it have been him?" Will asked.

"I don't know. I used to think I knew him, now I'm not sure about anything. He just seemed like a wild man yesterday. But your former friend Dodds doesn't care. He's not interested. He would barely talk to me."

He could almost detect she was shaking. He wanted to reach out to her but didn't. He said, "I don't know how else to push this. I wish I could get out of here."

She didn't miss a beat. "I can get you out."

Chapter Twenty-four

Half an hour later, Cheryl Beth wheeled Will out to the drive-up entrance to the neuro-rehab wing. She had signed him out for the day with the ward's patient coordinator—usually it was a privilege given for family members, so patients could spend a few hours outside the hospital. She made sure to take along all of Will's meds and some extra, just in case. The cold hit them when they came out the door. The temperature was in the low thirties, the gusts making it feel colder. Cheryl Beth had draped a blanket over Will because he didn't have a coat among his things. They would stop by his place and pick one up.

"Here's how we're getting you in the car," she said, opening the door and pulling out a thin board that measured about two and a half feet long. "This is a transfer board. I lied and said you had been trained in how to use it."

"Whatever it took to spring me." He smiled.

She instructed him on the use of the plastic transfer board, pushed his wheelchair close to the open car door, and removed the arm side closest to the car. She asked him to raise up while she positioned one end of the board under the seat of the wheel-chair and the other end on the car seat.

"This might not work," he said. "I'm pretty big, and I don't know if I can scoot that way."

She leaned down to him. "Do you trust me?"

He nodded. "Yes."

Cinching the gait belt around his waist, she coached him to move across the board and into the car seat. She wasn't a physical therapist and had never done this before. But it worked well enough. She held the belt from behind and he did the work. One inch out onto the board, then half his butt was on it, then he was moving into the car. He fell into the bucket seat and used both hands to lift his left leg in. Then he swung his right leg inside and pulled down the seat belt.

"Okay?" she asked.

He nodded, short of breath. Then she took the chair and transfer board and stowed them in the trunk. The newer wheelchairs folded with amazing ease and were not that heavy.

"Drive me around for a minute." He added: "Please."

It was not a demand. She could see the wonder in his face at actually being out of the hospital for the first time in almost three weeks. So she drove out of the maze of Pill Hill and into Clifton, around the university.

"I went to school there," she said. "I never thought I'd stay in Cincinnati. I thought it was very smug and insular—and I came from a small town. And it is all that. But I fell in love with it and stayed."

"Lots of people who come here say that," he said. "I always thought I'd leave, but I never did."

"So you're a native?"

He said he was.

"But you don't seem like one of those Cincinnatians whose families have been here for one hundred and fifty years and nobody else can really be accepted."

"No," he laughed. "They revoked my membership to the Queen City Club, and great-great-granddad didn't come from Germany." It was almost that simple among the establishment: the old English stock that settled after the American Revolution and the Germans that came in huge numbers in the nineteenth century. And the blacks. Will was working class. His father had been a cop. His mother had been a striver of sorts, or at least a dreamer for him, and she wanted him to go to college and not follow in the family business.

They drove and talked. She learned that he had gone to college, a rarity among Cincinnati cops of his generation and one that didn't exactly endear him to the old guard. He talked about that stereotype: the fat blond boys who grew up in Price Hill and went to Elder High School. There was always some truth to stereotypes. And what about her? She recited the thumbnail bio she reserved for first dates—thinking about it that way seemed strange. She had grown up in little Corbin, in the hills of southern Kentucky, where her father had worked for the L&N Railroad. She had been a fish out of water, couldn't wait to get out. Even so, she had married her high school sweetheart and he came with her when she took the scholarship to nursing school. But he had never liked Cincinnati, never felt accepted. They had divorced and he went back to Corbin.

"Any kids?"

"No." She was conscious of how her voice changed. "What about you?"

"A grown son."

"Really? Does he live here?"

"No."

The way he said the word told her she had scratched something raw. Family was usually a safe topic for conversation. But not always—she of all people should know that.

Will stayed quiet for several blocks. When he spoke, he was looking away. "He's not really part of my life now. He was a baby when I met Cindy, and I adopted him. We decided...well, she decided that she didn't want more children. But he had a rough time as a teenager. Drugs. The wrong crowd. And I was the bad guy, just from the job I do every day. Anyway, he was in Portland, the last I heard. I just wish he would call his mother once in a while."

"I'm sorry."

They turned from Clifton Avenue onto Ludlow, past the Esquire Theater, the restaurants and bars and chili parlors. Then

Cheryl Beth turned north into the neighborhood, with its old trees and substantial houses, where the tenured professors and old families lived decade after decade. The rolling ground was golden and copper with the fallen leaves.

"Where is your wife?"

"She left me. I don't blame her." He said it so simply she almost asked him to repeat it.

"Well, I sure as hell do. That's horrible!" She blurted it out and was instantly sorry. This was none of her business. She was already getting closer to this patient than she should. "I'm sorry."

"Don't be," he said. "God, this is a beautiful city. You almost forget it, just being in it every day."

"Especially doing the job you do."

"You learn to cope, or you go nuts and hurt yourself or other people," Will said.

Cheryl Beth thought that sounded a lot like nursing.

She had intended to stop at his apartment to get a coat. Will had other ideas and was very insistent about them. Knowing the way most of Cincinnati was built—old buildings erected long before there was an Americans with Disabilities Act—she thought it would be impossible. But Will had a loft downtown, on Fourth Avenue, and it had an elevator. They repeated the routine with the transfer board, traveled down the cold sidewalk and into the warm lobby of his building. It had been built in 1889 and rehabbed in the 1990s. They rode the elevator to the fourth floor and stepped into an airy, light-filled room. The wheelchair fit through the door with no problem. Will silently looked over his home.

It had potential, especially thanks to the tall, wide windows, but the loft wasn't much more than a large room filled with some boxes. The main room had two chairs and a desk. The upper level had a bed. The white walls were blank. Cheryl Beth smiled at the bachelor image. He probably had six-month-old takeout in the refrigerator. She didn't know how long Will had been separated from his wife, but this was obviously just a place to sleep and change clothes.

The problem was that the closet and bed were located on a platform two steps above the rest of the loft. He wanted to change clothes, put on a suit—"it'll help us get what we want." So he stayed down on the main level and called out to her what he needed: the charcoal suit, white dress shirt, blue striped tie, black leather dress belt, and black wingtips. "The collar stays are in the shot glass on the closet shelf," he said. Will had nice clothes and his shoes were highly polished. She brought them down, along with a shoehorn. He might need that.

"I'll sit up here on the bed," she said.

"I'm sure you've seen half-naked men before."

Even out of sight, she could tell it was an ordeal. He made breath sounds like a weightlifter and slightly moaned a couple of times. She tried to make conversation, but realized it would be better if she just talked. So she told him about her career, about pain management. He would respond as he could. She never saw patients after they left the hospital. Ones like Will would have lengthy recoveries and burdens to carry long after they were discharged. She knew this, of course. And working in the hospice was different—those patients had only one destination. Will still had a life ahead, but it would be totally different from what he had left behind when he walked in the doors of Memorial. Being here made it especially tactile. She looked around at the remnants of his old life and tears started to fill her eyes. She shook her head and they went away. Dressing took thirty minutes, but when she walked back down he looked quite sharp. He looked dashing.

"You clean up good," she said. He gathered up a pile of file folders and slipped them into a battered briefcase, then asked her to drape a dark topcoat over his shoulders.

He reached into the desk drawer and pulled out a bulky black object. Cheryl Beth was suddenly afraid.

"Will, I don't think…"

"Somebody's trying to kill you," he said quietly. He unholstered the pistol, hit a button, and a long object dropped from the handle of the gun into his hand. Was that the clip? Her father had only taught her to shoot a .22 rifle; she didn't know more about guns than that. Satisfied that it was loaded, Will slid the magazine back into the grip of the gun with a sharp metal snap. It was a sound that gave her a shiver of dread, but she said nothing. Then he slipped the gun and holster over his belt. He covered it with his suit coat flap and raised himself higher in the wheelchair. He read the concern in her eyes.

"Do you trust me?"

"Yes," she said firmly. "So what are we going to do?"

"The first thing I want to do is find a photo of Gary Nagle," he said. "Then I want to go visit our friend Lennie."

Chapter Twenty-five

Will bluffed his way into the Queensgate Correctional Facility of the Hamilton County Sheriff's Office. Cop-bitching always worked, especially with a deputy he had known for years. The round, hard face of Sheriff Simon Leis looked down on them from a framed photo. It seemed as if he had been in office forever, as a prosecutor, judge, and then sheriff, and, knowing Cincinnati, Will suspected he would remain in office forever. Si Leis would definitely not approve. The deputy looked over the wheelchair and dubbed him "Chief Ironside."

"You won't believe how far the DA is up my ass on this one. I had to leave the hospital early to prepare for this case."

"Fuckin' lawyers," the deputy said and signed him in. "I'd file a grievance over it, Chief." He looked at Cheryl Beth. "Who's this?"

"Cheryl Beth Wilson," Will said. "She's a criminal justice professor. Why she wants to study this stuff beats the hell out of me."

"You and me both." The deputy searched her purse. Then Will locked away his Smith & Wesson semiautomatic in one of the gun lockers, as he had done so many times before. The firearm felt heavier now. Everything felt different. The world outside was enchantingly vast, with every sight, smell, and sensation arousing him as it never had before. His apartment seemed surprisingly tiny. He had been confined to large spaces for so long. He was grateful he couldn't climb the two steps to the bedroom, because then he would see the bed and think of her. The blank institutional hardness of the jail corridors made forgetting easier.

They entered an empty interrogation room and waited.

"You lie well." Cheryl Beth smiled at him, but he could see she didn't completely approve. He offered her a chair but she stayed standing, showing a civilian's natural discomfort at being inside. He indicated she could pull a chair over to the far wall, closest to the doorway out. She did.

"So have you always been Cheryl Beth?"

"There were four girls named Cheryl in first grade," she said. "So I used my middle name and just kept using it. I like it."

"So do I," Will said.

Then there was a loud thud as the door in front of them was unlocked, momentarily emitting the unsettling noises from inside the jail. A pot-bellied deputy led in Leonard Leroy Corley, charged with assault. Will was momentarily bothered that the charge didn't specify "on a police officer." Lennie looked like a different man than Will had wrestled on the hospital floor. Besides the orange jail jumpsuit and shackles, he was clean. The jumpsuit looked amazingly like hospital scrubs.

"Want him cuffed to the table?" the deputy asked.

"No." Will looked Lennie over and went back to laying out his files. He took his time as the deputy sat Lennie down, and then stood two feet behind him, folding his massive arms.

Cleaned and calm, Lennie looked like he might have been a junior high teacher if the deck of life had been dealt differently, if his face didn't have a used-up and sorrowful expression. He sat in silence, his handcuffed hands in his lap, his eyes downcast in the prisoner's survival code: don't make direct eye contact.

"You can uncuff his hands," Will said.

"Hoo-kay," the deputy said, in a world-weary voice. He took the prisoner's hands and unlocked the manacles, sliding them into his belt. Lennie looked at Will for the first time. Cuffs-off was often the first transaction of goodwill in a prisoner interview. Lennie looked as his wrists, as if checking that they were still there. Will realized he was vulnerable, stuck in the wheelchair, as he had never been before in front of an inmate. It was a chance worth taking.

"Remember me?" Will asked.

"You hurt Lennie." His voice was high and childlike.

"You remember why?"

"No." He seemed genuinely puzzled. He looked over Will's shoulder. "Hi, Cheryl Beth."

"Hi, Lennie," she said in a shy, awkward voice. She added, "Are you taking your meds now?"

"Yes, ma'am. I feel better."

"That's good," Will said. He paused. "Lennie, you're in a lot of trouble. I'm a police officer and you attacked me. You might not have meant to do it. But it's a big deal."

"Didn't mean to..." He stared at his hands, folded passively on the table.

"You can help yourself by talking to me."

"I'll talk to you."

"That's good." Will opened one folder and began laying photographs out on the scarred tabletop. He set each one down individually, as if it were a card in a high-stakes game. They were shots of Theresa Chambers, Jill Kelly, and Lisa Schultz—all as they looked when they were alive. In a steady, calming voice, Will said, "I just want you to tell me if you've ever seen any of these women before."

He looked at each photo. "Pretty," he said. The man probably had the mind of a twelve-year-old, if that, like Craig Factor.

"Ever seen them?"

"Nope."

"Take your time. Take another look. We're not in any hurry."

Lennie bent over the pictures. Will tried to keep his mind from wandering. He had been in one of these rooms in October, talking to a prisoner who claimed the arresting officer had beaten him. It was a routine Internal Investigations case. Will had been standing that day, and he just fell over. One moment he was standing, and the next he had toppled to the left. The deputy probably thought he had been drinking. But it was the most dramatic sign of the tumor.

His feet were losing their ability to feel the floor and help balance him. He fell several more times, for no seeming reason. Looking back, the danger signs had started long before: a mysterious pain in his right side. Ultrasound gave him a clean bill and the pain went away. Or, it moved into his knees. That pain kept him up at night and the doc told him to lose weight. By the fall, he was having trouble walking easily, and still the doctor had no answer besides physical therapy. Two weeks after the fall in the jail, a neurologist had run a safety pin down his chest and belly, and he couldn't feel the pricks below his abdomen. They had sent him for an MRI the next day.

And yet, with his Scots-Irish fatalism, Will had known something was after him for years. He couldn't articulate it, and by the time it became a persistent foreboding he and Cindy had long since stopped talking about anything but the business of a marriage and the latest trouble of their son. What would it be: a heart attack, a bullet on a dark street? He knew time was against him and the knowledge had changed him.

Lennie spoke finally. "They're pretty. They wouldn't like me."

"Ever hurt a woman, Lennie?" Will said it in the same calm tone of voice and watched the man carefully. His mouth quivered and his eyes widened.

"No! Lennie wouldn't..." He held his hands up defensively and the deputy took a step, but Will waved him back.

Will slapped down an eight-and-a-half by eleven color photograph.

"Ahhhh!" Lennie gasped. Will could also hear Cheryl Beth take a sharp intake of breath. The photo showed Jill Kelly slashed to death in her kitchen.

"No, no...that's awful." Lennie shook his head and turned away. His shock seemed genuine. Will replaced the photos in a folder.

"Lennie, the bad picture's gone." The man still avoided looking at the tabletop. "Do you remember when you had the knife, when you were in the hospital?"

"The hospital's a good place. They help Lennie. Cheryl Beth helps Lennie."

She said, "But you had a knife, Lennie."

"I was afraid."

"Were you afraid of me?" Will asked. Lennie didn't answer. "That day we fought, you said something about the devil. Do you remember that?"

"No."

Now Will thought he was lying. Too many years of too many lies. He had perfect pitch for it. He leaned in close. A finger's length separated them. From that distance, the man still stank.

"Lennie, you talked about seeing the devil." Will lowered his voice. "It's okay, he can't hear us. These walls are too thick."

"No, I don't remember." He fidgeted, pulling on one finger, then another.

"You do, Lennie." He was whispering now. "Don't you want to help those pretty women? I know you do." He paused, made the distance half a finger's length. "Did you see the devil at the hospital, Lennie?"

The man slowly nodded.

"Where did you see him?"

"In the basement. I'm not supposed to go down there. But it's quiet and it's warm…"

"And you know all the hiding places, right?" Will said it as one kid admiring another's skill. Lennie nodded enthusiastically. He had specks of yellow in his eyes.

"You saw the devil in the basement?"

"Yes." His voice was a soft, serious whisper.

"How did you know it was the devil?"

"Blood."

"That's very brave, Lennie. That will help us." Will slowly opened another file folder and began arranging photos of ten different men. Some were suspects from old crimes. One was Judd Mason. Another was Gary Nagle—this had necessitated a trip to Cheryl Beth's house to retrieve the old lover's shot. She had been so embarrassed that she had actually turned bright red to admit she still had it. He had told her to leave the door open and come out immediately if anything seemed wrong. He hadn't known what he would do if he couldn't immediately shoot someone. Fortunately, the trip to her house had been uneventful, the new locks unmolested. And she had returned with a photo of Dr. Gary Nagle. Will couldn't see her with him. He looked like a weasel. Will set Nagle's photo alongside the other nine.

Then he turned over the photo of Bud Chambers.

Lennie made a sound like an animal that had been shot, a half whimper and a half last breath.

Will said, "Just point if you saw any of these men down in the basement."

Lennie's finger shook violently, but it rested on Bud Chambers' nose.

"You saw him in the basement, with the blood?"

"Yes." A whisper.

"Did you think he was the devil?"

Lennie nodded emphatically.

"What did you see?"

"Blood….everywhere. It was a sacrifice." He enunciated the word very clearly. "The devil needed blood. But I hid so he couldn't see me. Lennie knows how to hide."

The old homicide cop inside Will said, *fuck me runnin'.* Lennie had witnessed the murder. Getting a jury to believe Lennie was another matter, but for the moment Will had done as Bull had taught him so many years ago: had a theory, played a hunch.

"You're going to be fine," Will clapped him on the forearm, and let the deputy take him away.

Outside, Cheryl Beth finally spoke.

"That was pretty amazing, the way you did that. But as I recall that day, Lennie kept yelling that you were the devil."

It was only when he looked at her that he saw the broad, playful smile on her face. She was beautiful.

Chapter Twenty-six

They argued briefly at the car. Will said he wanted to try to stand by the wheelchair and let himself down in the car, instead of using the transfer board. Cheryl Beth was afraid—afraid he might fall, and that she was responsible. The sharp, cold wind was whipping around the buildings and there wasn't time to argue long. She let him try it. Before she let him stand, she cinched the gait belt tightly around his waist, locked the wheelchair in place, and grabbed the belt tightly. Her stomach tightened in anticipation as she looked down at the big man, confined to the chair. He took a breath and stood, one fluid motion. Then he pivoted slowly to the left and dropped himself down in the car seat. She pulled the wheelchair back to the trunk and stowed it.

"You're looking way too proud of yourself, Will Borders." She pulled out in traffic and waited for the car heater to get warm. He just smiled.

"I'm responsible for you, you know."

"And I'm grateful. And thank you for letting me try to do that. It's important."

She was grateful to be out of the jail, and drove slowly past the old industrial hulks and railroad bridges that nested above the untended streets southwest of downtown. High chain link fences were topped with rusty concertina wire. Seeing Lennie again brought back the awful fight in the hospital. Watching the way Will worked intrigued her—it was like a window into a totally different world. But it didn't make sense. It just didn't.

"What are you thinking?" he asked, noting her silence.

"Who was that, in the picture Lennie pointed to?"

"A man named Bud Chambers. A former cop. Bad actor."

"Chambers?"

"He was Theresa Chambers' husband—estranged husband. We always thought he did it. He was our first suspect."

Will told her about Chambers, while she remembered what Gary had said that first night, about the husband always being the prime suspect. She felt so tight inside, like all her organs had compressed together and were being wrapped around like the rubber band that propelled a child's plywood airplane.

"So you thought he would pick him."

"Yes," Will said. "But I had to do it right, run it with several mug shots. I've been wrong before."

"Really? You seem pretty sure of yourself."

He seemed abashed. She laughed. "It's fun to see you in your element." He was sensitive. That was a nice quality in a man, especially a cop. But she switched to a serious voice.

"Did you show him pictures of Judd and Gary?"

"I did. He just glazed over, like he didn't know them. The same with the other pictures. He only recognized Bud Chambers."

"So why didn't you arrest this Chambers in the first place?" Cheryl Beth asked.

"We worked it hard, and then we caught Craig Factor and the semen from Theresa matched."

"But you were never convinced?"

"No. I knew some corrupt cops were covering for him. It's not like this never happens. A few years ago, a cop was messing around with his wife's sister. The sister knifes the wife to death—her own sister. We always thought the cop was present at the homicide and covering for his sister-in-law. Some of his buddies—rotten cops—gave him an alibi. Then they hired a lawyer, a former corrupt cop himself, and he gets the cop off and gets a sweetheart deal for the sister-in-law. When I joined Internal Investigations the guy retired. He came up to me and said he knew I was going to get him, and he was right. So this stuff happens. It did with Bud Chambers."

"I just don't know."

"What don't you know?"

"I don't want to tell you how to do your job, but…"

"But?"

"I don't know…"

"Lennie's not the best witness, but he's a start. I can give this to Dodds and let him do the rest. I can spend my time learning how to walk again."

She wondered about that. The murder had seemed to animate him, transport him out of his troubles.

"I'm not convinced."

He seemed flustered, hunched down in the seat. "So, convince me otherwise."

"Well, first of all, Gary still scares me. It's like he's lost it. When he was standing in that room, swinging his hand like it was a knife, I could see him killing Christine in a rage."

"I understand, but I've never told you all the details about the Mount Adams Slasher." He went on to recount the similarities to Christine's murder: the folded clothes, the murder weapon hidden as if to taunt the police, and the amputated ring finger. By the time he was through, she had pulled the car to the curb and shifted into park.

"I know it's upsetting," he said.

"I've seen worse." She tried to toughen her voice. But she hadn't lived worse. She had lived all these "MOs" that night in Christine's office—alone—where she had been summoned by a message that nobody remembered taking. "It was as if someone wanted me to come down there. To witness it, or to be killed along with her?" That night's timeline telescoped in and out in her mind. "Maybe someone knew I would be back at the hospital that night. That's not brain surgery. I go back a lot—people hurt at night. Maybe it wasn't Christine who left the message for me at the nurses' station at all. Only, I spent more time with that patient, and maybe I was late getting down to the basement. My God, maybe I was meant to be killed, too. Why?"

Will adjusted his left leg. Even though he wasn't in pain, she could tell he was in constant discomfort. Finally, he said, "The only thing that joined you and Dr. Lustig was Gary. And the method of the killing would mean he killed the three other women, and planted the evidence that implicated Craig Factor. A cop could do it. A respected doctor? Talk about brain surgery."

"That's what he does for a living," she said humorlessly. "He's very bright. And he knows the layout of the hospital. He would know about the old morgue and the elevator. Someone is trying to kill me! What if it's him? What are you smiling at?"

"You." He paused. "You'd make a good detective." He wanted to say how happy he was to be out with her, how he loved her voice, with its light Southern accent that made her sentences sound like singing. It wouldn't be right to say any of that. "Cheryl Beth, if this were an ordinary homicide, I'd ask you what enemies you had, although I can't imagine you have any. I'd ask you why someone might want you dead. But this is the Slasher. If he's after you, it's because he thinks you witnessed the murder."

"I'm just not sure."

"You said, 'first of all.' What else?"

The car was starting to warm up. She unbuttoned her coat. "Judd Mason is another creep. There's the whole letter thing, and then he cornered me in the ER the other day…"

"You didn't tell me that."

"There's been a lot going on. He didn't really threaten me. Just acted creepy. Said he knew I'd been spying on him. But he said the strangest thing. He said that he knew I'd been told not to talk about the murder, but he said it in exactly the same language as the vice president of nursing had told me just after it happened. Ever have a boss who's a political weasel and got ahead for just that reason?"

"In the police? Never. All our bosses are selfless visionaries."

"Ha. Well, this woman jumped down my throat about being involved with Gary, as if that never happens in a hospital. As if I

didn't feel bad about it enough already. Then she says, I am not
to discuss Dr. Lustig's murder with anyone: colleagues, patients,
and absolutely not the press. Those are the same words Judd
Mason said to me the other day."

"Like he had some inside pipeline?"

"Exactly."

Cheryl Beth had been insulted when Stephanie Ott had
said it. It impugned her professionalism. But it also probably
meant that Stephanie somehow knew about the romance Cheryl
Beth had carried on for two years with one of the writers at the
Cincinnati Post. It had been the most satisfying relationship since
her divorce, and she had secretly indulged in every woman's hope
that it might lead to something—if not marriage, maybe they
could live together, really be a couple, *something*. She had tried
to keep the whole biological clock cliché at bay, all the time they
saw each other, but keeping hope at bay had been more difficult.
He had been smart and funny and worldly. He had been an
amazing, giving lover. A real catch. But it was not to be.

He had left town three years ago. She hadn't hated him—
they had too much fun. She did miss his company, miss the
hope, stopped listening to any sad songs. She missed him at odd
moments, seeing a street they had walked down, a park where
they had picnicked. He had introduced her to jazz and wine—
we are so much the product of our old lovers. She missed the
feel of his breathing on her shoulder as they slept together, and
the way he always made love to her in the morning, before he
left. Where Andy had lain atop her and humped, he would raise
himself on his forearms and look at her with an angelic smile,
and he had taught her so many positions. Damn, she hated
thinking about it, and yet many days it was a warm, immediate
memory. It did not last. Later, she realized how she had been
rebound-vulnerable to Gary Nagle. It was her fault. Damn it.
She kept all this to herself. Will probably thought she was a
floozy already. Her family certainly did. Her mother couldn't
believe she would divorce Andy, but then she couldn't believe

Cheryl Beth didn't want to live in that little town forever and just have kids.

"...*Absolutely not the press.*" It was as if they had been researching her life. But why? That was too paranoid.

"If it makes you feel any better, I don't have an explanation for the letter, either," Will said. "None of the other victims received letters. We do know that Christine had received threatening phone calls. Did you know that?"

"No." She didn't make an effort to drive. They sat stationary in the warm car.

"I've done some asking around," Will said. "Berkowitz used to be on the force, and I convinced him to help me a little. The hospital was very sensitive about the murder. They wanted the publicity shut down, which I can understand. What's unusual is that they weren't leaning on the cops to get results, to close this case. They just wanted it to go away. Dodds is working alone; his partner's on maternity leave. That was fine with them. Now that's odd. In my experience, the big boss would have been on the phone to the chief demanding that fifty detectives be assigned to the case."

"They just wanted it to go away," Cheryl Beth said.

"Berkowitz said something about accreditation?"

"Yes," she said. "The Joint Commission. They accredit the hospital. We just went through that."

"Berkowitz said something was wrong. Some major problems, and accreditation might be withheld. Did you know about this?"

"We've been waiting for word."

"They can't just conceal it?"

"It's public information," Cheryl Beth said. "But I guess if nobody asks... I can't believe they would try to conceal such a thing. You typically have time to lay out a plan to correct the problems. Hospitals can get partial or provisional accreditation. But Cincinnati Memorial? My God, we used to be the gold standard."

"Maybe the bosses are trying to figure out a way to put a spin on the positive and bury the rest. I guess big money was at stake. Doctor training funds, Medicare, Medicaid. Some big federal grant for a computer upgrade."

"The digital medicine project. Christine had stopped her practice to work on it."

"I learned something else about that. She had been reassigned to that basement office a month before. She had been working in the administrative offices. Berkowitz said she was moved. Why? In the police world, it would mean you really pissed off somebody powerful."

"That's exactly what Mason told me. She had been moved. He didn't know why." Cheryl Beth shook her head, processing all the new information. Then, "It still doesn't explain the threatening letter. Maybe Dodds found Mason's fingerprints on it. Are you really so sure your bad cop did this?"

Will was silent as she started the car.

Finally, "If I can't make the case to you, I sure as hell can't do it with Dodds. What would it take to convince you?"

"You're the detective. What other tricks do you have up your sleeve?"

He thought about this for a long moment. "Are you willing to try a long shot?"

Chapter Twenty-seven

They drove east out of downtown on Columbia Parkway, quickly passing the promontory of Mount Adams and the modern condo where a chief executive of Procter and Gamble was said to keep his mistress. On the left were the tree-lined hills with condo towers sprouting out at intervals, and on the right the broad Ohio River curved and dipped. One lonely barge was being pushed upriver by a tug. Will told Cheryl Beth about the time years ago when the river had frozen solid and he had walked across to Kentucky. But she quickly moved back to the case.

"Wouldn't the Mount Adams killer have kept the ring fingers as trophies?" she asked.

"Nobody knows about the ring fingers, so don't blurt that out accidentally with Dodds or he'll have a stroke."

"I'll be a good girl, and if he has a CVA, I'll help treat him. Seriously, though."

"That would be the profile," Will admitted, "and we never found them among Factor's things. We never even found the kind of tool that would do it."

"Surgeons have those instruments." She spoke more softly, staring straight ahead at the road. "Even a pair of heavy-duty bandage shears would do—they need to be able to cut off leather boots, whatever, in an emergency."

She was still sure the killer was Gary Nagle. Will was trying to work out how to deal with Darlene Corley. Her statement had given Bud Chambers his alibi. The night of Theresa's murder, Chambers had been on duty, except for a four-hour period that would have perfectly coincided with Theresa's time of death. Once Will and Dodds had established this fact—after days of stone-walling by other officers on Chambers' shift and even his watch commander—Darlene had emerged. She was Chambers' girlfriend and he had been with her, at her place down by the river.

"How do you know she didn't do it?"

Will laughed. "You'd make a good detective. How'd you get so cynical?"

"Old boyfriends."

"You deserve a lot better than that." He was instantly embarrassed he had said it, and continued quickly. "Now that you mention it, she'd be tall enough and strong enough. There's the little matter of rape. Craig Factor was arrested and the semen matched."

"But only one of the cases."

Right. They never really had a chance to sweat her. Neither detective believed her story covering for Bud Chambers. But it didn't seem to matter once Factor was in custody. Now Will would give it one more try. "Turn here."

They could have gone north, up Delta into Mount Lookout and Hyde Park, where even the sidewalks seemed to radiate graceful prosperity. But they turned toward the river, past a restaurant called The Precinct, which was once a police station. Another quick turn and they continued on old Highway 52, in the ancient neighborhoods that clung to the riverbank below Alms Park. They usually got the worst of it when the Ohio had its way, defying the most elaborate flood control attempts. You could see the water marks on some of the old houses. Will directed Cheryl Beth to turn again, and he immediately saw the three white police cruisers.

"Hell." He pointed to the porch of a tattered duplex. Half a strand of Christmas lights dangled off the rain gutters. Darlene Corley was sitting on the steps, her hands behind her, obviously handcuffed. One officer led a tall, rough-hewn man down the walk toward a cruiser. With stubble on his face and his dark hair poking out as if it had been shellacked, he looked as if he hadn't bathed for a week. He was handcuffed and cursing, walking down a weedy path and through an opening in a rusty, waist-high cyclone fence. The officer opened a back door and stuffed him inside, holding his hand above his filthy head to keep him from banging it on the top of the door sill. Will had done it thousands of times. He rolled down the window and beckoned the cop over.

"Hey," the young cop said when he saw Will's badge.

"Hey. What have you got?"

"Domestic. Briar thing. Boyfriend's going to jail for assault. The beauty queen up on the porch may be, too. When we got here she was waving an aluminum baseball bat at him and she hasn't been too cooperative."

"It's always on the domestics when cops get hurt," Will commiserated. "Her name's Darlene Corley. She had a prostitution arrest a few years ago, but I think she's clean otherwise. She's one of my CIs."

The uniformed cop nodded, new enough on the job to be happy to be spoken to like a peer by an older detective, to know about one of his confidential informants.

"Think you could bring her over here and cut her a break if she helps me? Otherwise, throw her under the jail. Hell if I care."

"Sure, sure, Detective…?"

"Borders, Will Borders."

The young man turned and walked back to the porch. Will was relieved that he didn't make the connection a more experienced cop might make between "Will Borders" and "Internal Investigations" and get all paranoid. He stood Darlene up and walked her their way. She hadn't changed much. She wore jeans, high heels, and a thick pink sweater with a bear stitched on it. But little about her appeared cuddly. She was both lanky and big boned—Dodds had called her "the roller derby queen"— and her face was cut hard, whatever her expression. Her long, unnaturally blond hair was poofed out.

"Hey, Detective Will. Long time, long time…"

"What'd you do, Darlene?"

"Damn Mike." She gingerly touched the gulf of purple and black spreading out from around her left eye. "He's my boyfriend. Long story. He's been drinkin' and every time he does he thinks he can beat on me, and he's got another goddamn think coming…"

Will held up his hand.

"The officer tells me you're going to jail."

"No!" She whipped her head back and forth. "I ain't done nothin'." She wailed. Oh, he didn't miss this part of the job.

"Here's the thing, Darlene. You might be able to help yourself."

Her drama ended instantly, her eyes intent on the potential transaction.

"I need information. You have it. If you help me, I might ask the officer to let you go, although the call is his." Will looked toward the young patrolman, who nodded appreciatively.

"Anything, Detective Will. Who's your partner with the pretty eyes? What happened to that fat nigger you used to run with?"

Will showed nothing on his face. They were words heard from whites more often in Cincinnati than the chamber of commerce types would admit. He had never used them, even though his father had, abundantly. His mother had disapproved. He waited for Darlene to realize her predicament. She was still handcuffed.

"So you'll talk to me?"

"Sure, darlin'. But not here on the street. I can't let my buds think I'm a snitch or something."

A plan emerged in Will's mind. "If the officer agrees, and you don't cause any more trouble… One more call, and you're going to jail. Got it?"

"Sure." She sulked.

"Then meet me under the bridge by the Serpentine Wall in an hour. I'll be sitting there. You'll find me."

"No problem." The officer took off the cuffs and she was beaming.

"Darlene."

"Yes sir?"

"If you stand me up, I'm going to make sure you do jail time."

Cheryl Beth drove silently, her chin set at a pensive angle.

"I'm sorry to put you in the middle of all this," Will said.

She shook her head. "I am in the middle. That was just a little too close for comfort." She pulled back on Columbia and sped up. "I grew up around people like that. I could have been one."

"I doubt that."

"I beat the odds. My dad died young. Railroad accident. I think he had some ambitions for all of us. We ended up nearly destitute. The church pretty much took us in until my mom could find work. All she wanted was for me to be a cheerleader in high school, then settle down, get married and have kids. I was the one who wanted to be an honor student and get out of town. I had several friends who got pregnant in high school. All my brothers are still down there. Lord."

He liked the image of her as a cheerleader, but kept that to himself. He admired the honor student part. His dad had only expected Will to do well at high school football and go to work as a cop. Going to college, much less at a fancy place like Miami University, was beyond his comprehension. And yet Will had come back home and joined the force. Maybe he hadn't beaten the odds.

◇◇◇

How do you want to play this? That's what he or Dodds would say to the other as they worked up a strategy before confronting a suspect or a witness. He found himself missing his old partner in spite of everything. Now it was up to him, even though he was constantly afraid the pain might break through, even though his body was a mess of constipation and foreign sensations.

They went through a Skyline Chili drive-thru and ordered a late lunch. Damn the short winter days. As the day streamed by, the time drew closer when he would have to return to the hospital. But the two cheese Coney dogs were ambrosia. Cheryl Beth ate two as well. Fifteen minutes later, they were set up.

Will wheeled himself into the riverfront park by the contoured mass of concrete called the Serpentine Wall. In the spring and summer, the area would be full of people and boats cruising the river. Today it was deserted. Downtown was behind them and the bridges soared overhead on either side. He found a bench that was easily seen and Cheryl Beth helped him scoot onto it from the chair. He was glad to be rid of the infernal transfer board, but his legs were feeling weaker. *Just hold out a little longer.* Then he instructed her to take the chair back to the car and stow it. She rejoined him and they silently watched the cold, swift, concrete-brown river flow past, and, on the other side, the old brick buildings of Newport and Covington. He thought about his morphine dream of dead children and quickly banished it. The park was one of his favorite places. Overhead, the American flags snapped noisily in the breeze, and the flying pigs looked cold up on their ornate columns. It wasn't long before he saw Darlene walking quickly toward them from the east, emerging from the shadows of an old bridge abutment.

"So what are we doin'? It's freezing."

"Have a seat." Will indicated for her to sit beside him. Cheryl Beth was on his other side.

"So you have a new boyfriend? What does Bud think about that?"

Darlene held her arms around herself tightly, shivering despite wearing several layers of clothes.

"Screw Bud." She said it like spitting. "I don't give a damn what he thinks."

"How come?"

"How the hell come? He's the one got me on the meth. Fucked up my life big-time. Then he leaves me. Haven't seen him for a year."

"Now, Darlene, you know anything you tell me can be used against you in a court of law."

"What? You're a narc now, Detective Will? That baby cop told me all that stuff. I've heard it before. Why are we out here? Can't we go sit in the car?"

"This won't take long." He fought to sit normally on the bench, so Darlene wouldn't know he needed the wheelchair, that he wasn't really on duty. That she wouldn't notice how his weak left leg fell out to the side, ever so unnaturally. He wanted to shift his weight every minute or two to ease the discomfort. He stayed still.

Darlene held her face in profile as she stared at the mesmer-izing river. It looked as if she had aged a decade since he had talked to her two years before. Her skin was pale and freckled, and now it was deeply creased. It bore a moonscape of small scars. She pulled out a pack of Camels and lit one, puffing on it nervously. The smoke mingled with the mist from her breath and it all came into his face.

"I just need to clear a few things up about an old case."

She looked at him and stubbed out the cigarette. "You mean the murder."

"Yes."

She lit another smoke and stared at the river.

"Been a long time ago. That boy went to prison. I hear he died there."

"That's right." Will watched the river and let her smoke and stew. The cold was on his side. He had never minded it. "You said Bud was with you that night."

"He was there. He came by most nights, when he was work-ing nights."

"You guys never lived together?"

"No. He wouldn't."

"He'd moved out on his wife. Seems like he'd want to be with a pretty thing like you."

"He said he needed his space, whatever the hell that means. Men say that. He'd come by some nights, some afternoons. We'd fuck and he'd leave. True love, huh?"

The Pain Nurse   189

"Who knows?" He waited, let the cold stab at her. Then, "Maybe he had a girl on the side."

She was inhaling furiously, the skin above her upper lip showing ribs of wrinkles. The river slapped noisily at the concrete and traffic droned on the interstate overhead. Quietly, he heard her say, "Son of a bitch…"

"I don't mean to upset you," Will said. "You know how some men are. Girl on the side here, girl on the side there, always too busy to spend much time."

"Son of a bitch." She said it louder this time.

"How'd you get on meth?"

"He brought it one day. Said he'd taken it off a dealer and it might be fun. It sure as hell was. Only he just drank Jack Daniels while I did it. Fuck, it wrapped around me like a snake…"

"When'd he do this?"

"Couple years ago."

"Before or after his wife was killed?"

She thought for a moment. "Before."

"So did you have to go out and buy it, once you got hooked?"

"No, he'd bring me some. I thought I had a real sugar daddy."

"You can get treatment." This was Cheryl Beth. Darlene lit another Camel and leaned forward to look at her.

"You sound like you're south of the river, pretty eyed girl."

"Corbin, Kentucky," Cheryl Beth said.

"I got people down that way," Darlene said. "Down by Bailey's Switch?"

"I know Bailey," Cheryl Beth said.

Will wished she hadn't gotten Darlene off track, but then he changed his mind. He knew how they'd play it.

"Darlene, about that night, when Theresa Chambers was murdered…"

"Yeah, yeah, Detective Will, you have a one-track mind."

"It wasn't really true was it?"

"What?" She hesitated just long enough.

"I didn't think so," Will said.

She twitched and huddled into herself. "He told me he'd kill me if I told you the truth."

Will told her she would be safe, and that moment he thought he could leap up and dance along the Serpentine Wall. She had come right out and said it.

"I had to cover for him, don't you understand?" She hugged herself tightly, staring down at the sidewalk. "He got me my stuff. I woulda died without it. He said he had a dealer under his thumb, that's just how he said it. And if I didn't do what he said, he wouldn't bring me my fix. Then when you guys called, he said he'd kill me if I didn't say things happened his way."

"So he wasn't with you that night?"

She shook her head.

Will asked her again and she nearly shouted "No!" then reached back in her coat pocket, pulled out the pack, and lit another cigarette. She was crying now. "Are you gonna arrest me? Take me to jail? I'm clean now. I got a baby now, Detective Will, please, God, don't…"

"Just tell me the truth, Darlene."

"It's going to be all right," Cheryl Beth said.

Darlene rubbed her nose and scrunched her face. "Who are you, girl? You don't have a cop face."

Will intervened. "What if I told you she was a witness."

Suddenly Darlene seemed to age another ten years and her face turned bright red before losing its color entirely. Even the veiny damage from her boyfriend's fist seemed to drain of blood. "Wha…? How is that possible? Oh, fuck. Bud said nobody could…" Her words became an unintelligible blubber with the occasional "they're gonna take my baby" coming through. Will put his hand on her arm and she fell into his shoulder bawling. He fought not to tilt sideways into Cheryl Beth.

"Tell me how it happened, Darlene. This doesn't have to go badly for you if you tell the truth."

"He just told me to tell you that he was with me. He said the bosses were after him, trying to fire him. I never knew anything about his wife being killed…"

"So you covered for him."

She nodded, kept crying. She was shivering and her teeth chattered from the cold. "But he said nobody would know, nobody would see us. I didn't know what he was going to do. I swear to God, I swear to God…"

Every nerve tensed in Will's body. He had used the word "witness" to describe Cheryl Beth. It had opened all the doors. He said, "So you didn't think anybody would see. Don't you want to tell your side of the story?"

She sat back up, miraculously avoiding leaving cigarette burns in Will's overcoat. She leaned out again to stare at Cheryl Beth.

"Bud brought that boy home. Bud was a kinky one, you know? We did some weird stuff, you know? He really liked it. But no way was I goin' to fuck some street nigger, much less a retard. Poor thing, looked scared as hell. Bud could do that to you. But he told us what to do." She gently touched her black eye. "I'm cold, Detective Will."

"Just tell it the way you remember it, Darlene."

She spoke slowly, the mist from her breath and cigarette smoke wreathing her head. "Bud told me to take off my clothes and get in bed and play with myself. 'Put on a show for him,' he said. And he had that boy sit in a chair and watch me." She hesitated, then continued. "Bud told him to jerk off in this plastic bottle he gave him. That's what we did. That's all we did. And Bud let the boy go. I just thought it was weird shit, you know? I said, 'Why you keeping his come in that bottle?' He didn't answer. Nobody was gonna get hurt."

She had pulled him through a door he didn't even know existed. He had a dozen questions, but didn't dare ask them. She believed Cheryl Beth had seen this. Will couldn't let her think otherwise.

Suddenly Darlene was talking rapidly, trying to purge it from her memory. "I never knew what Bud was going to do. I swear to God. That morning, he come by, all agitated. He said he found her body, Theresa. He swore to me that he didn't kill her, but he said he had to put that boy's come on her body because the other cops would frame him, say he done it because he was the husband and she had a restraining order against him and all. He told me what to say. God, I was scared! Fuck, it was hard keeping my head straight."

"So," Will said, "just to be clear, did you know who Bud brought home that night?"

"I never seen him before. Just said his name was Craig."

"The one we arrested for murder, right?"

"Yes sir."

"And when did Bud bring him home to you, when did you do this?"

"It was two nights before the killing."

"How do you remember that, what with the meth and all?"

She smiled, sniffled loudly. "It was my birthday."

Will stared into the opaque river and said nothing. The day was cold and dying. At last he spoke through the chill, "Darlene, you're going to have to give a statement. Are you willing to do that?"

"Yes. Yes, I am...just let me keep my baby."

He patted her arm and told her she could go. She stubbed out the last Camel, tossed it into the growing pile of cigarette filters on the sidewalk, and stood. She walked two steps and turned.

"I always liked you, Detective Will. Always thought you were fair. I never believed what Bud said about you."

It was a moment of premonition, the nanosecond where the bullet leaves the rifle and strikes a target even before its sound is heard. But Will asked, "What did Bud say?"

"That you killed Theresa."

Chapter Twenty-eight

Cheryl Beth was relieved for the physical effort of folding the wheelchair and lifting it into the back of her car. When she almost lost control of it, nearly tossing it into the air, she knew the level of her emotions. Yet she could say nothing once she was in the car. Will was on his cell phone, obviously talking to Detective Dodds. She could only hear his end of the conversation.

"Darlene gave it all up…calm down…never mind why I'm not in the hospital…"

She could hear the angry percussions of Dodds' voice coming through Will's phone, interrupting nearly every sentence, but she couldn't make out the words.

"Are you done now? She admits he wasn't with her the night Theresa died, and she explained how he planted the DNA evidence…of course, I Mirandized her…She's got a kid now, so you've got leverage…He turned her into a tweaker but she says she's clean now…She's in the same crappy little house, yes, she's there…You've got to get over there now and take her statement, get her protected, and get a warrant out on him. Pull him in for anything, just get him and hold him…I'm not trying to tell you how to do your job…Because somebody had to…You know where to find me."

She listened to Will talk, such enthusiasm in his voice. Her emotions were lava under pressure.

"Will Borders, you'd better the hell tell me what's going on because there's nothing I hate more than being lied to." She turned in the seat to face him, refusing to break eye contact, talking as adamantly with her hands as with her voice. "I've watched you these weeks as you've struggled and worked, and I've admired you. I never would have let you hurt as long as you did if I'd known and I stopped it. And then I got you out today, you go and get a damned gun, and this trailer girl talks about this man saying you killed that woman, and, God, you'd better stop lying to me right now! I'm sick of people lying to me! You'd better tell me what's going on right now!"

She threw it out as the words boiled out of her mind. One of the docs used to make gentle fun of her when she was that intense, the exclamation points shooting out of her, calling it "running hot." She was running hot. She stared at Will as he meekly put his phone away and reached down to rearrange his left leg. His eyes were wide.

"What do you want to know?"

"Did you kill her?"

"No."

"Then why did that girl say you did? Why did Lennie think you were the devil?"

"You think I killed Christine Lustig? That would be quite a trick."

"Don't play games with me," she snapped. "You know exactly what I mean."

"I didn't kill Theresa."

"How do I know that?" she demanded.

"I was with Dodds that night."

"But he said you lied to him. I heard you two, fighting in the morgue. He said you left homicide because he fired you, because you lied to him." She pushed herself back into the seat and stared out at the park. "What did you lie about?"

He sighed and adjusted his tie. "Theresa."

Something in the way that he said her name crashed against Cheryl Beth's anger and mistrust, leaving her off balance. She said, "Were you sleeping with her?"

"Yes."

There it was. Cheryl Beth looked straight ahead. The park was becoming a faded dream as their breath fogged over the windshield. It was growing cold inside the car, but she didn't make a move to turn the key.

Will's voice was drained of its previous excitement. "It was three years ago. I walked into a bar downtown. It was a slow evening and there weren't many people there. I walked between the tables and knocked her purse over, and I bent down to help her. We talked for a minute. She looked so sad. I'd never seen anyone look so sad. But there was this beauty, this grace, hidden behind it. So I sent a drink over to her table, and in a minute she came and joined me..."

"You were cheating on your wife?" She noticed he wasn't wearing a wedding band, but his chart showed a contact, Cynthia Holland, as his wife.

He gave a sour laugh. "We'd separated, again. She was seeing a man on the side. Or was it two?"

"So you and this woman..."

"Her name was Theresa."

His voice sounded as if it had hit a sandbar.

"She didn't want to get involved with a cop again," he said. "But we did." He spoke more slowly, pausing, his mind far from the cold inside of the car. "She'd never had anybody be good to her. Never had flowers sent to her. A car door opened for her."

"Her husband, Bud, he found out?"

"They were separated. I knew Bud Chambers years ago, on patrol. We weren't friends. The more I heard about the way he had treated her, I hated him. I checked him out. He was still a patrolman, never even made sergeant. He had a load of brutality complaints. But he was part of the ole-boy network on the force." He shook his head. "She deserved so much better. But it was, like, I don't know, once Cindy realized I was involved with somebody she suddenly said she wanted me back. I knew better, but it was hard. Cindy was the woman I'd married. But Theresa..."

He huddled deeper in his coat. "Her daughter kept pressing her to reconcile with Bud. The girl was, maybe, sixteen then. She didn't know any better, wanted mom and dad together. Theresa was very guilt-ridden about it. She said she was probably doing the wrong thing, making the biggest mistake of her life. But she told me she'd decided to try again with Bud. I didn't hear from her for almost a year. Then, the week before…" He swallowed hard. "Before she was murdered. She called and said he had moved out again. She'd thrown him out and gotten a restraining order. She said she didn't want for me to have to get involved in it. But she said she'd come over soon. We made a date. It was for the day after…after…"

He took a gulp of air. "We were the primaries. The first detectives called to the scene. It was a beautiful day. Like the first real spring day. I prayed she had moved, that someone else was at that address. But I knew. I knew." His voice slowed as he seemed to struggle to get the words out. "I knew he did it. I swore to her I'd make him pay, but I never did. I got him off the force, but he got away with it. And with those other girls he killed to cover his tracks. And now with Christine. He's a killer. Who knows why? Who cares?"

She asked why he didn't tell Dodds that he had been involved with Theresa Chambers.

"I knew how he'd react," Will said. "It would be a distraction, too. I knew Bud did it. And command might take me off the case—too close to the victim and all that. So I didn't tell him for two weeks, when the next woman was killed. When I did, he said he didn't want to work with me anymore. He never told anyone. We stayed together until Craig Factor was convicted and everybody said we were supercops. But our friendship was over. I transferred to Internal Investigations, to try to get some of these dirtbag cops off the streets." He paused. "That's what I told myself. I just kept seeing her face, seeing her dead…"

Cheryl Beth felt light enough to float away, felt wetness at the edges of her eyes.

"Did you love her?"

Will didn't answer. She could see him struggling not to cry. Men were funny that way. Most never knew the release of a good cry. She fought the impulse to take him in her arms. He was just a patient. She had hugged and comforted hundreds of patients. Why was she struggling? What was she struggling with? He leaned away from her, against the car door.

"Weepy Borders," he laughed and half-sobbed.

"What?"

"Long story."

Cheryl Beth tried to lighten her voice. "Did you have fun with her?"

"Oh, yeah," he rasped. "I never knew it was possible."

She started the car and drove slowly out of the park and into the downtown streets. As the defroster cleared the windshield, rain began pecking at the glass.

"You blame yourself."

He was staring out the passenger-side window as they passed Fountain Square, decorated for Christmas, an impressionist painting as umbrella-shrouded office workers and shoppers scurried across, the buildings dissolving in the rain. He stared past her into Garfield Park, magically lit by the ornate streetlamps. It was five thirty and full dark. Cincinnati still had the bones of the major American metropolis it once was.

"Let's just say when the tumor was found, I figured that God had given me what I deserved."

"How can you say that?" Cheryl Beth gripped the wheel tightly. "I grew up with that crap, and that's not the God I worship. Stuff happens, Will. Some gene betrayed you. It's not the Lord's punishment for anything you did or didn't do with Theresa. You're not to blame for what happened."

He laughed mordantly. "Well, I haven't had an erection since the surgery, so let's say I don't have to worry about women anymore."

They were stopped at a traffic light. Cheryl Beth turned to him. "Stick out your tongue. Go ahead, I'm a nurse. Stick out your tongue."

He did.

"You've got everything you need to make a woman happy."

The light changed and her tires spun on the pavement. She could feel herself turning bright red. That was a routine she had done before with spinal patients, a little bit of fun, strictly professional. Now she was burning with embarrassment. It faded only slowly as she drove up the hill on Vine Street and the windshield wipers revealed the sleet that was now coming down hard. She drove with extra care. The sleet clung to the hood of the car, slathered the street. If it froze… But she also drove slowly because she didn't want the day to end.

"Did you miss being a homicide detective?" She felt herself talking nervously, to break the spell that had fallen into the car.

"Some days," he said. "I loved my job. That may be different from a lot of cops. They start out loving it, showing up at work early, everything's new, they work past their shift without even thinking about filing an overtime slip. Later, it changes. A lot of them get bitter, hate everybody, marriages fall apart. Then they wait for their pensions. The best ones get in a zone. They know the job, the politics, how to put a case together and testify. They make friends off the job."

"Internal affairs must have been hard. Other cops don't like you."

"That's true," he said. "But there's a freedom to it, if you do it right. There are two kinds of Internal Investigations cops—the yes men, and the ones who believe in getting the facts and serving the public and your fellow officers. You want to make the bad cops go away and make sure the good ones stay. You have to be willing to ask important people embarrassing questions sometimes, and that upsets the bosses. But the chief has had my back."

Cheryl Beth gave him a gentle laugh. "You sound like an idealist."

Will laughed and shook his head. "An idealist and a philosopher. And a realist. That's a good cop. Dodds is that way, I give him that. But you can never let the idealist or philosopher part show, because you're surrounded by colleagues who believe the world is fucked. Pardon my language. They're the realists."

"That's too bad. Have you ever shot someone?" She was instantly sorry she had asked.

"I have no problem killing bad humans."

He said it dispassionately, then quickly asked about the politics of her job. "Me? I fight the bureaucracy, but mostly I try to put people at ease, make them laugh. Get them to trust me. I ask myself, 'How do you get people to do things they've never done before?'"

"You mean the bosses?"

"Bosses, patients, doctors, nurses."

Finally the neuro-rehab entrance became unavoidable, and she pulled under the overhang.

"Thank you," Will said. "I had…"

"I know."

"Tomorrow's Christmas eve. I couldn't get out to buy you a Christmas present, so this will have to do."

He reached in his pocket and handed her a piece of white paper. It was folded into the shape of a card, and on the cover were pencil sketches of a decorated tree and a pretty good likeness of Cheryl Beth in her lab coat and scrubs. "My best gift this Christmas…" was written in block letters. She opened it and read, "is no pain." It was signed, "Thank you, Cheryl Beth—Will."

"You drew this?"

He nodded.

"You're quite an artist."

"My dad said it was a waste of time. It's come in handy on a crime scene or two."

Now she was the one fighting back tears. "Thank you."

She unbuckled her seat belt and then undid his. "I can't let you take that inside." She pointed to the gun.

"There's a killer on the loose."

She gave a slight smile and shook her head.

"I'm a police officer."

"Well, right now the pain nurse is pulling rank." She opened the glove box and he reluctantly slid the holster and pistol inside. She closed it carefully and locked it.

"Do you trust me, Cheryl Beth?" He turned as much as he could to face her. He looked drained and yet still handsome. She leaned over and kissed his cheek.

"I don't know," she said, and opened the door to get the wheelchair.

Chapter Twenty-nine

Cheryl Beth took Will into the neuro-rehab unit, signed the paperwork that showed he had been returned to the ward, and went back to her car. The streetlights illuminated the sleet descending in thousands of vertical needles. Inside the car, she looked again at the makeshift Christmas card, then carefully tucked it into her purse. She smiled and shook her head. She would have to think about this man with his wavy hair and undercover idealism, his surface calm and inner fires.

She pulled carefully out from the overhang and waited while a black SUV sped past. She followed it as it reached the spot where the street hit an abrupt downgrade. Fortunately, she was driving slowly, deep in thought, letting several car lengths gather between them. Suddenly the red taillights ahead of her danced to the left, back to the right, and momentarily out of sight, only to be replaced by headlights. It was the same SUV. The hill had frozen and the vehicle lazily looped its way around and down until it crashed into a parked car. The muffled sound of smashing metal and composites reached her ears. She stopped immediately, called 911 and tried to back up. The road under her offered traction. Ahead was a down-bound street of black ice. She reversed the Saturn and drove around the level drive into the employee garage. She would work until the city came to put salt on the hill and clear away whatever other hapless drivers went down the slalom. She parked and double-checked

that the glove box, with its lethal cargo, was locked. Five minutes later, she was inside her cramped office, leafing through the
latest paperwork.

Cheryl Beth worried about her patients, especially at night,
even when another nurse was covering for her. They came as
impersonal consult sheets: a thirty-three-year-old male, motorcycle accident, with fractures of one femur, his pelvis, and elbow.
He denied he was in pain and refused to ask for medication.
When she talked to him she got little, but his body language
was a vivid storyteller, the way he didn't want to move, the set
of his face. He had a name: Ron Morton, he was from Dayton,
worked in an auto plant, and his dad had taught him never
to show pain, never complain. She could only gauge the time
between injections by the look on his face.

A forty-six-year-old female with ovarian cancer, metastasized
throughout her abdomen and liver. Her name was, with cruel
perversity, Hope—Hope Mundy and she wanted to live to see
her daughter graduate from high school. The doc had her on a
continuous morphine drip, which also left her in a stupor. When
it was cut back she moaned all the time, and the other patients
complained. Cheryl Beth adjusted the doses daily, sat with her
and listened, taught her how to relax through her breathing, put
cool compresses on her forehead.

The new consults came every day. Pain made people angry,
stoic, sometimes darkly comic. The woman in the busy ER who
had screamed, "Who do I have to give a blowjob to, to get an
epidural." Fortunately, Cheryl Beth had learned how to give
epidurals years ago, so no oral sex was required. Often they were
in the cruelest agony. They were grateful for the smallest things.
Some days she thought it would drive her insane, especially when
the suffering was caused by the hospital's inattention. Most days
she knew she could help them. Sometimes she caught addicts,
trying to scam new pain meds.

She always had the hardest cases: the most painful shootings, stabbings, chest tubes, spinal and lower back problems,
abdominal surgeries, and cancers. It seemed as if Will's job had

been that way, too. But his "consults" were dead people. His symptoms were "MOs." She was still on a high from the day: the latent danger of the jail, the way Will had elicited information from Lennie and Darlene. She would make a good detective, he had said. She doubted that. If she did his job, she would be too haunted by the ghosts of the dead and their very live, hurting families. She would be afraid of getting hurt. But just like her job, to do it well, he must have relied on skill, instinct, and, truth be told, bending the rules when it was necessary to help people.

She tried to think systemically about all she had seen and heard, as if it were a new consult. And she tried to listen to her gut. Will seemed so sure: the killer was this Bud Chambers. He was sure of it as a police detective, and surer of it as the avenger for the woman he had loved. It was still not so clear to Cheryl Beth. Her mind was branded with the memory of finding Christine—why would this man have killed a doctor he didn't even know? It was branded with the brief note she had dug out of Judd Mason's trash, written in the neat script. Obviously the police had found more about this strange, silent man—Mason was in jail for the murder. But, even there, she just wasn't sure, wasn't sure. What about Gary? He had lost his mind—enough to kill Christine? Yet she knew Gary's doctorish scrawl and he was incapable of writing as clearly as the script on the threatening note. Then there was Denise's self-described paranoid thought about the digital medicine project—it could have threatened any of the medical personnel at Memorial with something to hide, whether it was mistakes or stealing drugs.

And what of Will? She was growing too fond of him. But could he have killed Theresa in a rage? Was he capable of that? She had made mistakes judging men before, but it was hard for her to believe. It was impossible to believe he had killed the two other girls, and then somehow come right out of the ICU and murdered Christine.

It had to be Judd. Why else would he have retrieved the note and tried to dispose of it?

She leafed through the roster of the circulating nurses. Judd Mason had most recently spent two months in the pediatric ward. She grabbed her purse, turned off the lights, locked the door, and walked to the other side of the hospital, to the peds ward.

The hospital was emptying out for Christmas. Everyone wanted to be gone, and patients tried hard to get discharged. With visiting hours winding down, the normal crunch of people in the hallways was missing. The PA system, without its seemingly unending summonses of doctors and trauma teams, seemed more omnipresent by its silence. Only the most serious cases were here. Those, and the forgotten and abandoned. She waved and made small talk as she passed the nurses' stations, but nothing could stop the constricting in her throat and chest as she neared the bright blue-and-yellow doors. She would walk in briskly, say hello, and look over some of Judd's charts. If anyone asked, she would say one of the docs wanted her to double-check something. She would not look at the abundance of donated toys in the play areas and waiting rooms. She would not look into the rooms, or into the frightened, haunted eyes of the parents. She would avoid the doctors who had, as a matter of course, to tell mothers and fathers that their children were dying.

They had named her Carla Beth, after Andy's mother, with Cheryl Beth's middle name. After her, Cheryl Beth couldn't have another child; it had been a difficult delivery, a wondrous result. She had the wheat-colored hair that Cheryl Beth had as a little girl, before it had darkened, and she had loved unicorns and the color yellow and laughing. And Carla Beth was dead before her fourth birthday. And it was a story she would tell no one. It belonged to her. The grief and guilt and bottomless sorrow, the lock of her hair, her last expression—hers alone. Andy returned to Corbin, remarried, and had three children. Cheryl Beth stayed in Cincinnati. When people asked if she had children, she would simply say no. Every person in this hospital had been stunned by calamity, and why should she be different? She had to make the decision between sitting in a chair, staring at a wall, and waiting to die, or returning to her life helping people. But she could not work peds. She could barely stand to be in the ward.

She leafed through the charts looking for one with Judd Mason's signature. She found it on the fifteenth chart. The details of the case—she made herself skip over them. But the chart contained several pages written by Mason. The handwriting was not the same as on the note to Christine, not at all. She slammed the chart shut, shelved it, and nearly ran from the ward.

The Starbucks in the lobby was already closed by the time she got there. She was hoping to grab a cup of coffee that was better than the swill at some of the nurses' stations.

"Hi, there."

She knew she had jumped when she heard the voice, but she instinctively smiled as she turned and faced the young man. He was seated at one of the tables.

"I missed them, too," he said. "Seemed like a good night for a hot latte."

"Well, it's always something." Cheryl Beth stood there awkwardly. She knew this man. The young software millionaire. He had walked out of Stephanie Ott's office that day she had received her dressing down. He still looked like a college student on a pub crawl, this time wearing black jeans, a black turtleneck, and a black leather jacket. That jacket reminded her of what Christine had worn the last night of her life. Stretched out in the chair, the man was compact, with an unlined face, sleepy blue eyes, and a crop of moussed sandy hair.

"You're the one they call the pain nurse."

She introduced herself and he stuck out his hand. "I'm Josh Barnett. Care to join me?"

"For a minute," she said, curious. She still felt wobbly and was grateful to sit. "Not that anybody's going anywhere until they get salt on those streets." She nodded her head toward the front doors.

"I saw you at Stephanie Ott's office," she said.

"And I remember you as well." He looked her in the eye.

"Why would that be?"

"Well, don't be put off by this, but you're a very attractive woman."

She laughed and shook her head. He was nearly twenty years younger than she. But there was the irresistible allure of a compliment.

"Ms. Ott is quite the taskmaster," he said. "The accreditation process has them all jumpy." His expression was pleasant, but his eyes were deep like a friendly well; something moved far down, but she didn't know what.

Cheryl Beth leaned back. "So you're not from around here?"

"Oh, no," he said. "Silicon Valley. I'm not used to this kind of weather. If you don't think I'm out of line, could I ask if you were the nurse who found Dr. Lustig?"

Cheryl Beth sighed. "Now tell me how you would know that?" The edge was obvious in her voice.

"I've been working here, on a contract. People talk. I'd heard it was you. I was working with Christine."

"I see."

"It's a terrible loss for us," he said quietly. "And she was a wonderful person. Just a devastating loss."

"Makes me wonder why the hospital moved her down to that basement office. Do you wonder about that?"

"Well, the office was private, and I imagine she needed the quiet to get the evaluation of the project software done. We were under a very tight deadline to complete it."

He waited as a crowd of civilians walked past, bearing flowers and boxes in Christmas wrapping. "Did you know Christine, Cheryl Beth?"

She shifted in her seat, suddenly hot in her coat. "I did," she said, and slipped off the coat. She pulled out two of the new consults and studied them, ignoring him. For a long time she thought he might just stand and leave.

"I know this sounds weird," he said, a small smile lighting up his face. "But would you have dinner with me? I've been cooped up writing computer code for months and haven't had dinner with a beautiful woman." His eyes were different now. She had his full attention. "Maybe you'd show me your city. I'm not some weirdo Californian, I promise."

Cheryl Beth stopped herself from laughing. She was rusty with a gentle brush-off. He was an attractive young man with a sly and sexy smile. But she was not looking, and in any case she liked tall, big men. Maybe when she was feeling better she would tell Lisa this story and chuckle about it. "I can't," she said. "But you're sweet to say that, Josh."

"I mean it," he said. He reached into his pocket and pulled out a business card. She could see the logo SoftChartZ. Another reach produced a pen and he wrote something on the back of it.

"At least take my card. I put my hotel number on the back. Just in case you change your mind."

Cheryl Beth pocketed the card and turned away, eager to find Will so she could tell him about her sleuthing in the peds' records.

Chapter Thirty

Will had watched with apprehension as they neared the hospital, knowing his day out was ending. The hospital tower was illuminated by spotlights and it looked like a building from an old comic book, a perch for a superhero. It was just a box of the sick and dying, a base camp for perilous journeys and ascending prayers, and for now it was his home. He had watched Cheryl Beth walk away, seeing in those well-fitting civilian clothes her confident long-limbed strides, knowing she thought him a fool for giving her the Christmas card. Or she thought worse of him. And as she walked out the door, he felt the almost supernatural buoyancy that had kept him calm and functioning after the tumor was diagnosed, through the first days of dismal prognoses and dire worries, through the surgery and days of pain, through Cindy's final jettisoning of him, through the murder investigation—he felt it disappear.

He asked the aide to give him his dinner in the large rehab room. He couldn't bear to take off his suit and get in the cursed bed yet, even though his legs and back ached and he was battered by exhaustion. So he sat alone in the room, feeling the cold seeping through the windows, and surveying the precise little scoop of mashed potatoes, three tablespoons of corn, and two slices of meatloaf. He had enough money to buy a Diet Coke, which he used to take his pain meds. This was his life now. He had lived twenty-five years on the other side of the crime-scene tape and the emergency lights, a quarter century where his badge gave him a pass anywhere in the city. That was gone. Tomorrow or the next day, he would have to endure a visit from his brother and his family, bearing gifts they probably resented giving. He would have nothing to give in return. And the day after that, and every day he was given, he would assess every little pain or change in his body with the knowledge that it might be nothing, or it might be catastrophe. Theresa's face and then Cheryl Beth's hovered in front of him, her kiss still warm on his cheek, as he lapsed into sleep.

The next image that broke into his consciousness was J. J. Dodds. Will shook his head to clear away the medicine haze and was fully awake.

"Detective Dodds."

"Detective Borders." Dodds sat in a chair turned backward, his blue, polka dot tie hanging over the chair's back. "I risked my neck on the ice to bring you good news and bad news. Which do you want first?"

Will pushed himself up in the wheelchair and said he needed good news.

"Darlene is in protective custody, her kid, too. She gave Chambers up. We've reopened the case and we've got a warrant for his arrest. I think we can get him for the three women in Mount Adams."

All this, Will thought, and Dodds was not angrily berating him for interfering.

"So what's the bad news?"

"He's gone. We sent a tactical unit to his apartment and he wasn't there. We've got it staked out."

"Where does he work?"

"He's some kind of independent security consultant, so he works out of his place. We're running down family, friends. So far, no Chambers."

"Hell." Will's mind pulled out of its depression and began plotting how they could find him.

"There's more," Dodds said. "Darlene said Chambers has a cabin down by Rabbit Hash. We never found it before because it's in his father's name. It's empty right now, but we've got Kentucky State Police sitting on it. If he doesn't show up there in the next day, we're going to execute a search warrant. What do you want to bet we find some very interesting things hidden down there?"

"That doesn't sound like bad news."

Dodds' mouth turned up in an imitation of a smile. "That's because there's more bad news."

Will pushed away the food tray and waited.

"Your girlfriend's been lying. I always had this gut feeling about her."

"What girlfriend? You mean Cheryl Beth?"

"She was with Dr. Lustig the night she was killed."

"Oh, bullshit."

"Real shit," Dodds said. "Dr. Nagle said he saw the two of them talking and drinking at a bar on Main Street the night the doc was murdered…"

"He's just trying to save his own skin, since he doesn't have an alibi anymore."

"Will you let me finish? Thank you. After you so industriously had this girl Amy Morton come back and say she lied about Nagle's alibi, well, I brought him in for a chat. He's very full of himself. Know what he calls himself? The Two Million Dollar Man, for all the surgeries he does. But he tells me he was on Main Street that night and saw the two of them together. Unfortunately for your girlfriend…"

"She's not my girlfriend," Will said through a sour mouth.

"Unfortunately for your girlfriend, I took their pictures to the bar and the bartender and one of the waitresses positively identified them. She was with Lustig that night."

Will stared into the table, ran his hand lightly back and forth over its smooth surface, and felt himself breathe. His stomach was now the home to a heavy, spiky rock. How could she have lied to him? "So what are you saying?"

"Motive. She was Nagle's lover and Lustig's rival. Opportunity. There could be an hour or more between the time Cheryl left the bar and the time she claimed she found the body. And she's been lying to us."

Will rubbed his temples, feeling his head start to ache. Was it a headache because Cheryl Beth had lied to him, or a brain tumor? Finally he shook his head and forced a laugh. "Reach, reach, hell, your arms are long."

Dodds ran his hand across the top of his head, as if searching to see if any hair had escaped his daily shaving. "There's some weird shit going on at this place, and she knows what it is. I still like Mason for killing Lustig. I'm keeping his ass in jail. But maybe Cheryl Wilson is in on it, too, and this Nagle asshole."

"Her name is Cheryl Beth."

"Mason's fingerprints are on the threatening letter. He also has a knife collection. Have you seen him? He's one of these no-affect types—you don't know if they're just fucked up or a killer. I say a killer."

"What does he say?"

"He says he was in love with her, that the letter was clipped on the windshield wiper of his car one day at work, after Lustig was killed. Nice try, but the stamps had been canceled. He had to have taken it from Lustig's mailbox to cover his tracks."

"Unless somebody steamed the stamps off a canceled letter and applied them to the letter found with Mason."

Dodds snorted. "Let me guess. Damn, Bud Chambers. He's killed everybody in Cincinnati! But it could still have been your girlfriend, Cheryl *Beth*. She could be the killer."

"I thought you said you liked Mason!" Will's angry voice echoed in the large, empty room.

"He's involved. Hell, maybe they were all sleeping together. We've seen stranger shit. Stuff like that even happened in the department."

"And they somehow found out the confidential information on the MO of the Slasher to do it? Give me a break. You know this is the Ring Bearer again."

Dodds mouth tightened and they locked eyes. Finally, "You can find anything out on the Internet now. Maybe a patrolman told his wife, who told her girlfriend, who told…I don't have it all worked out yet. Maybe I need to check into the hospital so I can be as good a detective as you."

Will sat in the acid of betrayal, silent. Dodds just watched, with his preternatural patience. Will's heart banged against his chest wall as Dodds' cell phone rang. The conversation was brief.

"Dispatch," Dodds said. "Hospital security asked if I could meet Berkowitz down in the basement."

"Lustig's office?"

"Yep."

Will stared through the blackness of the windows, now accumulating ice around their edges. "Have fun."

"Fuck you very much." Dodds stood up. "But you're working, too. Quit feeling sorry for yourself because you're on the job and coming with me. Back to the murder room, Detective Borders."

Will put his hands to the wheels and rolled toward the doors. "Just like old times, Detective Dodds."

Chapter Thirty-one

Cheryl Beth checked in on several patients, and each time she looked out the windows to survey the streets outside. From the promontory of the tower, nothing seemed to be moving on Pill Hill. She could even see a clot of red taillights at the foot of the street where the SUV had slid. Several blocks through the trees came the yellow pulse of lights, salt trucks, but so far she was stuck at the hospital. There were other ways down, but they all involved hills and she would not risk it. Cincinnatians became hysterical in even modest snowstorms. An ice storm on a city of hills was, as her grandmother would have said, a gracious plenty of a mess. If worse came to worst, she could use one of the cots the on-duty trauma teams slept on.

She noshed on the remains of a Christmas party on Five-West. Most of the nurses and docs were already gone. She was still in civilian clothes with her ID card hung around her neck by her red lanyard. She smiled attentively as a young nurse talked about her little girl's part in the Christmas play. From somewhere down the hall, she barely but distinctly heard a small choir singing carols. *Hark, the herald angels sing...* The sound filled her with longing. She wanted to find these singers and listen.

"Hey."

She turned to see Lisa surveying the remains of the food. "I am such a carb and sugar slut," she said, picking up a piece of cold pizza. "Thank God they didn't order in Aglamesis' ice cream." Her lean, tall body seemed to show no ill effects from her addictions.

"What are you doing here so late?"

"I'm trapped like everybody else." She munched contentedly, but her eyes looked tired. "I gave notice today."

"What?"

"I'm going to University. For years I thought I could make a stand here and make this place better. I'm just ready for a change."

Cheryl Beth hugged her. "Who's going to maintain the FDN list and keep me up to speed on all the gossip?" She felt like crying, even though Lisa was only going a few blocks away.

"You should come with me," Lisa said. "They'd love to have you."

"I know. Maybe not so much now that I'm the slutty nurse who was involved in a murder."

"Oh, please. It just makes you more interesting. Anyway, you're the most straitlaced person I've ever worked with. Not that the degenerates at this hospital are a good yardstick." She stopped laughing and cocked her head. "You're wheezing, babe. Asthma acting up?"

"I guess." It was true. The cold and the stagnant Cincinnati air were hell on her lungs. She reached for her inhaler and the business card that the young man from SoftChartZ had given her fell out, fluttering down to the floor. It landed face down.

"Shit!"

"What?"

Cheryl Beth picked the card off the floor and read the hand-written message on the back: "Westin, room 560. I'm on West Coast time so am staying up late. I'd love to have company." She turned the card to the front, which introduced Josh Barnett, Chief Executive Officer, beneath a SoftChartZ logo.

Lisa had been hovering, watching. "Way to go, Cheryl Beth! You will have such fun, and you'll have that wonderful funny walk in the morning that happens after…"

"Stop!" Cheryl Beth nearly shouted. "You don't understand. Now I remember. This is the guy you said was sleeping with Christine."

"Young and strong." Lisa's smile was so broad it nearly broke her face in half.

Cheryl Beth held the card in a shaking hand, the paper nearly searing her skin.

"Don't be afraid," Lisa said. "It's no questions asked, rules of the road…"

"His handwriting." Cheryl Beth was almost talking to herself. "It's the same handwriting as on the note in Mason's car. I swear it's the same."

"What are you talking about?"

Cheryl Beth tried to explain as Lisa cocked a hip and rested her hand on it, looking at her as if she were a crazy woman.

"This was never some random murder," Cheryl Beth said. "Christine somehow…" She tried to work through it, feeling light-headed. It seemed impossible that the baby-faced tech executive could be a killer. But so many millions of dollars were at stake, and the hospital was already in trouble. "This is why Stephanie Ott was so strange, why the hospital tried to keep this quiet. Why they moved her office down to the basement. Now I understand why Christine was so crazy that night…" To herself, she thought, *now I know why she held me so tight and kept asking, "Can I trust you, Cheryl Beth? Can I trust you…?"*

Lisa put an arm around her. "You need to go home, babe, or take a cab to his hotel once the roads clear."

"Ladies." Dr. Carpenter sidled into the room, his voice booming. "My two favorite healers."

They moved apart and greeted him. Cheryl Beth stared into the face she had known for so many years and wondered, *who can I trust now?*

"Is my timing bad?" he asked. "Sorry if I interrupted."

"Just women stuff," Lisa said.

Cheryl Beth stuffed the card back in her pocket just as her pager buzzed: the main switchboard.

"You have a call from Detective Dodds, to meet him down in Dr. Lustig's office, uh, former office."

"Now?"

"The call just came in."

Cheryl Beth put the phone back in the cradle. She was excited, but she was also afraid. Why did Dodds suddenly want her? And why there? Maybe she would ignore the page, try to make it home through the ice. Then she would, what? Think it through... Maybe... She shook her head. It wouldn't work. It wasn't right. Just then, she saw one of her favorite guards pass on an intersecting hallway.

"Don!"

She ran and caught up with him. "Could I ask a favor? Would you walk me down to the basement?"

"Now?"

She said now, and they headed to the main elevator bank, talking about the ice storm. He said the radio was reporting wrecks and impassable streets all over the city. "We're pretty much cut off for awhile," he said. "I guess the ambulances have chains. But I haven't seen one of those for an hour, either..." She was barely listening. The downward movement of the elevator was making her ill. As it left the fifth floor, as the car deviated from its normal run to the lobby, the lighting seemed to change and darken, the buttons looked filthy and worn, the walls pocked with stains and creases, gravity making her feel heavy, as if her body would crumple in on itself.

The elevator car settled and a deep mechanical thud came from somewhere far above them. Don just shook his head and they stepped into the hallway. The single bank of fluorescent lights was starting to go out. Its insistent flickering made them look like characters in a silent movie. It made the beds and big supply carts parked against the walls cast trembling, diabolical shadows. Her body was wound tight and her lungs felt small and fragile. She finally used the inhaler.

"You sure somebody called you down here?" he asked.

Then they saw the light streaming out of the office. "I guess so." Twenty more steps and she looked inside to see Dodds and Will. At the sight of Will, she smiled spontaneously.

"It's okay, Don."

"You're sure?"

She said yes and thanked him. Then she watched as her Danskos again crossed the threshold into what had been Christine's office. Dodds was sitting in Christine's chair, all but concealing it with his bulk. Will had wheeled himself to the far wall by the desk and they both looked surprised.

"What are you doing here?" Dodds said. "And where's that guard going?"

"What?" She appraised the expressions of both men. "You called me. I got a page from the switchboard to meet you here."

"It didn't come from me," Dodds said. "We were told to meet the hospital security chief down here. Where the hell is Stan 'Don't Call Me David' Berkowitz?"

Cheryl Beth stepped into the room, feeling an awkward chemistry from the two. Will barely acknowledged her.

"Well, since you're here, maybe you'll tell your boyfriend here why you lied to him?"

"I didn't…" She got the words out, but her insides were tied up with dread.

"We've got time until Berkowitz gets here, so tell him, tell us," Dodds slowed his voice into a falsely friendly tone, "why you were at a bar with Christine Lustig the night she was found murdered."

"I…oh, shit. I know what you're thinking. Will, it's not…" Her eyes stung with tears. She tried to speak, but was wheezing again. She looked at Will, searching for a connection, but his eyes were opaque.

She pulled out the card and handed it to Will. "Look at this."

"Just tell me the truth, Cheryl Beth." Will spoke for the first time, and his voice was taut with emotion. His face looked troubled and distracted.

She said, "Look at the back of the card, the handwriting. It's the same handwriting as on the threatening note to Christine. But it wasn't written by Judd Mason. It was written by the head of SoftChartZ. He made the threat! What if Christine found out something about the project? Something that could get her killed?" Dodds looked through her, bored. She got angry. "You called me down here, so at least listen to what I'm telling you!"

"I did not call you down here," Dodds said. "But since you're here... You were with Lustig in a bar on Main Street the night she was murdered." He went on to give her the very same warning she had heard in a hundred police shows: silent...used against you...lawyer...do you understand?... She wasn't really listening. Will looked pale.

"This isn't right," Will said suddenly. "We need to get out of this basement right now..."

Will's premonition was instantly telegraphed to Cheryl Beth and she instinctively reached for him, to wheel him out of the room. In that same second the walls shook with the sharp noise of the door slamming shut. They were closed in.

They were not alone.

Chapter Thirty-two

Bud Chambers leveled the SIG Sauer 228 at them. His hands were encased in latex gloves. The weapon was graphite colored, accurate, and reliable. It could be chambered to nine millimeter or .40 caliber, but what did that matter right then? As Will remembered, it was a favored semiautomatic of the feds and could hold fourteen rounds. Chambers wore green scrubs, a white lab coat, even a hospital ID card clipped to his left pocket. His shoes were covered with the kind of footlets they wore in surgery. The better to avoid tracking blood, perhaps. He had been hiding in the same dead space behind the inward-opening door where Will had stayed that day when he had snuck behind Dodds into the office.

Somehow, deep in the premonitory brain cells that told him something was stalking him long before the tumor came, somehow he always knew it would end this way.

"Ah, ah, ah!" Chambers flexed the semiautomatic at Dodds, holding it in both hands. "Don't even think about it, fat man. You!" He cocked his head at Cheryl Beth. "Reach in his coat and get his gun, and do it slowly."

The room was crushed with still silence.

"No," she said.

"You'd be amazed how soundproof this room is," Chambers said, pulling his thick eyebrows into a dark overhang above his eyes. "Nobody's going to hear you. The hospital's shut down by the ice. Don't try to be a hero, honey."

Cheryl Beth spoke in a quavering voice. "Fuck off."

Chambers took two quick steps and his left hand flashed toward her face, instantly sprawling her over the desk. She let out a cry and Will tried to raise himself out of the chair.

"Sit down, cripple." He spoke without taking his glance or gun off Dodds. "I'll take that." He grabbed Josh Barnett's card out of Will's hand, glanced at it, and slid it into his pants pocket. "What a fucking little moron." His gun arm stiffened and he snarled at Cheryl Beth. "Now get that goddamned gun!"

"Just do what he says," Dodds said quietly.

She pushed herself up and reached into Dodds holster, pulling out his Smith & Wesson nine. Her left cheek was bright red. "Slow," Chambers commanded. "Now hold it by the barrel and hand it to me. Thank you." He stepped back, placing Dodds' weapon on the bookshelf against the far wall.

"Now get the backup piece on his ankle."

Will groaned inside. The bastard was too thorough. Cheryl Beth knelt and retrieved the five-round .38 Chief's Special from the ankle holster on Dodds' right leg. Chambers repeated his move, placing it on the shelf beside the larger semiauto.

"Stand up. Up!"

Dodds slowly stood. Chambers ordered Cheryl Beth to take the handcuffs from Dodds' belt and shackle his hands behind him. She did it slowly, glancing at Will. He wished he knew what to telegraph to her. He wished he knew how. The handcuffs clicked into place.

"Back up to me, Dodds." The big man slowly complied and Chambers used his left hand to ratchet the cuffs tight. Will watched as Dodds' temples and mouth reacted. "There," Chambers said, a smile creasing his puffy face. "That's the way I like 'em with dangerous Negroes, nice and snug. Now go sit again." Dodds eased into the chair. "Lean back, get your feet off the floor. If your feet touch the floor, I'll kill you."

Chambers turned the gun on Will now. He had never been on the receiving end of a gun barrel without having a weapon in his hand. His insides felt as if they were liquefying.

"Now just because I don't trust the cripple, and he's so dressed up and all, I want you to open his coat and pull up his pants legs to make sure he's not packing." Cheryl Beth complied. Will wished his service weapon hadn't been locked away. He would have pulled it long before now.

"You're always in the way, Borders," Chambers said, gesticulating with his free hand. With the gloves, he looked like a malevolent clown or a cartoon character. "This was going to be a simple plan tonight. Just tie up a few loose ends with Detective Dodds and the pain nurse here, and I'd be gone. Two birds, one stone. Once again, you've mucked it up."

Will's brain was a riot: every rampaging channel of training, thought, and instinct asking how to get out of this. How to play for time.

"Where were we?" Chambers said. "Oh, yes. You were about to tell these fine ossifers why you lied about being in the bar with Christine."

Cheryl Beth stared at him, almost in a daze.

"Sit down," he ordered, and she slid against the wall between Will's wheelchair and Dodds. He aimed at Dodds. "Keep your feet up!" To Cheryl Beth, "Why were you there?"

"I ran into her!" Cheryl Beth set her jaw and Will could see moisture forming in her eyes. "I didn't plan it. I got off work and wanted a drink. I went inside and she came up to me. She wanted to talk. So we got a table."

"What did she want to talk about?" Chambers said, his voice impatient.

"Gary."

"I don't believe you."

"Gary and I…"

"I know all about you, Cheryl." Chambers slid the pistol into his lab coat, its outline falling heavily into the pocket. "I've watched you. I've been in your house. I've been in your fucking underwear drawer. You ought to buy more black. I know you stopped seeing Gary months ago, so she didn't want you for that. She had plenty of her own distractions. She didn't give a damn about his."

"She wanted to know what it was like between us," Cheryl Beth said. "She wanted graphic details. I thought she was very drunk and very distraught, and I just tried to calm her down."

"Bullshit!" As he shouted, she jumped.

In a quiet voice, he said, "This is just business. Tell me what I want to know and everybody gets out alive."

"There's nothing to tell!" Tears were tracking down her cheeks now and her voice broke. "Christine seemed very upset, but not at me. She was all over the place. I'd never seen her like that."

"What did she say about the hospital?"

"Nothing."

He ripped her up from the floor, delivering a brutal open-handed blow to her face. Then he shoved her down to the floor. She rose on her haunches and charged him.

"You son of a bitch!" Her fist connected with his nose before he got hold of her. He pushed her hard into the wall and she slid to the floor.

"A little fighter." Chambers used the sleeve of his lab coat to wipe the trickle of blood from his nose. "Get your hands off her, Sir Galahad." Will had reached out to touch Cheryl Beth. He slowly pulled his hand back into the confines of the wheelchair.

Chambers loomed over her. "She talked to you! She gave you something!"

"No."

"She did. She gave you something before she came back to the hospital."

"She didn't! And don't you think you've made me cry, you bastard. I cry when I'm mad!"

"What did she give you?"

"Nothing."

"Where is it?"

"What?" she yelled in frustration.

"Have it your way." Chambers pulled out the gun and approached Will. He felt the steel against his temple. It was smooth and surprisingly warm.

"Don't hurt him!" she said. "You want to know what she did that night? You really want to know? She said she was afraid she might lose her job and she didn't know who to talk to. But then she slid next to me and held me, crying. But then she kissed me. She had her hands all over me and kissed me, told me she wanted me to come home with her, she didn't want to be alone. I freaked out and left. *That's* what happened. When she left word for me later, I was afraid she was going to start all over again."

Chambers seemed momentarily confused. "Well, I'll take you with me and we'll have plenty of time to get to know each other and talk. I'll find out where you put it."

Dodds said, "It's all over, Chambers. We know everything. We have a warrant on you. We know about the cabin at Rabbit Hash. Make it easy on yourself."

Chambers gave a low chuckle, the dimple in his chin deepening. "Spoken like a true professional. But you don't know much of anything." He laughed louder this time, watching the gun as if it would share his mirth. "You know what? They told me I wasn't smart enough to be a detective. That's what the bastards said. But here I have the two supposedly best detectives in the Cincinnati Police, and you've been five steps behind me all the way…"

"So you killed Christine," Will said, "just like you killed the others."

"Now you're only four steps behind."

"But Christine was a hit," Will said.

Chambers stared at him, unsure of whether to put away the gun again. He kept it in his hand but let his arm fall. Will continued, "It's 'just business,' you said. You were paid to kill Dr. Lustig. You framed Judd Mason. But since you've always been a narcissistic fuckup, Marion, you couldn't do a simple job. You had to imitate what happened on Mount Adams. You think you're an artist. You had to give this one your signature strokes, right, Marion?"

Chambers' right cheek twitched at the mention of his given name.

"You wanted to get back at us, get back at me," Will said. "You killed two women to cover up the murder of your ex-wife. You took their ring fingers as trophies. You killed Christine for money, but you didn't close the loop." He fought to control his fear, make his voice speak in a slow disdain. The deep anger he felt made it possible. "Marion, Marion… Something's still out there and your masters want you to get it."

Chambers leaned casually against the wall near the door. "I have the right to remain silent."

"It's about SoftChartZ," Cheryl Beth said. "That's it. Josh Barnett gave me his business card tonight. He wrote a little note on the back. It's the same handwriting that was on the threatening note I saw with Judd Mason."

"You're pretty good, honey," Chambers said. "The software is hopeless. They can't make it work, and when that comes out the company is done."

Will said, "SoftChartZ needed the continued cash flow coming in from the hospital while they were frantically trying to debug the software. They needed this to look like a success, so they could win contracts from other hospitals, keep it going."

Chambers clapped very slowly. "Very good, Detective Borders. Why else would their stock be a hundred dollars a share? All these morons buying into the future of digital medicine. My ass. The lady doctor realized it was a sham and she was going to go public. They had a problem and wanted somebody to solve it. Good old Berkowitz told Barnett to talk to me. Berkowitz just thought they needed help with a security breach."

"Kind of funny," Will said. "The software company hired a hit man with a bug inside his fucked-up hard drive."

The low chuckle rumbled out of Chambers' chest again. "They offered to pay me in stock. I took cash, and it'll be off-shore waiting for me. Unfortunately, they're pretty sure the doc made a copy of some incriminating documents and gave them to someone for safekeeping. Obviously I've got to get them back to get paid. What are you doing, Borders?"

"It's hot." Will undid his necktie and tossed it to the floor. He didn't want Chambers to use it later to choke him. Chambers wasn't paying attention. He returned to the shelf, put down the SIG and retrieved Dodds' nine millimeter Smith & Wesson.

"Do be comfortable," he said. His tongue flicked out of his mouth. "I lied. I wanted the two of you down here tonight so I could kill old Dodds here. You know how many cops eat their service weapons. The despair of the job and all that. And I was going to take a little road trip with Cheryl here and get the information I need. Hell, if I was in the mood, I was going to stop by your room," he looked at Will, "and smother you with a pillow. Sleep apnea's a real problem. Then I'd be free and clear. It was all going to be nice and neat, no loose ends. Mason would still be in jail for killing the lady doctor. But you had to show up again, Borders."

Will fought back the panic smashing against his chest. "I just have an asshole detector and have to follow it, Marion." Chambers glared at him with hate, his eyelid nervously fluttered, and suddenly Will felt a strange calm inside himself.

"After I take care of Dodds and handcuff Cheryl, you and I are going to settle up," Chambers said. "This will be pleasure, not business."

He strode to Dodds, chambered a round in the pistol and, using the gloved clown hand, brought it up to his temple. At that instant, Will used every molecule of his adrenaline to launch himself out of the chair. With a sharp exhale, he shot straight out toward Chambers, who desperately tried to re-aim the gun at Will. But they were now too close. Will's legs started to give way—*damned legs, damned spinal cord!*—but not before he fired a savage uppercut with the heel of his hand.

It connected with the base of Chambers' jaw with a snap and bony crunch, and he lurched backward onto the floor. The nine came out of his hand and slid all the way to the door. Will fell forward like a bag of potatoes, breaking his fall with his hands. He fought to disentangle himself from the footrests of the wheelchair. He relied on his strong right leg, using his right foot as a hook to catch the left and pull it free. Then he was flat on his belly, trying to crawl an eternal distance to the gun.

"Will, watch out!" Dodds yelled. Chambers was on his hands and knees, slowly shaking his head. Then he stood and advanced on Will. "I'm gonna kill you," he slurred. His shadow was over Will when glass shattered. Chambers wobbled to the side. Cheryl Beth had grabbed the Tiffany lamp from the desk and struck his head. But it was not enough. He delivered a brutal backhand and Cheryl Beth careened into the wall, hitting her head. Her eyes were closed and she didn't move.

Pain exploded in Will's side and a second later another kick came. Bright lights flashed around the edges of his eyes…he thought he was going to throw up. He fought to breathe. The foot came again and Will deflected it, getting the surgical footlet in his hand. Then his scalp erupted in fire. Chambers pulled him up by his hair and smashed him in the eye. He went momentarily blind, felt dizzy, and his cheek and eye socket burned in agony. Something felt loose in his face. Chambers was cut and bleeding from the lamp. The look in his eyes was the devil's, the last look those women saw, that Theresa saw.

He picked up Will and shoved him into a cabinet. Another cascade of pain blasted through his back. Will was showered by a mass of used needles and other medical flotsam. The red hazmat disposal box had come down on him and split open. He tried to get to his knees, every joint aflame, but Chambers kicked him again. Will fell backward into the footrests of the wheelchair and he was trapped. Chambers spun wildly around, as if another adversary might appear. Then his eyes focused on the floor in front of Will.

"Goddamn." He bent down, pushed aside the spent needles and picked up a computer disk. He looked as if he had discovered buried treasure. "This is where she hid it." He stood and glanced back at Will. "I'm done now."

He put the disk in his pocket and his right hand changed to metal.

"He's got brass knuckles!" Dodds yelled, trying to stand. Chambers slashed toward his face and Dodds collapsed back into the chair, then toppled to the floor.

Chambers turned to Will. "You're not good enough to use a knife on. Now you're gonna pay."

He only needed two steps forward to start dismantling every bone in Will's skull. It was just enough time.

Will twisted, screaming in agony. He fought to keep from passing out as he found the fanny pack attached to the side of the wheelchair and inside it the smooth, slim steel cargo he sought. He turned back just in time. As Chambers started to swing his fist in a wide haymaker, Will pressed the button on the switchblade. One second later he plunged the blade into Chambers' right thigh.

The man emitted a sharp scream and tried to retreat. But Will now had hold of his leg, and as Chambers tried to step back, he carried Will with him. Will slammed and twisted the knife into the muscle, found bone, brought another shriek. Chambers fell on his back and Will climbed up him as if scaling a deadly escarpment. Will's left leg was thirty pounds of dead weight, cramping. Chambers flailed with his brass-knuckled fist but Will grabbed his wrist, twisting it as hard as he could. The knuckles fell out with a clank. He held both Chambers' hands to the cold floor.

Will felt the body under him writhing madly. Veins now standing out in his forehead, Chambers strained to use his good leg to push himself toward the door, toward the gun. His other leg spasmed ineffectually. The pasty skin of Chambers' face reddened deeper every second. Will slid across his torso and smashed his right fist into Chambers' nose, spewing blood like a fireworks burst.

"Kind of hard to move, cripple," Will hissed, "now that things are a little more even between us." He rammed his fist again into Chambers' right eye, drawing more blood. "You like to hurt women, don't you, Marion?" Will didn't recognize the sound of his own voice. He reached behind him, twisting the knife again, and the room was filled with a sound as if an animal was being tortured. "How's it feel to pick on somebody your own size, cripple?"

Chambers spat a viscous mix of blood and mucus into Will's eyes and freed one fist long enough to connect with his jaw. Will wobbled, dizzy, but couldn't be easily dislodged. Yet in an instant, Chambers' hands were around his throat, trying to crush his windpipe. The room tilted before Will put his fists together, made a V with his lower arms, and rammed them into Chambers' grip, breaking it.

He pulled in sweet air and his hands now found Chambers' throat. He slammed his head against the floor and dug into the soft, warm flesh of the murderer's neck, connecting with the harder tissue of his windpipe.

"Will Borders, don't you dare kill him!"

It was Cheryl Beth, shouting at him. "You've been given the gift of life, and don't you dare throw it away over him, over the past."

Will stared into Chambers' eyes, rage meeting rage, his fingers turning into a vise.

"You have a life to live, damn you!" He felt her on his back, trying to pull him off. "People need you!" Then her soft hand touched his cheek. "I need you."

As if a spell had lifted, he released Chambers' throat and heard him gasp for air. He lay unconscious but breathing.

Will fell backward onto the floor, and Cheryl Beth held him. "I got you. It's going to be all right now…all right."

He reached for her, brushing aside her soft light-brown hair, gently caressing around the scratches and bruises on her lovely face. "For you, too, Cheryl Beth," he said.

"When you two kids are done with this sentimental crap, would somebody mind un-cuffing me?"

Will looked over and Dodds was awake, wiggling himself upright.

In a moment, they helped Will into the wheelchair. He was a mess and everything hurt. On a scale of one to ten, his pain was a ten.

He felt fine.

To receive a free catalog of Poisoned Pen Press titles, please contact us in one of the following ways:

Phone: 1-800-421-3976
Facsimile: 1-480-949-1707
Email: info@poisonedpenpress.com
Website: www.poisonedpenpress.com

Poisoned Pen Press
6962 E. First Ave. Ste. 103
Scottsdale, AZ 85251